Starlight
In The Ring

T0159479

Starlight
In The Ring

H. N. Quinnen

**TOP HAT
BOOKS**

Winchester, UK
Washington, USA

First published by Top Hat Books, 2014
Top Hat Books is an imprint of John Hunt Publishing Ltd., Laurel House, Station Approach,
Alresford, Hants, SO24 9JH, UK
office1@jhpbooks.net
www.johnhuntpublishing.com

For distributor details and how to order please visit the 'Ordering' section on our website.

Text copyright: H. N. Quinnen 2013

ISBN: 978 1 78279 532 2

A CIP catalogue record for this book is available from the British Library.

Design: Stuart Davies

Printed in the USA by Edwards Brothers Malloy

We operate a distinctive and ethical publishing philosophy in all
areas of our business, from our global network of authors to
production and worldwide distribution.

To my beloved Nikki, 'my friend'.

Author's note

This book is entirely a work of fiction based on South African historical facts, covering the period of The Apartheid Era from 1948. It is written carefully, to inform, inspire and entertain the readers. I am aware that there are people who might have suffered during and after that period of conflict – those who were for the laws and those who were against, who may still be alive; therefore to respect their dignity, I have used the language I believe to be politically correct throughout. In order to protect their privacy, all the names identifying settings, characteristics, dialogue, structure and details, other than those clearly in the public domain are fictitious. The story is reconstructed for this purpose. Any resemblance to real persons, living or dead is purely a coincidence. The moral of this story is that of perseverance.

Acknowledgements

A million thanks to Nicola Quinnen, my daughter, for her love and encouragement when I was writing this book; you've been an asset throughout my life.

To Richard Gibson - for your love, support in every possible way and patience.

I owe gratitude to Mike Willmott of Shrewsbury Words for all his help reading every line of this manuscript.

For her critiques and encouragement, Carole Manship, Editor of GEM Magazine, "thank you".

My editor Autumn Barlow.

Top Hat Books, an imprint of John Hunt Publishing and the whole team that made this book a reality - John Hunt, Catherine Harris, Maria Barry, Mary Flatt, Nick Welch, Stuart Davies, and Trevor Greenfield.

There are other people who played a very important role, helping to research for the content of this book and to get this work to print – thank you Stivie.

Preface

S koonfontein farm, where I live happily with my parents, and cared for by the farmers, is my home. Of course I've faced many challenges there and elsewhere, one after another every so often; who doesn't after all?

The apartheid laws, around which this book are based have taught me valuable lessons as has my interaction with many people; this knowledge supplements my teacher training in South Africa. I learned to be a good citizen, work hard, obey all the laws, and resolve issues through peaceful means and negotiations only.

I write about these experiences and cover each of the 16 laws in every chapter of this book. Before the start of each chapter, I write other people's views about me, and also some extracts from my diary or journal about my thoughts at different times. This is to keep reminding you, the reader, about me, Betty Baker.

I've gotten familiar with the beauty of life and also its challenges, and have chosen to focus on the good reports I've often received from these people. However, when the laws restrict me from having my chosen lifestyle, especially the love of my own choice, education and career, it hurts so much. I escape to other countries. My story covers various experiences, living in three countries, learning new cultures and best of all, enjoying myself.

I've had some happy days while my life journey has been very long and rough; I've chosen to keep my commitment to 'doing things as I am told' by adults – a common catchphrase I often hear daily in my community. I know also that some things do change for better, when adults give good guidance.

When you love the people around you, you become so familiar with their actions, whether good or bad, and get used to their lifestyle. It may seem odd to say I've seen unpleasant situations, too; I've lived in fear, facing uncertainty, and near death situations, and yet I continue to love every one each day. How can I hate these people? Nelson Mandela told the Nation, including me, to reconcile *with them*. This is the message that this book carries forward.

But it certainly wasn't always easy...

Chapter 1

The Wedding

August 1975

Eventually, I arrive at my dream destination. Whispering softly to myself, and shaking my head, I say, "Huh, Betty Baker, is this really you? Has your dream ultimately come true?" Trying to come to terms with the day's programme, I tap my chest with my index finger for assurance. I've reckoned this amazing day would happen, but I haven't known when. However, it's been a long wait. Nevertheless, the most fantastic and overdue day of my life is just about to unfold.

The vintage, cream Daimler decorated with a triad of colours - gold, crimson-red and lily-white ribbons - gradually pulls in front of the weathered church, in Kettlewell, a small village near Skipton, in North Yorkshire. To me, it appears neglected – neither plastered, nor painted: it's just bare stone! In front of the church, the thick mist is swirling around. Within the mist, three doves flap their wings gently, before one descends onto the cracked windowsill.

My flower girl, Polly, page-boy, Dean, the maid of honour, Donna McArthur and four bridesmaids get out of the Daimler to make a guard of honour. Two are standing on the right side behind Dean, and the other two are behind Polly, all facing this magnificent, ancient stone-built village church. I wait in the car contemplating the tall bell-tower, the cross above it, the large archway, and the stained-glass windows, wondering which century it was built in. Suddenly, my thoughts are interrupted, when Donna re-appears, opening the car door on my side to help me out, fulfilling her role as a maid of honour. I manoeuvre my body gently, stepping out of the car, but moving with some difficulty, as Donna lifts up the three-metre long train fastened to my white wedding dress. Fully covering my face with the veil, she then gives me the enormous, pretty bridal bouquet of fresh lilies, red carnations and roses. They complement the gold of the bridesmaids' dresses.

My silver tiara and the veil adorning my head make me feel a bit stiff. However, nothing can upset this day for me. The foggy atmosphere, with a glimpse of sunshine glowing through the clouds, brightens my spirit. I feel the cold breeze though, but I ignore it because of my excitement. With Donna on my right, we walk in between the bridesmaids, positioning ourselves just behind Dean and Polly.

"Betty, smile!" Donna commands, in what I think is an unpleasant tone for a day like this.

"I can't smile, Donna - I'm sorry," I whisper back, gently shrugging my shoulders. I wonder what's disturbing me. I try to laugh, then realise the congregation have been waiting since 9.00 a.m. We're running late. The time is about 9.34 a.m.

Donna notices that as the bride today, I'm not cheerful enough. She mumbles firmly this time, widening her big brown eyes, "Betty, tell me, what's the matter with you?"

I murmur back, "I'm trying to look happier, Donna, but we're so late. I'm feeling embarrassed about what people might be thinking of me. First impressions are very important. They stick in people's minds. I'm so sorry if I am a disappointment to you. Anyway, we've tried our best after the late night of preparations. I hope people won't mind this slight delay."

"Not to worry, Betty - this is your big day. They should wait patiently," Donna says, smiling sweetly in her bright way.

Eventually I smile back, adding a wink. We all walk slowly up to the church porch. Donna discreetly peeps through the door, and signals to Melanie to start playing the bridal-march. The guests stand up, and some face the entrance. Holding onto Donna's arm, we walk gradually down the aisle towards the altar. About halfway, I look further up to the front, catching sight of my fiancé. We both smile at each other.

I look to my left through the veil: the seats are all filled with people of various nationalities, a rich variety of faces and costumes. I lift my head up, and manage a smile; only I know of my personal difficulties. I guess the congregation will accept this gesture as my kind of greeting. With me clinging on to Donna's arm, we take a few steps forward, and stop again. This time I raise my head to my right. The congregation is so multi-racial. A couple are taking turns carrying a baby who looks like me. I stand there stunned, until I feel Donna's grip pulling me forward. Blinking several times, I turn my head, slowly to look forward. We move further up to the altar, passing the front rows; and then Donna and my fiancé exchange positions.

The music stops. The effect of the resulting quietness engulfs me for a moment. My legs feel weak, and my knees wobble a bit. Forcing a smile as my gaze is roving about behind the pulpit helps me control my nerves. Two ministers, Reverend Andrew Fleming and Reverend John Harris are ready to share officiating at our wedding, standing in front of the altar.

The Reverend Fleming, dressed in a white and purple robe, with a big gold cross and tassels hanging from his neck, steps forward. He says in his eloquent, deep, resonant voice, "Good day, friends, and welcome! I was going to say something unkind, but as I can see, in Africa, we celebrate 'African-time'." He refers to our lateness jokingly, but it still causes my mind to sink. "However, in Africa, this fog wouldn't have happened, so we can't blame that beautiful continent. Let's rather say that some things are worth waiting for."

I hear people giggling, and then a roar of laughter from a few. Surprisingly, he knows about 'African time'. I'm too nervous to appreciate this joke. I feel a bemused smile spread across my face.

He makes another joke that amuses the congregation, saying, "So, let us sing our hymn, and it is the only one to sing. Therefore, you'd better sing it heartily. The bridal couple chose it, and we sing all the verses."

I'm a bit confused. Should I join the laughter, or just maintain my dignity, as the focus of the day? I haven't had formal, traditional classes for a marriage ceremony. I laugh at the jokes, smiling frequently.

The music starts, and the congregation stands up and sings, *'Let there be love shared among us'*. As this is my favourite hymn, I sing it passionately, with my eyes shut. It's over quicker than I thought it would be, and I wish we could sing it again. I want to say, "Please, sing from the first verse one more time." However, I catch the sparkling eye of my husband-to-be, and want the next fifteen minutes to hurry.

Reverend Fleming steps forward, wiggles his shoulders, and says the opening words of the *Book of Common Prayer* Office of Holy Matrimony, leading up to the climactic lines:

"The union of husband and wife in heart, body, and mind is intended by God for their mutual joy; for the help and comfort given one another in prosperity and adversity; and, when it is God's will, for the procreation of children, and their nurture in the knowledge and love of the Lord. Therefore marriage is not to be entered into unadvisedly or lightly, but reverently, deliberately, and in accordance with the

purposes for which it was instituted by God. Firstly, it was ordained for the procreation of children, to be brought up in the fear and nurture of the Lord, and to the praise of his holy Name. Secondly, it was ordained for a remedy against sin, and to avoid fornication; that such persons as have not the gift of continency might marry, and keep themselves undefiled members of Christ's body. Thirdly, it was ordained for the mutual society, help, and comfort, that the one ought to have of the other, both in prosperity and adversity, into which holy estate these two persons present come now to be joined. Therefore if any man can shew any just cause, why they may not lawfully be joined together, let him now speak, or else hereafter for ever hold his peace."

There's stillness, before it's interrupted by a small muffled sneeze. This bit disturbs me. I feel unease. As I hold in my breath, clenching my teeth, my tummy rumbles, and then aches. I feel anxious, and the butterflies flare up more violently, as I remember the *Prohibition of Mixed Marriages Act 1949*. This law prohibits the marriage of Europeans to anyone of other races living in South Africa. The groom, knowing the harshness of the regime, from where I had made my escape, reassures me in his soft voice, "You're in England now, my darling. Don't be afraid. You're safe." I sigh gently, releasing the breath I've been holding in.

Reverend Fleming, looking at us, repeats.

"Therefore if any man can shew any just cause, why they may not lawfully be joined together, let him now speak, or else hereafter for ever hold his peace."

He keeps quiet for about a second, giving us the opportunity to respond. He repeats the last bit, adding, *"or else hereafter hold his peace."*

I hear a loud burst of applause from the congregation.

"With this in mind Sir, I ask you to repeat after me," he says. "I do solemnly declare that I know not, of any lawful impediment, why I may not be joined in matrimony to Betty Baker." Reverend Fleming asks me to repeat the same statement.

Clearly, confidently and audibly, looking at my fiancé, I say the words after him. "I do solemnly declare that I know not, of any lawful impediment, why I may not be joined in matrimony to this man."

Then the Reverend Harris bows his head, praying fervently, leading the congregation:

"Almighty God, unto whom all hearts be open, all desires known, and from whom no secrets are hid. Cleanse the thoughts of our hearts by the inspiration of Thy Holy Spirit, that we may perfectly love Thee, and worthily magnify Thy holy Name, through Christ our Lord. Amen."

I add an additional line of prayer, in my mind: *Pardon all those who prevented us from enjoying our marriage-life years ago. Give me the power to forgive them too. Amen.*

I look up at my fiancé, and imagine the thoughts passing behind his hazel eyes. I guess he is thinking about the Apartheid Law that prohibited us marrying while we were in South Africa. I look at him smiling, and wonder if this is a genuine smile.

Sadly, my family isn't here to witness this remarkable day. How could they be present? They have no legal right to leave the country. They don't have a passport. Should they wish to hold a Bantustan passport - a slim booklet with a green cover, permitting free movement within other South African homelands only - they might get it, if they apply based on their ancestors. However, it's invalid for travelling outside the country; therefore, useless for attending my wedding.

My parents had lost their South African Citizenship, as I had done, when the government passed the *Bantu Homeland Citizens Act* in the 1970s. The United Nations declared sanctions against South Africa, because of these apartheid laws. So, European and other African countries have no 'official' relations with her and the homelands. This is sad for a country that was once a British colony. I divert my mind from these unhelpful thoughts.

Today is the one, unique day for me to enjoy the beauty of life. We can both make a commitment to love each other fearlessly, and publicly promise to stay together forever.

Betty, forget South Africa, and move on, I say to myself, trying to encourage myself. No, I can't forget. My eyes water with tears.

It's practically impossible, at the moment. *No, Betty, not today*, I say again, trying to stop my thoughts about the awfulness of my past. I blink rapidly several times, closing my eyes tightly for a few seconds before looking up to the vicar. Today is the day my dreams come true; I suddenly realise just how true this is, and finally smile.

Reverend Fleming speaks loudly from memory with his trembling voice, "One Corinthians, Chapter Thirteen says, *'Love is patient and kind. It is not jealous or boastful. It is not arrogant and rude. It does not insist in its own way; it is not irritable or resentful. Love does not rejoice at wrong, but rejoices in the right. It bears all things, hopes all things and endures all things. Love never ends.'*" I sense a pleasant atmosphere after hearing a burst of applause.

Vividly, I recall the events that led to my fiancé – now my bridegroom – returning to England, prior to his intended time. We take our vows, and Reverend Fleming proceeds:

"Do you take this woman to be your lawful wedded wife, to live together in the estate of marriage? Will you love her, honour and keep her, and forsaking all others, be faithful to her so long as you both shall live?"

"Y-Yes – I will," he replies, stammering, lowering both his shoulders to relieve tension, and looking into my brown eyes, with a wavering smile.

We're both submerged in a vast ocean of an incredible love and deep physical passion that penetrates into our souls. I hear someone in the congregation giggling. He is not supposed to say 'yes' at this point: he's obviously extremely excited.

Reverend Fleming turns to me asking, "Betty Baker, do you take this young man to be your lawful wedded husband? Will you live together in the estate of marriage? Will you love him, honour and keep him, and forsaking all others, be faithful to him so long as you both shall live?"

"I will – Sir," I reply, with respect for a clergyman, gazing into his face, my eyes taking in his strong jaw line and well-formed, straight nose. I've waited and travelled from very far just to be with him. I realise that I'm loud. We exchange the rings, saying, "With this ring I thee wed."

"A very authoritative bridesmaid told me to do something customary in this country. She said that at this juncture I have the prerogative of saying they can kiss each other," says Reverend Andrew.

We finally kiss each other before the congregation for the very first time. Our lips meet. The physical attraction is so powerful, as though the internal fireworks display is a full-on explosion. My knees shake in alarm; I push my husband gently away. I hear applause from the congregation; perhaps we're inconsiderate towards our onlookers. The photographers take countless pictures, with numerous flashes everywhere. What a day! Life is wonderful.

Reverend Fleming is now excited, as he returns to the altar to encourage us, saying,

"For some people, it seems as if marriage is the contract of escapement, and then they start playing with time. No wonder it becomes boring for them. Unless there is growth in a continuing relationship, you can indeed become disenchanted easily. Treading water in any relationship is tedious in the extreme. A bonfire relationship is just the infancy of love, and the beginning of trust. You should say to each other, 'Oh my darling, what a long way we've come! What a journey we're determined to go on; growing and deepening our preciousness and togetherness.'"

"Yes, that's true," says my fiancé, nodding quickly and repeatedly in agreement.

"Shh!" I'm overcome by mixed feelings of joy and tiredness, and just want him to keep quiet.

It seems Reverend Fleming senses that he has no need of 'preaching to the converted'. So, he quickly draws the sermon to an end with a blessing, inviting us to the rectangular table covered in a white tablecloth with a fresh vase of flowers on the right-hand side of the altar, to affirm our commitment by signing the marriage register. The bridesmaids also come along to offer their support.

While my husband signs the register, I look around, my heart bubbling with joy, admiring the rough stones sticking through the walls. To me, it's a beautiful, unusual design.

We both finish signing, and then the witnesses add their signatures, as Melanie continues playing the organ. Issuing the certificate, the Reverend Fleming concludes the ceremony with, "Go forth and multiply."

"What 'multiplication'?" I exclaim, thinking he is referring to having many children. My husband pats my shoulders slightly, saying in his soft tender voice, "Hmm, don't worry, darling."

The procession leaves during the playing of another song. My husband and I come out to jubilation, applause and confetti throw. My new life starts. The ecstatic faces all around are a reflection of my own. We get into our car, and we're driven to a beautiful park for photographs, before heading for the reception at the Golf Club.

Cars are already parked in the car park, behind the building. Some guests and friends are already seated, while others are having drinks in the bar, waiting for us to join them. We wait at the door for the DJ to start playing the music. This time we go into the hall dancing; some people stand up while clapping their hands. Most people are smiling. Perhaps they have never seen such a kind of dance, because it's the South African beat. My husband and I love this rhythm immensely. We've had lots of practice. Sometimes he loses it, but soon he catches up. We dance until we reach our seats. The best man, Frank Warden, delivers his witty, but very sincere, speech.

Finally, he says, "Today has been a wonderful day for everyone here. This is truly an international gathering – not because the groom is European and the bride is African, but there are people from various parts of the world. People from England, Wales, Zimbabwe, South West Africa and other parts of Africa are here." I hear a round of applause, and see the people waving their hands. Frank continues, "We have people from Asia, United States of America, Brazil, Ireland, Poland, Canada, Finland, China, Germany, Japan and Sweden, all coming together."

"Yeah!" Another group shouts, clapping their hands. There is a sense of unity that shows us life's possibilities. And then he proposes the toast.

"So, ladies and gentlemen, let's raise our glasses to the bride and groom!"

All raising their glasses, the guests say in a chorus, "To the bride and the groom!" The crowd, having filled this hall up to the door, start chatting among themselves. I look around, admiring this beautiful gathering. I like what I see – what appears to be a changing world, where humans live together, value each other, and race or origin are not a determinant of anything. That subject is not even mentioned here.

The servers bring in various delicious foods, including the foreign dishes, such as couscous, pizzas, samosas, wraps, rabbit and all sorts. I just can't get over what I see – people from many different races sitting, eating and chatting freely together. We have our first dance of the evening together. Later, other people join us dancing to all kinds of music. We can't stay longer. We soon vanish discreetly to prepare for our two-week honeymoon in Cyprus. Our flight departs from Heathrow Airport at 8.30 a.m. the next day.

To Miss Betty Baker – A small token

Thank you for being Brian's Year 1 teacher. You have been splendid in helping him overcome his writing difficulties in the early days. He has done so well. He enjoys coming to class each day. I thank you for all your help. Brian is achieving a very good standard in his education. Thank you again.

Mr Jasons
A Parent

A message of appreciation handwritten on a card - from Betty's Folders

Chapter 2

At Skoonfontein

November 1960

It's been very hot all morning at Skoonfontein Farm near Burgersdorp. As the afternoon approaches, clouds fill up the sky, darkening the atmosphere. I hear rumbling thunder, and then the lightning strikes. I can smell rain.

My mum had told me to watch out for those thick, dark clouds appearing over the mountains, as this indicates heavy rainfall or storms shortly. "When you see them, abandon what you do Betty, and get closer to shelter. Lightning is dangerous. It kills. You must be careful."

She was the daughter of poor farm labourers, plunged into her miserable marriage to my dad after turning sixteen, wedded without her consent. She had just learned to write her name and surname, something she finds difficult to do these days, resorting to signing her signature with a thumb-print.

The farmers benefited from marriage between labourers living nearby, to retain their skilled labour market. They wouldn't entertain fornication by any means. My mum, blessed with worldly wisdom after finding herself in this awful predicament, crying for months, finally settled down, becoming a devoted wife to my dad. She had no choice.

She never knew she wouldn't return to her own parents' labouring farm that Saturday afternoon after visiting her aunt living on another farm. Ten strong men approached her randomly, grabbing her hands saying, "Come with us." She resisted, struggling to break through. When she refused to walk properly, three men carried her on their shoulders. The other seven sang loudly, clapping hands, hindering her scream from being heard. They arrived at Skoonfontein about four o'clock in the afternoon. Her eyes were blood shot, swollen from crying.

Immediately, my granddad sent a messenger to my mother's parents saying, "Don't search for your daughter, Gladys. We've got her here. She's now our son's wife, Benjamin's." The messenger dropped them a bag of corn, sugar, tea and coffee, offering 'dowry' – the bride price - before vanishing hastily, leaving them in deep dismay.

My mama, quite timid and hunched up in obesity, is careless about her appearance. She gets so occupied with both her and 'Baas' Jimmie's families, that sometimes she forgets my name. The farm-workers use this Afrikaans word, 'Baas' meaning 'Boss' to address all the European male farmers respectfully in situations like this.

She is an ambitious mother for her family, a sensible hard-worker, quite popular among other farm labourers with her humour expressed in a deep low rough voice. Although she is withdrawn, she makes herself available to younger women confiding in her for counsel.

Her appearance improves when she's at work, because she is obliged to wear the clean uniform. This is contrary to when she's home: there, she wears clothing made from the white flour sacks, and my dad's old jumpers.

She likes telling me both fascinating and dreadful stories about my maternal and paternal grandparents. These are mainly about their lives in the olden days. She also touches on those of other natives living near Burgersdorp and Aliwal North farms.

However, her forehead creases slightly as she blinks rapidly to hold her tears; and then, a faint smile vanishes from her face completely. Extreme sadness replaces it as she remembers my paternal grandfather, Mvula Nkomo (meaning Rain Cow), a farm labourer for Baas Jimmie's dad, Walter Douglas.

Walter struggled to call my granddad with his indigenous names. So, he gave him the Caucasian name, Baker; he was often seen carrying his baking pot, baking his own bread. That's how my dad became Benjamin Baker, the names he cherished. This is a common trend in South Africa.

Born and bred in Skoonfontein, my father resembles his dad in every way possible, his six foot height, baldness, short temper, and above all loyalty to his master, Jimmie. His body is well-built like an athlete's. His farm jobs require such a physique. There's a lot of running around, carrying heavy bags of cement or crops, and he is always rushing. Often he is dressed in his filthy, sweat-smelling patched blue overalls and black Wellington boots: my father works night and day.

He has little time for himself and the family, often on stand-by for availability for as long as Baas Jimmie needs him. One can tell this from his cracked, hard dirty hands, eyes clogged with sleep, and scruffy long beard. I sometimes wonder how he managed to have the two of us. My dad is compassionate when unprovoked, and likes to have other children around helping us with these unending farm errands.

Being the youngest in our family, I often wonder why my appearance is different from my parents' and my sister's. They are all brown skinned, yet mine's very light. I'm referred to as 'a goat among the sheep', in addition to other names. My family has black coarse hair, and mine is a bit thin, wavy, long and brown. There's no doubt, I have mixed-race features in me. I have a slim body with brownish eyes and protruding nose, more like a European's.

I could easily be classified as 'a Cape-coloured', an official term for people born from natives and European 'parents'. However, as both my mum and dad are natives, I can't get this identity. How I bear such features is still the mystery to be resolved. Rita, my cousin, joined my family from the age of two. We are often together in whatever we do.

On this day

We're out collecting cattle from the field. It's our turn. We set off earlier due to the day's unpredictable weather. We run all along, competing against each other until we reach the camp.

"The person who reaches the bridge last will marry Brother Bravo," I say, taking the lead. When we reach the place, the next person says the same and names the place. This game, 'Brother Bravo's wife' speeds us up, and I love it. In reality, there is no person called Brother Bravo. He could be a character from a book. We get there without feeling the tiredness that usually follows a long walk.

The grazing fields are quite a distance from home, and it takes some time to gather the cattle. Strangely, today when we get to our field, there are no cattle. The field is ring-fenced, and the gate is properly shut as usual.

We walk around the fence trying to establish how they might have escaped. We come to a gorge. The fence seems to have been deliberately cut. *Who could do this awful thing? And what would be the motive behind it?* I think of many things. However, I couldn't be certain my guesses were right. Baas always says, "Be vigilant – we have enemies around here." At the same time, he never reveals who they are. So, 'our enemies' did it, perhaps.

As we stand there wondering what to do next, the lightning flashes, and the rumbling thunder follows. The rain pours heavily. We walk around, foolishly not knowing what to do. We carry on searching, ignoring the rain for a little while. It gets heavier, making it difficult for me to see the way. The water starts dripping from my clothes. Feeling soaked from head to toe, I struggle, dragging myself, trying to speed up. I brush off the rain from my eyes with my hands, to be able to see the way. Different thoughts cross my mind.

If we return home now, Baas Jimmie Douglas will be extremely annoyed with us. "Where is my herd of cattle, Betty?" he will ask aggressively. He might lash out; I know him. What shall I say to calm him down? He can be a monster, demanding things to be done his way throughout.

Jimmie, with his wife Theodora, and their only son, Mark, own this farm. They inherited it from Jimmie's parents. Jimmie, the giant with big, blue eyes and grey moustache is frightening. He has a distinctly loud, hostile voice, and never laughs with farm labourers. He is short-tempered, and very unpredictable. He maintains his dignity in that scary, intimidating way. He wears clothes according to seasons. Two things that make him special – he hates lazy people, and swears a lot. He never enjoys seeing people sitting down or sleeping, except at night when all the jobs are completed and the animals are asleep. However, I still believe he is a really nice man, generally. Where would I be, should he not have given me and my family a home, made of bricks, instead of just shacks like houses for labourers in other farms?

I imagine the conflict, if we return home without finding the cattle. I can't provoke him. I dislike hearing him swear when he is angry. Though no one ever challenges his behaviour, he shouts non-stop, calling all the bad names he thinks of. He usually leaves me emotionally scarred after a conflict. I have to live with these scars as I cannot erase them.

"Where have the cattle gone, Rita?"

"I don't know," Rita replies, clenching her lips, eyes opening widely, and shrugging her shoulders.

"Huh, we're in great trouble today," I suggest, feeling uneasy, confused and frightened with wobbly knees, shivering from cold.

"No, I don't think so," Rita replies hesitantly, with her eyes gazing about, searching. Our pace slows down for a while, and then gradually improves.

"For goodness' sake, we must find his cattle, Rita. That will cheer him up. We can't get away with it." Feeling heartbroken and dismayed, I shout loudly at the top of my voice:

"Betsy!"

'Betsy.' I merely hear a faint echo.

"Buttercup!" I call as loud as I possibly can.

'Buttercup.' I hear an echo again.

I stand on the riverbank, looking down and across the river, hoping to find clues for missing cattle. My eyes look between the bushes, under the dancing leaves of the willow trees, towards the cliffs, and at the foot of the mountain. I wonder why Baas' cattle can't respond to my voice today, and come to me running. "Stanford, beautiful Stanford, come to me!" I plead, in desperation, with my whimpering voice, and with tears in my eyes.

"Ferdinand! It's time to return home!" I say, running out of words, and getting tired of screaming. My head starts pounding.

There's no sign of the herd of cattle. I always call once or twice before they recognise me, and then come running and bellowing. However, not today – all I can hear is my echo. Suddenly, Rita and I plunge into the dirty deep water swimming across the river. We reach the other side, force our way through the wet thorn trees. We walk across the barns, towards the rocks, expecting to find the herd of cattle.

"Ouch!" I scream, as a thorn pricks my face, tearing my skin deeply diagonally. The blood flows down my left cheek, just below my eye. I wipe it off with the back of my hand, feeling very hurt without imagining the bruise I have. It would have been worse if it had pierced my eyeball.

I lean over the fence, exhausted and confused. My heart throbbing loudly, I fear the worst. "I'm responsible. What will I tell Baas?" I say to Rita, who is also panting from tiredness. "Shall we go home, and continue searching tomorrow?" I'm deeply stressed and confused. It's hard for me to make a firm decision and stick to it, as a similar memory bombards my thoughts.

"No, we can't go home without them. Where will I run to?" I've tried very hard to forget about this terrible incident over the past three years, but it is impossible. It's stuck to my mind. Whenever I think about Baas' reaction when angry, I remember what he did to my friend, Raymond Barton. Then, sadness and fear engulf me. Tears start flowing, and I weep uncontrollably.

On that day, Baas Jimmie waited until we put out our lamps, leaving our house dark. He was certain we were all asleep. However, he was wrong. I wasn't. Lying still, with my head covered with only a small opening left just for my eye to see what he was doing, I watched every move he made.

Trying to be still by breathing gently was difficult. I couldn't continue for any longer. It got better when I opened my mouth. However, the more I tried to suppress my breathing the louder my heart pounded. Could he tell I was awake? Just in case he looked at me, I lay motionless like the dead, giving him no chance to be suspicious. I was like the other children in the room.

My Baas trod carefully in silence, trying to locate Ray, the oldest of us all at that time. This task seemed difficult for him. There were many children sleeping on the hay mattresses on the floor. Someone was snoring loudly. Baas uncovered their heads simultaneously. He stood above Ray's head calling, "Ray! Ray! Get up… now!"

"Hmm?" Ray replied in a slurred tone, clearly still in deep sleep, turning over to face the other side. I felt a chill slip down my spine. Afraid to move, I held my breath. My eyes blurred with tears. To gain visibility, I wiped them off gently with the corner of my blanket that I held tightly onto.

"Bloody hell!…Why are you here when my Daisy isn't? You're happy to enjoy your sleep, at my loss? No boy, you can't, get up!"

There was silence for a moment. Ray delayed, probably still recollecting his mind from the deep sleep. And then he tried explaining, "I'm sorry, my Baas. I went all over, searching…" Before he finished his sentence, Baas Jimmie interrupted him, completely ignoring his lengthy explanation.

"Shut up, lazy boy… ignorant boy! " shouted Baas Jimmie.

Ray, complying with the order, kept quiet for a while, and sat up, holding on to the blanket.

"I'm sorry, Baas!" he bleated eventually, staring at Baas Jimmie, caught up in a trap. Baas uncovered his blankets, leaving him naked.

Poor Ray had no clothes on, but I couldn't tell at first, as it was usual for all of us children to sleep half-naked or naked. I heard the whip-sound as he whacked him - one lash - two lashes - and three lashes, all on his bare body. He resisted for a while. It must have been difficult to endure such pain.

"Aaargh, my Baas!" Ray finally screamed in agony, staring at him motionlessly, with his tearful eyes.

"Silly boy!"

Baas Jimmie yelled, waking my parents and other children up. His loud noise disturbed the whole house. My parents put their lamp on, illuminating the living room brighter than his bouncing flimsy torch-light. I saw them standing by their bedroom door, my mum hiding slightly behind my dad, with nothing to say or do. They couldn't dare to challenge Baas Jimmie, not even in their 'own' home. They were just helpless poor labourers, in need of a roof over their heads, and food to feed us and themselves.

Ray couldn't take it anymore. He leaped out of the door like the football goalkeeper diving to intercept a score. My heart sank. Trying to hold tears and control my breath was difficult for me.

"Hey, Ray! Get back here!" Baas Jimmie screamed, attempting to catch him. Fortunately, he missed him, but dropped his torch, instead. He delayed picking it up; and then a chase started. This time he was extremely angry, hissing like a snake. He left our house, slamming the door behind so loudly.

My parents stood there for a while before returning to their bedroom. My soft-hearted mum wiped her eyes, and blew her nose with her flannelette nightdress sleeve every so often. I knew she was crying. My heart, filled with sadness, really ached. I couldn't tolerate seeing my mum cry. Under my blankets, hopeless, I felt angry and frustrated with what I witnessed. My eyes filled up with tears. I wiped them off, this time with the hem of my blanket. Soon, it became wet also, and I pulled another dry corner of my blanket to wipe my cheeks. I sobbed quietly. The pain I felt was so unbearable. However, when my tears stopped flowing, I pretended to be asleep.

Firstly, I heard the running footsteps outside - a chase was on… and then they disappeared in silence. I was trembling under my blankets, wondering what Baas would do to all of us on his return. With my eyes soaked in tears again, my hands sweating and my body shivering, I heard my heartbeat pumping louder than usual. I felt pity for Ray, and disgusted with Baas Jimmie. However, I preferred him compared to his son, Mark Douglas - the 'small Baas,' who would never say a word to me. I found his presence intimidating. He would stare, making me feel uncomfortable.

My parents returned to the dining room whispering between themselves. I could hear the sound of my dad's deep voice, though. They stood there probably confused and feared for their lives. My mum's right hand moved across her face every so often. I guessed she couldn't stop crying. I sat up saying, "It's all right, Mama." I got up, stood by her side, whispering and comforting her from the distress she displayed. "We'll be a successful family one day."

"Shh, Betty," my mum mumbled, with eyes opened wide, tapping her index finger on her lips.

"Mama, I hate this," I said softly trying to sound persuasive. "It's unfair."

I know how she felt about Ray. She has always cared about people generally, especially the orphans. The hurt she portrayed in her voice and appearance broke my heart. My parents returned to their bedroom talking softly to each other. I went back to my mattress to lie down. Our house was dark again. Without realising, I fell asleep.

The first thing I did the following morning was to look around for Ray's clothes. His brown pair of trousers was lying by the door. The white t-shirt he wore that afternoon was on his pillow. It seemed he tried to grab some of his clothes, but he couldn't manage it before escaping. He was under too much pressure.

I looked on the floor, and noticed some dry bloodstains. I followed this blood-trail outside, and behind our house. The grass was long. I couldn't guess which way he escaped. I thought he could go for ever, and never return. These thoughts triggered the pain I felt when I heard him cry. I returned home, weeping, but hoping to hear Ray knocking at the door, calling my name.

This didn't happen. The next few days passed, and still no Ray. Three more days went by without Ray at home. My hope faded after six months. Years went by. Sadly I never saw him again. This incident has stayed with me. Where did Ray go? What happened to him? This was the memory that haunts me now, as we search for the missing cattle.

"Rita, I am not returning to our house tonight. I know Baas Jimmie will be mad."

"Wait, Betty, I have a plan."

"What is it, Rita?" I ask, hopelessly dragging my feet due to tiredness.

"Betty?"

"Huh?"

"Could you listen to me carefully, please?"

"I'm getting soaked, Rita. Come on, what's the matter?" I murmur, feeling irritated and slowing down.

"Let's go back that way!" Rita says, pointing with her wet index finger.

"Yeah, we could jump over that fence. And go through those bushes to avoid using the usual route home. In case someone is there to get us," I suggest.

"Yes," agrees Rita.

"We could stay in the bushes behind the dairy, until all lights go off and everybody is fast asleep. And then, we could walk quietly behind the shop to the stables. The young mare, pony, and donkey should be asleep. Also Ringo's stable may be empty, and that would give us good shelter until tomorrow. We'll see Janice on her way to school, and we'll follow her as usual."

"Where shall we wash and get clean clothes from?" Rita asks me, compliantly.

"We should be all right with what we've got on – no one will notice dirt," I reply.

"If they do, we can make up a story for them to believe. Everybody knows kids love messing about in the sand, and they do get filthy."

"We might be able to wash our faces from the duck-pond," I suggest.

"We should be fine," agrees Rita.

Oh my Lord, I have another long walk to school: out of the stables to the duck-pond, past the old cow-folds on Mr Grey's farm. I go down the river, up to the footpath, and through the tall grass of the meadow – keeping a good distance away from Janice, my older sister, because she will send us back home. I don't want that.

Dad might be pleased to know that we got ourselves to school and may forgive us for not finding Baas' cattle. He loves children who go to school after all, 'after organising Baas Jimmie's stock, though.'

We follow our proposed route, and reach the stables safely. We make our beds on the floor using every filthy smelly rag we could find. We both cuddle to keep warm. I turn around, trying to sleep. I feel the cold, early-morning breeze. Horses' blankets aren't meant to warm humans. They have a rough texture, just good enough to stop the draught.

I wake up. I must have been asleep just for a short time. My feet are freezing. I try warming them up by rubbing them with my hands; this doesn't last. Therefore, I soon give in, and start sobbing uncontrollably, with tears running down my cheeks. I control my chattering teeth with difficulty. My nose gets blocked – I unblock it, carefully avoiding disturbing Rita. She is better off asleep.

With my mind filled with hurtful thoughts, I ask myself several questions: *What are we doing here? What is it about this farm-life? Why are my parents so attached to it? Do they really like this kind of life? How did my grandfather get to Skoonfontein? Why don't we live in towns or cities? Does my dad like driving the cattle to the fields every day? Does he like milking the cows, ploughing, planting corn, hoeing, delivering milk and cream to dairies in Ladysmith?*

I'm tired of cleaning the dog-kennels with choking, gagging filth all over them. I hate watering the pigeon-loft, feeding the pigs in the sty and chickens in their shed, collecting the eggs from the hens, watching peacocks and turkeys walking around all day. Why spend my time learning about farm-life, if I can never own one?

No, I'm sick and tired of this situation, I say to myself.

I don't want any more lingering about the farm, going from barn to barn, loading hay for horses on a wheelbarrow, watching ducklings and ducks swim in their pond all day, and mama mixing flour with yeast, salt, and water, kneading the dough and leaving it to rise before baking homemade bread from the Missus's coal stove hot oven for them. I've had enough of Baas Jimmie screaming, at my family. This is disgusting!

What good will these do for me? As I ask myself these questions, I hurt more, and feel internally bruised – not surprising for a ten-year-old farm-girl.

I close my eyes, hoping to sleep again. I just can't. I turn around to check on Rita. She's fast asleep, snoring. The floor without a mattress and a saddle under my neck is hard. This keeps me awake for a little while.

I hear a cough from the stables behind the wall. *Could this be a man?* My heart beats faster, and it hurts. *No, it can't be* – not at this time, in the stables; *who could this be?* I dismiss my thoughts. I hear a shuffle and a cry from a deep voice appearing to be that of a man in trouble. *Who could be around here at this time?* I wonder. Now wide awake, I look across at the stars. Their light comes through the gap above the door, brightening the stable we're in. Rita rolls over, at the same time as the man sneezes. This might have disturbed her from her sleep.

She opens her eyes and sits up.

"Rita!" I whisper, filled with fear.

"Yeah!"

"I think there's a man in the stable next to us. He seems to be in trouble. He is crying – listen!"

"What, Betty?" Rita stares at me , yawning, and then realises we could be in trouble again.

"Shush!" I'm worried that this person might hear us and come over, so I ask her to listen carefully again. I'm too tired to tiptoe or go on the hay bales to peep. My heart aches, and I lack the courage to do this. Ignoring this disturbance, I whisper to Rita: "Do you know why we're living here?" She doesn't respond. I continue speaking.

"Why don't we move to townships in Queenstown, Somerset

East, Worcester, Beaufort West and even Newcastle? Dad could get work in the diamond mines around Johannesburg. Life might be a lot better there."

The man coughs, and then sneezes again. He murmurs for a long time. I listen, hoping to hear what he says. The man starts crying again, saying, "I'm starving; I have no one to help me. It's hard to be an orphan. Why did my mum die? Why did my dad leave me - only to suffer?" The cry of this man at this time disturbs me. I wonder who could this be, and why is he here? Men don't cry. I heard this saying many times.

Rita interrupts my thoughts, saying, "No, moving into townships is impossible. We have laws here. Your dad explained it all. We can't just live where we like."

"What?" I ask, sternly surprised with what I hear.

"We must obey the *Natives Land Law* of 1913, just two years before your dad was born. And the *Natives Urban Areas Law* that got through Parliament in 1923 is still active. It's illegal for us to buy land from the Europeans, and also to live among them. Where would we get the money from to relocate, anyway? You know we are very poor. We shall need Baas and Missus to keep us here on their farm, and provide for our needs," Rita spouts these facts in such an authoritative way, as if she is an agent.

"Ah, you talk like the government now so you can join them if you like. So, where should we live then?" I ask, turning around to sit on my bottom.

"We have certain areas reserved for the natives. By law, we should only live there, or be stuck here," Rita replies. "We can't do much about it. It's the law. We must obey the laws. If we don't, we go to prison. Your dad says this so often."

I put my head down, feeling powerless, and weep bitterly.

"Laws...what are they for?"

"Ha-ha, they are there to favour and protect certain people," Rita laughs grimly.

"Err, Rita?"

"Yeah."

"I now know what I want in my life."

"What is it?"

"I want to be clever. I'd like to be a teacher, like 'Mistress' at our school, and help people."

"You are joking. How will you do that? You need a lot of help yourself. Stop wasting your time."

"But for now, I'd prefer to be like Alvin, Edna and Harris."

"Why would you like to be like others, Betty?"

"They have a better life than me. Jonny, their older brother works in Johannesburg. He sends them nice clothes and shoes. They wear them to school; and they look bright and happy. After school, they go home and kick their balls - real balls. They don't wrap around old rags and stockings, and pretend it's a ball, like us, and they have no sheep and goats to worry about, or their mummy telling them to feed their boss' chickens. I want to be..."

Suddenly, I hear the cockerel's crow. So, it's early morning, and very soon my mum will wake up to prepare morning coffee for Baas and Missus, and lay breakfast in the dining room for the whole family after that. Samson and Howard will be getting the tractors ready for ploughing. What will Dad do? Will he go look for the missing herd of cattle, or us?

Some months later

I like going to school: it's fun, and enjoyable. I love reading and writing. My school is close to my home – about four miles. It's a good walking distance on sunny days. I cope fairly well with it but it's not like there is any other choice. Perhaps, authorities aim to make farm schools accessible to as many children of farm labourers as possible. I'm used to walking sometimes bare foot for hours. The only problem is that some days I get to school late, and this is not fun.

Mr Parker punishes all the latecomers by the gate. We have to run several times as fast as we can around the field, until he is satisfied that we have learnt the 'punctuality lesson'. I feel sad, though, when he chases the slower children, flogging them with his rubber-whip, like Baas Jimmie's. I hear the screams of agony behind me, and know that Mr Parker is close by.

"Mama, I must be in school early. I'd like to be there when the bell rings." Although it's a loud buzzing sound that makes me jump.

"Get up earlier, then. Hurry up, and leave at sunrise."

"No, that's too early!"

"You want to be in school, when the bell goes, isn't it? That's the best way of doing that. Go to bed now."

As I walk away towards my bedroom, I hear Mummy calling my name. "Betty, is your homework done?"

"Yes, Mum, I've done it. It was easy. It didn't take me long."

"Go to sleep then. Good night!" Mum commands before disappearing into her bedroom. She soon returns and asks another question. "Is your uniform ready? There's no time to do much in the morning."

"Yes, Mum," I reply, yawning from tiredness.

Knowing my mum, she will only move away when she is sure that I've done it. She always says that urgent things must come first and then the rest can follow. I'm working hard to get this right.

"Don't worry, Mum. Teachers won't check uniforms. We're busy practising for our physical education competition and English orals," I say, hoping to get rid of her quickly.

"Betty, do your best," says Mum, walking away.

"I will, don't worry, Mum."

I lie on my bed and find it difficult to sleep as I think about what I must do to be selected for the Orals. Only the top three children in our class will do English oral examinations externally. This ensures Mr Parker's teaching practice is moderated. I've done very well this year and I should get in. English is my favourite subject after all. I'm good at reciting all the poems but I must stick with Julius Caesar.

The following morning I get up early to prepare for school. I walk all the way alone today. As I enter the school-gate, the bell rings for the start of the lessons. I run quickly to my classroom and sit down. It's registration time.

"Good morning, Dennis," says Mr Parker, lowering his chin, opening his eyes widely to look above his brown-framed glasses which rest on his nose. Dennis gets up, replying promptly, "Good morning, Mr Parker."

Mr Parker calls Harold, Dorothy, Paul and then, "Good morning, Betty Baker." I shake my body, pretending to be getting up. "Present, Mr Parker," I reply with attitude, hoping to amuse the class. I regret my actions.

Most children start laughing loudly. Worried, I look around and notice that some children are quiet after all. They didn't get my joke, perhaps. Mr Parker puts down his glasses on the table staring at me. "What's amusing?" he asks in his loud croaky voice. The class responds with silence, and then starts to murmur loudly. I sense trouble. Everybody knows Mr Parker's immediate reaction when upset. So, I get up as I should have done and look down, feeling ashamed. Mr Parker bangs his hand on the table, screaming, "Silence!" Suddenly, everybody in class goes quiet.

"Tell us your story, Anne Barnsley. What's amusing?" This time Mr Parker is holding up his glasses, nibbling on them.

Anne shouts loudly, "The names, Barker and Parker rhyme, Sir."

"Yes, Anne, that's correct."

Our teacher appears disappointed, after realising that Anne isn't silly after all. She remembers the rhyming-word lesson we had yesterday.

We start the English lesson straight after registration. I hear my name and realise I've been called to recite. I get up and stand far from my desk, allowing myself enough space to move around and act. I know my recitation by heart, so I recite from memory:

Friends, Romans, countrymen, lend me your ears!

I've come to bury Caesar, not to praise him.

The evil that men do lives after them…

I recite all the verses, changing the tone and pace of my voice, as I say the last two lines:

My heart is in the coffin there with Caesar, until it comes back to me.

I end with a sad expression on my face for the loss of Caesar. My classmates clap their hands. Mr Parker gets up, nodding and saying, "That's good!" However, I don't need anybody to tell me it was excellent; I'm already convinced it's great.

Mr Parker says, "Very good" again. He sends me to a Standard Five class with over forty children to show them how to recite a poem. I leave our class, smiling, and knock at the door. The Standard Five class teacher welcomes me in.

"Yes, Betty Baker, what can I do for you?"

"Mr Parker has sent me here to recite my poem, if that's all right with you, Sir?"

"Okay, you go ahead," he says. "Could you all stop what you're doing, and listen?" This time, as I'm unfamiliar with any of the children, I recite the verse even better. Again, I receive a big round of applause. I leave the class, feeling good about myself. I return to my seat, and Mr Parker cannot control himself: he bounces joyfully. He sends me to the Standard Six classroom to show me off yet again. I go and do even better than before. Today, I've received attention for my hard work. I return to the class, and thank my teacher.

"It's my pleasure," he says, grinning. As I turn around to sit down, he calls me back. "Betty, come and see me before going home today." I'm not frightened this time. Surely, he should have good news for me. So I do as I'm told. He gives me a letter for my Dad in a blue sealed envelope.

"Make sure your dad gets this letter today - or else..." he says.

"Yes, Sir," I nod, receiving it with a smile on my face.

I know I know very well what he would do if I disobeyed him.

Believing I'm carrying good news to my parents, I take the letter and run away. I try to catch up with my school mates, who come from the farm on the other side of Baas Jimmie's.

I run down the hill, cross the river, pass the church, cross the stream and catch up with them. We walk together past the tennis courts, and around the foot of the mountain. All the way home, my heart is filled with joy, but I keep it to myself. My mind is in an unusual state – I don't often feel like this. This is not a state of mind I often experience.

"Teacher's pet!" John teases me.

I don't react badly to this. Instead, I respond with a cool smile. I reach my home, and wave good-bye to them as they continue with their journey.

I go straight into my bedroom, and change into my home-clothes. Then I go to the kitchen to look for food. My Mum asks me to serve myself and as I finish eating my food, my Dad arrives back from the farm. I can't wait to give him a cup of tea, his meal and the letter. I know he wouldn't welcome any news from me, until after he's eaten.

Finally, he opens his letter, and reads it aloud. It says:

Dear Mr Baker,

It's my pleasure to inform you that Betty has been selected to represent our school at the English Oral Competitions in town. I'll go with her next Friday; please make sure she gets to school by 7 o'clock. She should wear the full school uniform and have her packed lunch. We shall walk from school at 7.30 am and should be back by 5.30 pm.
Yours faithfully,

Mr O. Parker

"Well done, Betty, keep up the good work!" Dad says. That's the only reward I get from him, yet it means so much to me. I can't ask for more: a hug, a kiss on my cheek, a seaside holiday, 'Well Done!' stickers, or certificates of achievement. However, I should motivate myself because it's about my future. I could give myself a pat on the back if I like. I smile.

"It seems a thorn is stuck, piercing deeply into the sole of my foot. When it is untouched, I'm okay. I can limp around, getting on with daily activities, just like other people do. I force a smile, as nothing amuses me. When something touches my foot with the thorn, accidentally or on purpose, it bleeds and I feel intensive pain from within, leading me to cry. Around the pierced part of my foot, my flesh has grown almost covering the thorn. Therefore, I can tolerate the hurt, and I'm accustomed to it. However, beneath I have a deep oozing wound."

from Betty's Diary, 5th December, 1973

Chapter 3

Ups and Downs

February 1961

It's 10.00 pm. I'm in bed reading my favourite comic 'SHE', struggling to see the words in the dim light from the tiny paraffin lamp, made from a baby-food tin and a wick. I've been reading the series of this comic about a woman's self-defence tactics. I find her powers and high kick absolutely fascinating. I feel drained. My eyes are red, nodding every so often, but I'm determined to read it until the end.

"Betty, why's your lamp still on at this time?" Mum asks me kindly, pushing the door, and walking into my bedroom. "Aren't you going to school tomorrow?"

I stop reading, thinking about what to say. Then I reply, "I'm going, Mum - you know that I like school."

My mum, humming her favourite tune, opens the drawer of the chest, looking for something. She takes out a towel, turns around, and blows out the lamp. It gets pitch dark instantly.

"Good night, Betty," she says, leaving my room, and then shutting the door behind her.

"Good night, Mummy," I say, closing my eyes, hoping to sleep.

I stay awake for a little while, thinking deeply about the comic. I wish to be like this woman, and kick everyone who hurts me. I think about my first target, imagining myself releasing my high kick on his chest. Due to his height, I'd have to approach from a distance, skip and then deliver my kick that would undoubtedly bring him down. Hopefully, he'd respect people.

Suddenly, my heart leaps with joy as I remember tomorrow's school timetable: I'm ready for the History test. I know the dates we'll be tested on - the arrival of Jan Van Riebeeck at the Cape in 1652, the second Anglo-Boer War 1899 until 1902, and so on. The afternoon is cool, with Mistress Marlene Overton's needlework lesson. She's fine. Without realising, I fall into a deep sleep.

The next morning, I jump out of bed to make the morning tea for my parents in the kitchen. I like them to have it before my mum goes to work in the Big House, so that she has no desire to have theirs. That's what I do when Rita's gone back to the boarding school.

When the kettle boils, I fill the washing basin with warm water to wipe myself with the flannel before putting on cream and combing my hair. It's easy to comb it because it's soft. This is the requirement for boys and girls in our school. I prepare myself breakfast – bread and tea, and then walk quickly to school.

I enjoy all the morning lessons. The bell rings for lunchtime. My friend, Marcia Bush, has brought a bag full of fried dumplings. I help her sell them, and we both eat the leftovers.

The bell rings - it's the start of the afternoon session. I wash my hands thoroughly and quickly before rushing into our needlework room. Mistress Overton is already waiting in front of the classroom.

"C'mon girls. We've got a lot to cover today!" she commands.

I join the queue from the end. All the girls are holding their hands up high, ready to show the teacher that they are clean, as we walk inside. She always sends back anyone whose hands are dirty.

I'm surprised. We aren't told off today, for anything. Usually, she has a go at us, for getting there late, or for whatever reason she finds at that time. We all sit down quietly, waiting for further instructions.

"Could the monitors give out sewing please?" Mistress Overton asks.

Both Loretta and Constance get up, go to the sewing cupboard and give out our bags. They then sit down. Miss Overton introduces the lesson.

"Today you are going to learn about 'gathering'. Gathering is different from making pleats," she says, holding her demonstration bag up. "Start with backstitches." She demonstrates on her bag, but I'm too far away to see what she's doing. I'm sitting at the end of the second row of desks. I can't dare to mention this, because she would scream at me. I'm certainly very frightened of her. It's difficult to know what her next move will be. She laughs for one minute and the next minute she stares at you, and shouts. Mistress continues:

"When you have sewn through to the end, come to show me," she commands.

I pick up my bag, sew the first stitch, and then I remember to backstitch. So, I carefully go over the same stitch once again, before sewing through to the end. I follow her instructions precisely. Mistress will be pleased with my work, I think, as I get out of my seat to show her. I join the long queue from the back, as usual.

My turn comes, and I give her my bag, with a gentle smile of satisfaction. She picks it up, looks at it, and then pulls the thread from the end to make gathers. Sadly, the whole thread comes off. She never says a word. She just slaps me very hard on my left cheek, and throws the bag in my face.

My cheek feels very hot. I see the bright flickering lights, as I stagger about a bit, finding it difficult to see. I stand still, confused, while Miss attends to Constance and other girls. I'm very good at controlling my anger. I manage this well this time around.

After a little while, I pick up my bag to return to my seat. My eyes are flooded with tears. I try to hold them back, but fail. I lower my head, weeping silently, wiping off my salty tears with my palms. I do this quietly to avoid provoking my teacher to anger. She'd go berserk if I cry aloud. Sitting down, I wish I was dead. However, I pretend to be fine, hiding my broken heart.

I'm thinking, *Mistress this is your entire fault. You didn't explain the purpose of backstitch, and what would happen if we didn't do it securely. Should you have told us, surely I would have done it properly.* I wish to explain, but I can't. Children aren't allowed to prove adults wrong, especially their teachers. I stare at her. The sorrow is unbearable within me.

The bell rings for home-time. I hand in my bag to Connie and walk towards the door. Before stepping out of the door, I turn and stare at Miss, who seems to be ignoring me. I return to my classroom to grab my school bag, and walk all the way home, alone. I am not keen on catch-up with other children, as we usually do. I greet my dad by the gate of the Big House, "Hello, Dad." I walk past without saying much. My dad likes talking to me, finding out the day's news.

"Have you got any good news today, Betty?" he asks me, hesitantly.

"No, there's none today, Dad," I reply, walking away quickly.

"What has been good today?" he insists.

I reply, "I'm sorry, Dad, I can't say much about school. You know that I like school, generally."

"So, what happened actually? I need to know Betty."

"I'll tell you later, Dad. I want a good future when I'm old. I have to put up with this kind of school life. I can't stop going to school. If I do, I'll miss out on education. That will be bad for me, because I'll have to do hard labour for the South African Europeans. This is the worst thing I could ever do." My voice fades, slowly whispering the last words in the sentence. My dad senses something has gone terribly wrong with me.

I turn back, and run to my dad, screaming loudly, "Daddy!" and throwing myself into his arms. Tears mixed with mucus dribble down my chin. I bury my face under my hands, closing my eyes tightly as I take a deep breath, controlling myself.

"It's all right, Betty. Please don't cry. This hurts me," my dad says, hugging me. This works. I stop crying, and cling to him, knowing very well that he's unable to protect me, for now.

In October, the same year

We are in our History class revising question papers, preparing for end-of-year external examinations. I am sitting on the front row, my usual place in this class, to avoid my teacher. He asks the children sitting at the back too many questions, perhaps to encourage their participation. I'm happier when he leaves me alone, and takes no notice when I'm not paying attention.

Feeling proud of himself, he usually says, "In the future, you will remember me for helping you define your careers." He enjoys parading in front of the class. Mister Lyndon, a tall man with a hunch-back, bald with a long scruffy greyish beard, smells of some kind of odour from the tobacco he smokes through his pipe. He is unpopular with most of the children.

Slowly, he makes a few steps towards a wide-opened window; a cold breeze comes through. Grinning slightly, his forehead crinkles. He raises his eyebrows, creasing it more. He does this, when he is very upset.

I take a deep breath, suppressing the fear in me. I have no reason to be afraid. I stare at him striding from around the window to the door of the classroom. Suddenly, he turns around. "Who made that noise?" he asks aggressively, in his deep voice.

Most children ignore him; others laugh loudly, provoking him further. Vincent Hunter even bangs both hands on his desk, until he wobbles in the aisle with his eyes full of tears from laughing.

"Children, tell me, who caused this bad smell?" he asks again.

The class is chaotic, with everyone in denial. All I could hear is:

"It's not me! It's not me!"

"Why look at me like that?"

"Don't you dare to try to accuse me!"

Some children have their hands on their noses, and others are waving their books in front of their faces, trying to keep the smell away from them.

"Someone with bad manners did this," Mr Lyndon says, looking threateningly at Patricia sitting next to me.

"No, Sir, it's not me!" exclaims Patricia Paddington in her high-pitched voice.

"You are going to tell me who it is," Mr Lyndon commands, looking at his stumpy stick, moving his hand around, feeling and bending it. Shuddering from a wave of fear, I put both my hands on the desk, and then on my lap, feeling uncomfortable. His heavy breathing along with his ugly appearance is unbearable.

"Are you going to tell me the truth?" Sadly, no one responds.

"You have no right to interfere with my work," he insists in his efforts to find the culprit. He makes his last dramatic move, and then turns around sharply before reaching the door.

"Right, I know what to do," he says, walking towards the first desk of the front row, rolling up his sleeves. "Okay, children you have a choice – to tell me the truth, or remain silent about this for ever."

As he is about to hit Terence Rook, sitting at the start of the first row, and continue beating everyone else, his usual practice, someone shouts from the back, "Sir, it's Betty Baker!" My God! I turn around to see who calls my name, but I can't tell or recognise her voice either. Everybody appears cool and innocent.

"No, teacher, it's not me!" I plead. It's too late.

Shivering, I watch teacher Lyndon's next move through the corner of my eyes, my stomach lurching violently. I feel virtually defenceless. Already in tears, I see no escape in continuing defending myself. It's useless anyway. He doesn't listen to children. He walks towards me in silence. His eyes are opened wide as saucers. My anticipation of his next action is right.

He whacks me repeatedly on my shoulders with his knobbly stick. I respond by looking at him in silence. I feel a rain of lashes from this stick on my chest, head and face. With my eyes in floods of tears, I get up. By this time, he is hitting me everywhere throughout my body. I can't cry. I try to shield my eyes and head with my hands, as my teacher repeatedly hits me. I hope he is going to stop, but he doesn't. I move backwards towards the door. I can hear a roar of laughter from my classmates.

He continues beating me until I am outside the classroom.

"Silly girl!" he says, shutting the door with full force behind him, leaving me outside like a dog in an African village. I stand with my back by the wall for a while. When my eyes start watering, I stare deeply holding my tears until they flow, first gradually. I then let go, just like some babies do, constantly wiping off my tears with my white shirt's sleeves. As my legs start aching, I sit down on my bottom.

Engaged in deep thoughts, I fail to understand the reasons for the suffering of an innocent child like me. I know children aren't allowed to let out wind – it's bad manners – my teachers told me that. When adults do it, children aren't allowed to laugh – it's horrible, and I know this too. I always play by the rules, although I don't sometimes agree with them.

I wouldn't do it. And even today, I, Betty Baker, confirm I didn't do it. I defend my innocence. Through this experience, I learned that the innocent children could suffer in a similar way as bad boys do.

Teacher Lyndon has failed to conduct his investigation properly before causing me such pain. What shall I do? I look at my arms, with visible stripes. Anyone can see where the stick has hit. I have cuts and bruises, and I'm bleeding. I bury my face under my hands, crying again. I have no clue what my face looks like.

The bell rings - it's time to go home. Frightened of what teacher Lyndon might do when he appears through the door, I remain outside until the last child has left the classroom. My teacher re-appears from the door, staring at me. He walks past me, and then turns around, shaking his index finger, pointing and shouting, "Never again, Betty Baker, do you understand me, you silly girl?" I don't reply, but look at him with my swollen eyes full of pain and sorrow. He walks on slowly, until he eventually disappears around the next building. I see him no more.

I return to my classroom, put my books in my bookcase and rush out. *Am I coming back here tomorrow?* Several thoughts cross my mind. I remember that I dearly want education, so I must be prepared to get it at whatever cost. *What kind of education am I getting?* I ask myself this question, knowing very well: it's the education that the natives get, that is inferior to the education of the Coloureds and Europeans in South Africa.

The school is quiet, as most children have gone home. I walk slowly towards the school gate, down the hill and across the river. I jump over the stream, and I keep going my usual way, but not to catch up with my schoolmates today. I reach home and go straight to the kitchen to meet my mum.

"Hello, Mum," I say, sitting down on the chair.

"Hello, Betty. You took longer to get back today. Is everything all ri…?"

Before she finishes the sentence, I burst out into a loud cry, like a pig going for slaughter – a bitter cry.

"What happened?" says my mum, looking at me shocked. "Betty?"

I keep quiet, and continue crying. "Who attacked you? Did you get involved in a fight? Who could do this – beat you up like this? I can only help if you tell me. Oh my God! Betty!" my mum cries bitterly, covering her eyes that are filled with sadness. She can hardly look at my face. She drags her feet about the kitchen, wandering aimlessly. I look at her face, imagining her inner pain.

"Betty, did you get involved in a fight? Betty, tell me, please?"

After a while, I stop crying. The silence is remarkable: Mum is just looking at me, waiting for my answer.

"It's my teacher, Mr Lyndon – he beat me, Mum," I say, wiping off tears and mucus, coughing and blowing my nose.

"What did you do to him?"

"Someone accused me of flatulence."

"Did you do it?"

"No, Mama – I'd never do that in public."

"Tell me the truth, Betty."

"Mum, I didn't do it. Believe me, God knows this."

Looking at my mum, I could guess her feelings. I'm her daughter and in pain. She is hurt. I can sense her internal cry. However, what can she do? There is absolutely nothing, unfortunately.

The teachers have authority to do as they like, in the name of 'educational interest', to see their children succeed. Mum tries to wipe off the dry blood from my wounds, and gives me tablets to stop the pain. She serves me dinner, and then sends me to bed.

"You can't go back to school until you look and feel better," she says, watching me walking slowly towards my bedroom door. She follows me into my bedroom, helping me to change into my pyjamas. She assists me into bed, tucking me in. She kisses me goodnight on my forehead, and closes the door behind her.

I don't mind being away from school this time, because I have my textbooks in my suitcase to study at home. Whether my parents contacted the principal or not, I'll never know.

My parents are concerned about my future, so they will encourage me to return to school, when I feel better. In spite of the handful of brutal teachers at school, I still miss my friends and I look forward to being with them again.

Two days later

I get up to look for a book from the bookshelf. Missus gives us old books when she's clearing up their study room. So, we have many books. I choose a fiction book, and then return to bed, and start reading it for pleasure.

It gets darker. I get out of bed again, searching for the matches to light the lamp. I realise that it has run out of paraffin. So, I light a candle instead.

We always keep some candles for emergency, like tonight. The candlelight, although it is also not bright enough for reading, will have to do for now. I check it's fixed properly in the candlestick, and leave it on the old dresser, that we got from Missus. I really like her: she gives us many things. So, the light shines from behind, as I lie down on my back, reading.

I feel tired, and drift into a deep sleep.

I wake up hearing my mum's hysterical yelling as she uncovers my blankets.

"Betty, wake up! Wake up! Fire!"

When I open my eyes, I see flames spreading rapidly all over me. With my heart beating faster, I jump out of bed, screaming. The room is dark, and full of thick smoke. My face and body feels very hot. Inhaling the smoke through the nose is difficult and my throat has a kind of burning sensation as my rasping breath is loud in my ears. I'm suffocating, struggling to breathe, as my pyjamas are on fire. My mum pours a bucket of water on me. The flames disappear. She pushes me out to the living room while my dad is doing all he can, extinguishing the remaining flames. After a long battle with the fire, everything goes quiet. The clothes on the dresser have burned to ashes. I am lucky not to have died in this fire – what a narrow escape!

There are no fire-fighters to call on for help around Skoonfontein. The nearest Fire Brigade station is in Burgersdorp, quite a distance away. Our house is also very far from the Big House, so we can't even tell Baas Jimmie and Missus. It's better that way, though, because their concern is bound to be for their property. I may have got my parents into terrible trouble, inviting brutal beatings from Baas perhaps.

My dad hates it when Baas hits him, and treats him like a child. He's already told my mum, if this happens again, we'll have to move out. What happens if they fail to extinguish that fire? I may have burned down Baas' servants' quarters, and I myself too.

The burnt bedding is a constant reminder of that disastrous night. My parents didn't beat me up, just because the accident happened while I was reading a book, something they are fond of. "Education is your only inheritance, Betty," Mum always tells me.

Therefore, I strive to learn new things daily, and I always try to achieve my best. I have hope for a better future.

One unforgettable Friday

Teacher Russell Hamburg is a man of average height, well-built, with a big tummy. He has dark hair and a long, scruffy, clumsy beard. His eyebrows are thick, and he frowns, as he quickly marks our Mathematics test books.

"Right, when you hear your name, get your book and go outside," he says. He calls thirty-nine names, and finally says, "Betty Baker." I get up from my desk, and walk towards him to get my book. He appears upset. I don't know why; however, my guess is that many of us have failed the test. He is the last person to vacate the classroom. He stands by the door, his large brown eyes wide.

"Thirty out of thirty!" he calls out. Steven, Walter, Virginia and Gloria walk towards him by the door, show their books and go in.

"Twenty-nine!" Martin, Maria and Suzanne walk towards the door. They put their books on the floor. My teacher picks up the cane he got from prison recently, bends it and hits in the air to test it.

Martin goes first. He lifts up his right hand towards the teacher. "Take it," the teacher says, beating him. He receives a lash on the palm of his hand, and goes in.

"Next!" calls teacher Russell. Maria goes, and then Suzanne. Those with two errors get two lashes and so on…

I'm still outside, shivering. I'm looking at my classmates, crying aloud bitterly. Those who fail to hold hands up properly don't escape. They are beaten everywhere. My turn comes.

"Five." I walk forward, ready to receive twenty-five lashes. I put my book down and stretch my right hand up towards my back with my fingers pointing backwards. I really don't want him to hurt my fingers. My teacher flogs me, until I lose count. When I fail to keep my hand up, he hits me anywhere. I cry, cuddling myself like a ball on the ground. He stops when he is satisfied.

November 1962

Our class is learning to write English essays. We edit our own work in the presence of our teacher, with a cane in her hand. It's my turn to read my story out loudly and clearly. She expects me to identify and correct my own mistakes. This is very difficult for me, because English is my third language. For every mistake I fail to spot, she strikes me hard. By the time I finish reading my story, I'm groaning in pain. My book is wet with tears as I return to my seat. Most of the children are crying today, as we have made many mistakes in our stories. We are all ordered to resubmit by the next morning. Next day, I'm first to arrive at school, followed by my teacher.

"Betty, bring me your composition book," Mistress Shirley Copperfield commands.

"Yes, Mistress," I reply, hoping for the best. I take out my exercise book from my bookcase. "Here, Mistress," I say, handing over my book with a smile. She takes, and marks it without my involvement this time. That's my reward for arriving early on that day.

January 1963

It's the beginning of the academic year in South Africa. I'm in our house at Skoonfontein. My end of Standard Six results arrived yesterday: I've passed, and will definitely be going to Blythewood with Sharon Hurst, my friend, to start in Form One. I call her 'Shah'. We've been best friends ever since I started at Skoonfontein Primere Skool.

"Betty, you must pack your clothes."

"Okay, Mum. I can't wait to travel with Shah and her parents to Blythewood High School."

"No, you aren't going there."

"What?" My heart sinking, I look at my mum.

"You're going to Butterworth High School."

Immediately, my eyes feel up with tears. "No, Mummy, I didn't apply to go there. I want to go to Blythewood with my friend, Shah."

My parents don't consider children's views. I have no choice. They have made their decision, and I know it's final.

I pack my uniform, clothes, canned stuff, spices and tomato sauce in my metal trunk. I fill the mattress cover with soft hay from the garden, and roll it into a small bundle, ready to catch the 5.30 a.m. bus to Butterworth High, a residential church school. I prepare another provision trunk for a week - putting in cakes, bread, meat, squash, etcetera, from Missus. I go to bed earlier.

I board the bus at about 5.30 a.m., arriving at the hostel six hours later. The matron shows me my dormitory. Unpacking my clothes, hanging them on the wall, and making up my bed, I have no clues what to expect in a combined secondary and high school.

As days go by, more students arrive, and our dormitories are filling up. Every so often I meet a new face. On this particular day, after supper, Sister Fatima, one of the old comers, summons all the newcomers to the Common Room.

When all of us are in, Sister Fatima shuts the door, and then says, "I welcome you to Butterworth High School. I hope you will enjoy your studies, and learn about the activities here. You will be called 'Tails' until the 1st of April. This is a special day called 'Fools' Day'." She pauses. "Until then, you are not allowed to look at the faces of the 'oldcomers'. If you do, they will come around you and say, 'Eyes down, Tail!' Don't be offended with this. It's the common practice for every newcomer. The best thing to do is not to be 'cheeky'; otherwise, they'll make you jump up and down for ages. That's enough for tonight. Good night, Tails," Fatima, the head-girl says.

"Good night, Sister," we all respond in a chorus. She holds her thumb up – a sign for 'okay' – and leaves us.

I return to my dormitory, having mixed feelings about the treatment. *Will I cope?* I hang my jacket on the wall, fold the rest of my clothes, and put them in my suitcase. I put on my pyjamas and get into bed. I stay awake, thinking. The lights go off.

The waking-up bell rings at 5.00 a.m., the next day. I sit up, and one of the prefects starts singing the Lord's Prayer, 'Our Father, who art in heaven.' I join in. Some prefects walk around between the beds looking for 'offenders' - those who aren't sitting up and singing during prayers.

As we sing, 'Amen', I jump out of bed quickly, and rush outside to collect my water, which I hid in the nearby bushes. We aren't allowed to keep it inside the dormitories. I can't delay getting out, in case someone steals my water. I get to the bathroom to wash myself. Good gracious, I have space - but the bathroom starts filling up as I'm about to leave.

I return to the dormitory to make up my bed. I ensure the four corners are pointed, and the bed is not descending in the middle. This is very difficult to do with my hay-mattress, but I manage well in the end. All the beds are covered with white bedspreads, or white sheets.

I put on my new school uniform – a white shirt, a pleated gym-dress, a gold tie with black stripes, and a gold girdle around my waist. I wear my black and gold striped jacket, black socks and shoes with laces. I go outside to brush my teeth. Prefects are watching every move in this quiet and tense environment.

At 6.00 a.m. the lining-up bell rings, and I go outside ready for breakfast. Everyone is quiet. You could hear a penny drop. The whistle goes, and the students walk all the way, down the slope, jumping over the furrows to the dining hall. The prefects are walking by our sides carrying notebooks and pens, recording offenders' names whenever necessary.

The dining hall is a very old, unused stable, built with stones. I walk in. Before sitting down, I put my dish and mug on the table. Everyone does the same. Our tables are long wooden sheets placed on triangular prism stands. When everybody is in, again one of the prefects starts to sing the thanks giving song. I close my eyes and sing:

"I thank you, for the food we eat
I thank you, for the world so sweet.
I thank you, for the birds that sing.
I thank you Lord for everything.
Amen."

We all sit down. The waiters come in, some carrying buckets of cornmeal porridge and hot water with sugar. Others are carrying trays with brown bread. This is done very fast. The prefect bangs the table, giving a signal to go outside to line up again. This meal is enough to keep me full until dinnertime at about 3.00 p.m.

The lining-up bell for going to school goes. I join the queue, a very long one, although we are standing in pairs. The prefects inspect if shoes are shining, and we are in full uniform. Breaking all these rules is a punishable offence. I am not very good at shining my shoes. However, will she notice?

I watch her walking slowly towards me. I hold my breath hoping she will walk past. I'm wrong. She stops by me.

"What's your name?"

"Betty," I reply, my legs and voice shaking.

"Speak louder, girl – what's your name?"

"Betty Baker, sister," I say, raising my voice. I remember the warning – not to be cheeky. She writes my name in the Punishment Book. We walk quietly all the way to school. Then the prefect shouts, "Dismiss!"

We hang about the school grounds waiting for the bell to ring. Some children are completing their holiday-work, while others lean against the wall chatting.

"Betty, you should use old stockings to shine your shoes," Dora advises me.

"Okay, thanks – I didn't know that," I reply, with my voice still trembling.

The bell rings for the start of the school session. We all go to the Assembly. Mr Jerry Water, the Principal, comes out of his office carrying a Bible, and reads, "St Matthew Chapter 5 from verse 3 to 10:

"Blessed are the poor in spirit, for theirs is the Kingdom of heaven....

Blessed are the peacemakers, for they shall be called children of God." Then he sings, "Our Father, who art in heaven…"

We all join in until we sing, "Amen."

He says, "I'd like to welcome all the new students here to Butterworth High School. I hope you will enjoy your studies, work hard, and achieve your education. The teachers are here to teach you, and you have come to learn. We have rules, and you must obey them. Your class-teachers will call you. Follow them to your classroom; and have a good day!"

I listen carefully for my name to be called. When hearing, "Betty Baker," I walk quickly to our line to join my classmates. Our class-teacher leads us to our classroom. I sit quietly at the front desk. The old students bring the exercise-books and textbooks for those who have paid their book-fees in full. Baas paid my dad in advance. So, my family will be receiving a reduced income, while paying back the loan. I get all the books required for Form One.

I look across to my right-hand side. A girl is sitting alone at her desk, a bit further away from me. I approach her.

"Hey, why don't you bring your books over here, and sit next to me," I say, confidently.

"Yes, thank you, I could do," she says, picking up her 'bookcase' and moving to sit next to me. She quickly opens it to get a book out.

"What's your name?" I ask her, my voice loud in my eagerness to make friends

"Charlotte," she answers softly, but fidgeting with her book as she asks. "What's yours?"

"Betty Baker."

"So, where do you come from?" I ask her firmly, looking at her face hoping to get her full attention. This works out. She turns slightly looking at my eyes.

"My home is at Soweto Township in Johannesburg. And what about you?"

"I come from Skoonfontein Farm near Burgersdorp – Baas

Jimmie's."

We talk for some time, getting to know each other better. I get on well with her. I'm happy that I now have a friend, and by the end of the day, I call her 'Lottie'. The bell rings for home time. We walk together all the way. Lottie tells me all about her family - that they work for the Europeans.

I'm interested in her talk, as we have similarities. I had thought those who work for the Europeans in cities have a better life than the farm-workers do. I want to hear more. I have many questions for Lottie, but I need to wait. We have time anyway.

Lottie and I always look out for each other. We fetch water from the river, hand-wash and iron our clothes together.

In May 1963

"Lottie, I'm sleeping by you tonight," I say.

"All right, Betty," she agrees happily. I return to my dormitory, change into my pyjamas, and go to Lottie's dormitory. Whispering under the blankets, she tells me about her family life - her parents and the treatment they receive from their bosses.

One of the incidents that strikes me is about what happened to her family one morning. She keeps quiet for a little while; I encourage her to tell me about it.

"My mum was doing domestic work for the Europeans, who lived in a very Big House with a garage and servants' quarters at the back. I was in the servants' quarters. My dad was helping the Baas' son, Graham, repair one of their cars."

"Uh huh," I say, nodding my head to prove that I am listening.

"My dad was inside the car, taking instructions from Graham under the front bonnet, when he heard him say, 'Brake!' He pulled up the hand brake. When Graham said, 'Okay,' Dad then released it. My dad later told my family that he heard Graham say, 'Okay.' Therefore, he released the brake. Unfortunately, the car rolled forward."

"What happened then?" I ask.

"My dad pulled the handbrake, just on time as it was about to crush his head."

"Oh!" I say, imagining the situation.

"Graham was very angry. He got out from under the car, opened the boot, took out a black rubber whip, and flogged my dad, who was already out of the car, standing by the boot."

I sigh, finding it difficult to deal with what Lottie's family had gone through. I now realise this practice is happening in Johannesburg too.

Lottie appears to be struggling to breathe, and she starts sobbing, a single tear slides down her cheek, and then she cries loudly.

"What did your dad do then?" I ask, feeling sorry for this family.

"He stood still, shielding his body with his arms, until he realised Graham was hitting him continuously. That's when he cried loudly. Graham's dad rushed out of the house, and his son was still beating my dad. 'Graham, stop it!' he shouted. He stopped and returned the whip to the boot. His dad patted him on his shoulders, as if he was saying, 'Well done, son.' That's when my dad grabbed his jacket and walked back to our Soweto home. I followed him, as he walked briskly all the way. When we arrived at our Soweto home, my dad was still crying silently, saying repeatedly, 'Never, never to be treated like this in my life again.'"

"Lottie, I don't like to hear this. So, people in the townships also experience such a horrible life too?"

"Yes, Betty. But it can't continue like this; somebody should do something, to stop it."

"Mmh, I know; some of our heroes have tried, and died. We should always remember them. They died for our cause. Others are still fighting."

"Betty, what's our role in this?"

"What do you think, Lottie? We may not be able to reverse the past."

"You're right, Betty. But we could work to change our future, so that all South Africans live together peacefully. We must do this."

"Of course, Lottie," I agree, feeling the wetness of tears in my eyes. I can't control myself. I cry alongside Lottie. We talk, comforting each other until we both fall asleep.

On Saturdays

Saturdays are 'Manuals Days'. After breakfast, we all go to the hall. The prefects read names from their Offenders' Books, while the Matron is standing in front with her whip. There are various means of punishment. Some children's punishment is beating, cleaning the surroundings, bathrooms, toilets, scrubbing dormitory and hall floors, or sometimes two of the punishments together. So, the school doesn't employ cleaners here.

On this particular Saturday, I am not lucky enough: the prefect calls my name, and reads my offences. "Betty Baker: unpolished shoes, sleeping during studies, and late for supper." The matron says, "Five lashes and cleaning the surroundings." I walk forward boldly, stretching the palm of my hand. She gives me five lashes. I don't cry this time. I just go outside to collect the tools - wheelbarrow, spades and rakes. Three other girls join me. We sing as we clean up the surroundings, and then return the tools after that.

I enjoy my studies. Lottie and I make friends with Nancy Castle. She comes from Guguletu Township in Cape Town. I feel great to have friends who come from the townships near the cities. We stick and study together. We're only allowed to go home during school holidays at Easter in April, winter in June and summer in December. Other opportunities for going home are possible when we owe books, school fees or boarding fees: I don't have these chances. My dad pays my fees on time from his advances. Baas Jimmie is very helpful in this way. God bless him.

* * *

I've been at Butterworth High School for some time, and have adapted well. As a responsible adult, I've learned to endure the pain inflicted during punishment. Some days are better than others: we do enjoy ourselves.

This Saturday evening, there's some entertainment going on - a Beauty Contest. I'm not asked to compete, as certain height is required. Lottie and Nancy are in it. The competition starts at 7.00 p.m. with live music. It all goes quiet, and then fifteen contestants walk in, smartly dressed in short bright-red attires. All the girls are wearing high-heeled shoes, and glittery jewellery. They are almost the same height - a lot taller than I am – perhaps that's why I wasn't selected to participate. I stop my thoughts from drifting away from this activity.

The first girl appears, and we all clap hands for her. Other children stand up to get a clear view of all the contestants, as they parade in the hall. They all walk, and stop, each with a different pose. Spectators are asked to encourage them with another round of applause. They are all beautiful, I think, but my eyes are on my friends, Lottie and Nancy. I want them to win. It's Nancy's turn.

She comes out wearing a big smile, and having an authoritative walk. She poses in all the corners, and then disappears into the dressing room. Other girls also reappear to parade. Then Lottie walks out confidently in an unusual style in comparison to Nancy; she walks, swerving her shoulders to the centre of the hall, kisses her hand, show the audience a 'big five' before waving to all of us, including the judges at their table. She has a big crowd cheering her up. We are invited to dance while the judges are deliberating. The city girls do various dances, and are better than me. I copy them as if I'm a dancer. The music stops after some time, and everybody is asked to take their seats. This is the end of the Beauty Pageant. The judge announces the winners. He says, "Number three is …Brenda Date."

She gets up, walks happily to the front, and with a massive smile to receive her prize.

"Number two two is…Doris Burnham." She wears her sweet smile, and walks to the front to receive her prize also. The announcer takes his time to call Number One. Then he goes. In my heart I hope it's going to be Lottie.

"Number one is…" and keeps quiet as if he doesn't know the winner. And then he calls, "Darlene Granville." She receives a big round of applause, as she walks to the front, keeping up with the musical rhythm, to receive her prize.

I look at my friends sympathetically, wondering how they feel, and what I could do for them. I get up, run to the front and give both a hug. This seems to give them some comfort. "You should be proud of yourselves for trying," I say, kissing them on the cheeks. They smile at me.

"Good, Nancy," I say confidently. They both look at me, as if they say, "Not really, Betty." I continue saying, "enter the competition again next year, you might win? If at first you don't succeed, try again." I recall one of my favourite mottoes.

Whether they listened and got the courage, I can't tell. They disappear into the dressing room to change, while I wait for them, thinking of how to cheer them up. It's bad to lose, but if you don't get involved you don't win or lose. We walk back to our dormitories, laughing at the funny stuff during the parade.

"Good night, girls," I say.

One Monday morning

I get up, get ready for school, and check my school bag to ensure I've got my Mathematics book. My first lesson is English, followed by Mathematics, Afrikaans, and then playtime. After lunch, I have Latin, History and a double lesson of Domestic Science.

Mr Larry Wilson, my English teacher, took my composition book to mark over the weekend. I get it back. I'm pleased with the comment written in red ink – 'A really strange dream' – and 'A' grade. This has made my day. I should aim for high grades in all my subjects.

My teachers take notice of me, as I make progress in my school work. I continue working hard until we break up for the Easter holidays.

In July 1963 we discuss The 1948 Apartheid Policy

The winter holidays are over. I am back at Butterworth High School. Lottie, Nancy and I are in the Common Room, chatting. I tell them how wonderful it was to help out my mum and dad with her jobs in the Big House.

"It was great! It kept me busy throughout my holidays." I then fall quiet, expecting an exciting response from my friends. Surprisingly, I get none; instead, they exchange glances, as if something was wrong.

"What? Work for free in Baas' house during the holidays!" both Nancy and Lottie exclaim.

"Oh, that's how things are there."

"Do you like it then – working for nothing during the holidays, while we're having fun, relaxing and going to the cinema?"

I think about this question, seriously; do I really like it?

"You know what - the whole thing seems a bit oppressive to me," Nancy says.

"Of course, girls, you surely must have heard that in 1947, when the National Party won the elections, they introduced many laws, oppressive to the South African natives?"

"In 1947 –mmh - that's history. What has that got to do with us now?" I ask, really wanting to hear more.

No one answers me; both girls are quiet.

"Oh, Betty, you mean you don't know what's going on? Wake up, girl! Those laws are still in force, even as we speak. In fact, the government is making things harder, with newer laws to restrict us even more," Lottie says.

"Yes, they deny us all human rights, including a high standard of education," Nancy says, rubbing her nose.

"Really," I say, encouraging them to keep speaking.

"Betty, in Cape Town, things are bad at the moment. I'm worried about my family."

"Uhuh."

"It's sad to say, some people might lose their homes. I'm not sure if we'll keep our house in Guguletu," says Lottie.

"What?"

"Yes, they keep sending people back to the villages where their ancestors originated," explains Lottie.

"What happens to those who are born in the townships then?" I ask.

"Huh, our leaders know the smartest way of doing it," says Lottie, giggling.

"Oh, what is it then? I'd be glad to know," I say.

"They came up with various categories for the natives requiring the right to live in townships permanently. In Section 10 of the Act, it says: 'Those people born in a town or city and have lived there for fifteen years or more can acquire the right to stay.'"

"Okay," I say, nodding.

"Those who have worked for more than fifteen years without breaks and those who have worked continuously for the same employer for ten years at least, also have residence rights," says Lottie.

"So, you mean that the people who haven't given this service to their employers are denied the right to reside permanently in their own country? That's tough!"

I bury my face behind my hands, listening to my hard heartbeat, reflecting on what I've just heard, and preparing myself for what is coming next. This is too much for me to take in.

Nancy, who has been silent for a while, suddenly says, "My mother heard her Baas, Van der Merwe, talking about the education transformation for the natives that's needed."

"What's going to happen to our education?" I ask.

"He said Dr Hendrik Verwoerd's ideology of apartheid was right."

"What's that?" I ask – wanting to know what the basis of this dreadful ideology is.

"His view was that it is misleading to teach the natives like us to acquire knowledge about life beyond our communities. There was no benefit in showing us better opportunities enjoyed by the European communities, while we aren't allowed to enjoy it," Nancy explains.

"Huh?" I ask, nodding my head, surprised.

"According to Verwoerd, I must be taught from an early age to understand and accept that I'm not at the same level with the Europeans. They are '*above*' me," continues Nancy.

"Who tells all the teachers what to teach us and how?" I ask.

"The government does this, by 'modifying' our syllabus, allowing it to stop us from aspiring to high positions in any society, within our country and abroad," Nancy replies. "We're only learning the skills necessary to help other natives, and also those we need for doing menial jobs for the Europeans, or under their supervision. Can't you see the things we're learning? We spend more time learning Arithmetic and the three languages."

"Oh, is that the reason for learning both English and Afrikaans?" I ask.

"I think so; we should be able to speak with either an English or an Afrikaner Baas, when they employ us," Nancy replies.

"Oh dear, that sounds odd to me. Education shouldn't have limits. The government should prepare us to live and work anywhere in the world," I respond, feeling a stir of ambition within me to prove the lawmakers wrong.

"Forget it, Betty, this is South Africa. While the Europeans are in control, they might do whatever they choose for their benefit," says Nancy.

"No...Stop – you're talking about politics!"

"So, what?"

"You know this is not allowed. Are you trying to get us into trouble?" I raise my voice in panic at Lottie and Nancy, after realising that we've now crossed the red line. I get up ready to walk away.

"Shush! Make sure no one ever hears you say this – yes, it's politics," whispers Lottie, tapping her index finger on her lips.

"Betty, come back here!" Nancy calls to me. I return to sit down with my friends, hoping I haven't upset them. Lottie and Nancy explain the importance of understanding the issues that affect us, and that I shouldn't talk to anyone else about the Apartheid Laws. I listen, nodding every so often.

"I'm sorry; I shouldn't behave like this. My parents banned this kind of talk at home, our lives depend on Bass Jimmie, who is the Government," I reply, thinking about what I've just heard. "And what happens to the Europeans who don't agree with the Government's laws?"

"Well, they have a choice to accept the job, or leave it. Should they take it, they are obliged to abide by the country's laws too," Nancy explains.

"Well, girls, what can we do about these laws? I personally need more information about them," I say, and then change the topic, to talk about the upcoming netball tournament.

In September, the same year

I am at school for afternoon studies. It's noisy in the classroom, and I find it difficult to concentrate. I just can't continue reading. Some children are talking about something that seems interesting, but they are in disagreement. I close my book, and move to the back of the class to listen.

The talk is about the 1953 Bantu Education Act. The debate is about the pros and cons. Wow, so many children know about these laws! The children who live outside urban areas know a lot more than those who come from rural areas and farms. These don't have a clue, and have nothing to contribute – just like me.

So, I pull my chair to sit down and listen. I'm amazed the more I hear, but I keep quiet throughout the discussion. This strengthens my determination to see the change in South Africa. Meanwhile, I cannot yet break the laws. How will I manage to contain myself, when I know very well that these are designed to hinder me? I must surely obey them, because should I fail to do so, I might go to prison. My dad warned me. I return to my usual desk, and bow my head down. The bell rings. I collect my bookcase, and walk slowly back to my dormitory.

From now on I think more seriously about many things: my punishment and pains endured at school; the hardship my parents are facing; trying to earn a living from Baas Jimmie and getting pocket money while I'm studying. Yet this 'education', it appears, aims at keeping me inferior to people of other races for the rest of my life.

My concern is about my teachers, especially the natives. *Do they really have advanced subject knowledge,* I wonder. *Or they are here to reinforce the limitations?* I have no one to answer my question.

So, I conclude that unless I teach myself independent learning skills and explore other avenues, I may never succeed in helping bringing about the change that is desperately needed in my community.

I think about the European teachers, and wonder how much knowledge they are imparting to me. *Do they stick to the Bantu Education Curriculum, or do they go beyond it?* I can't tell, for I know no other way to make a comparison. I have a lot to accomplish – going beyond what I'm taught. I start using my pocket money to buy books. I buy an Oxford Dictionary and novels, and spend most of my spare time reading. I find some words difficult to pronounce, and use my knowledge of phonetics to try to learn the correct English pronunciation phonetically. For example: 'kidney' reads as 'kidni', 'greedy' reads as 'gridi', 'scale' as 'skeil', etcetera. I'm really determined to learn. Before I realise it, it's December: the year is over. Tomorrow is the last day of the term. I'm returning home to Skoonfontein for the holidays, having learnt a bit more about South Africa - my beautiful country!

I've searched for a suitable word to describe my life in South Africa, and emerge with none that completely satisfies me. Many words could do – dehumanised, trapped, resentful, misunderstood, disbelieved, terrified or violated. But these words aren't enough to paint the whole picture of my feelings. I'm thinking of the right word. Will this situation ever change? This has been my rhetorical question, to live hoping for change and help myself survive. However, some days are different.

From Betty's Diary, 20th January 1964

Chapter 4

The Apartheid Laws

January 1964

I'm still at home in Skoonfontein Farm for holidays. My mum is sitting outside, chatting to other people from the nearby farms. They have finished eating their meals – dumplings and roast lamb. Lots of dishes are left on a tray for washing up later. I help myself feeling very pleased to have such a lovely lunch today.

It's bad of me to be happy because Baas' sheep died delivering a lamb. Whenever an animal dies, Baas gives it to us to eat. We have loads of meat and we're also able to share with other farm labourers. Well, I can't help it; one man's meat is another man's poison.

We're having a kind of a celebration today with our visitors sitting outside having a barbecue, although my parents are unable to entertain them fully. The smoke is thick in the atmosphere, and the smell of barbecue is mouth-watering. Sadly, my Mum and Dad are unable to stay with our guests; that's a shame.

They pop in to see that everybody is all right, eating meat, peaches and drinking homemade ginger-beer, and then return to their usual farm-jobs. Baas should be happier since they are not neglecting their duties. A bowl of yellow peaches is put in the middle of the circle, for those people who want to help themselves. Aunty Rose starts singing songs in her distinctive voice, one after another, and the others join in. I stand by the door listening and watching them sing *Happy Skoonfontein* and dancing with sweat dripping down into their eyes. They don't seem bothered by this, as they wipe it off with the back of their hands. Others blow their noses, and wipe off their hands on the grass or their clothes.

Happy Skoonfontein! Home to our Elderly!
We love you; we thank you.
Happy Skoonfontein!
I'm happy for Skoonfontein, ha-ha-ha! I'm happy for Skoonfontein,
oh-ha-ha-ha! Happy Skoonfontein!
We're happy with you!
Here to stay; and to die.
Happy Skoonfontein!
I'm happy for Skoonfontein, ha-ha-ha!
I'm happy for Skoonfontein, oh-ha-ha-ha!

A young man, half naked, with a red cap on, is playing an accordion. He plays with his eyes shut but manages to press all the buttons, playing a beautiful melody. The farm-workers appear happy, dancing many different kinds of dances. I'm fascinated with one where they form a circle and then take turns dancing in the middle, doing all kinds of tricks, lifting their legs up, one after another. Some men are great at vibrating their bodies from their legs to their shoulders. Women tend to concentrate on moving their waists.

"Huh, what are you doing?" The volume of the music is so

high and to make things worse some people are aiding the rhythm, yelling, "yep, yep, yeah." I shout louder, "No" putting my right hand under my chin, surprised as Uncle Dover goes behind Aunty Maud's back, moving his waist towards her buttocks and then drops his upper body to the right and left. They receive a round of applause. I find it absolutely disgusting for grown-ups to dance like that. Uncle Witvoet turns his head, waves at me, before filling a glass with ginger-beer. He finds a space and sits down drinking.

Both men and women take turns beating the drums. These are made from cut diesel containers, and then covered on both sides with dry cattle skin. They paint them bright colours and attach a strong string to go around the neck and hold them up. Women shake improvised tambourines. They dance alone and in pairs, gently smacking each other's backsides. They are very loud. It's a real happy day in Skoonfontein for them.

As for me, I know what I want – to be in school daily and hear Mistress Barlow shout, "Children, read your books. You need the best possible education!" Miss Barlow is a tall skinny lady with a friendly, echoing voice, sharp nose and grey curly hair. She often wears dark-brown attire and high-heeled shoes and never misses wearing her red lip stick. Her black-framed spectacles suit her long face. She is my outstanding teacher and I always miss her when we are apart.

I haven't been in Miss Barlow's class, in Butterworth High School for two weeks, since the term started because I'm not well. I'm home, sitting down hearing my family members talking, laughing and shouting. I hear footsteps going in various directions, the cluttering of plates, mugs and spoons. I can't see anything – it's very dark. "Mum! Are you there?" I ask, seeking assurance after hearing her voice. "Is the storm coming, that it's so dark?" There is no response to my question.

"Mum, when is daytime coming? What is happening in Skoonfontein? Why is it so dark? I want to go to school," I ask my mum after noticing the endless darkness. Mum doesn't answer me but I can hear her talking to a visitor. I guess I'm disturbing and maybe even embarrassing her. Children aren't supposed to interrupt when parents entertain visitors in case they hear adult secrets and pass them on. That would get them in trouble!

I want to read books, but I can't, and I'm upset. Is it still at night? But why is it so long? I love daytime, being out on the farm doing my favourite things; playing with my baby dolls, Ruby and Clifford, which I made with sticks and old rags in my playhouse behind our home. I feel someone grabbing my hand, saying, "come and sit outside for fresh air." And that's my mum for sure. I follow her, and as soon as I step my foot outside, I feel the heat of the sun on my skin.

"It's very hot out here. It's lovely." My mum and Rita exchange hands; I hold onto Rita's hand as we both go further away, perhaps by the bushes behind our house.

"Sit here," says Rita. *Our playhouse is still there, fortunately*, I say in my mind. Rita says, "I'm going to gather firewood to cook dinner for Ruby and Clifford, Betty. Please wait for me right here. I'll be back soon."

"All right, but don't be long – our children like soup and bread, don't they?" I hear Rita's footsteps and then it's quiet.

She returns and passes Ruby to me to feed. I rock and pat her gently, pretending to feed her bread and milk. We play together for a little while and then return to our house when the sun goes down and it gets cooler.

Strangely, the dark continues, and I wonder what's going on. I'm used to working, or doing my own stuff. So, I get up and walk, hoping to get to the kitchen.

"Oops!" I've bumped into the metal chair. I turn around, stretch my hand forward, hitting the washing-stand corner. After striking the corner of the wooden table, I cry as I fumble, hoping to find my way around the house. Why will no one tell me what is going on? I start to get used to being moved around and having people doing everything for me.

That same evening I hear my mum suggesting taking me to the doctors. *Yes,* I say to myself. *But, what if I never see again?* I don't want to be a burden on others. How will I read the books? "No!" I say aloud, feeling agitated with my thoughts and situation.

I hear the car stop by our door, and my mum talking, and I recognise Missus' voice. My heart fills with joy as the car starts moving forward, my mum taking me to the doctors. I can remember the silence in the car all the way, until it stops, and the door opens. Somebody helps me out into the surgery. I hear the Doctor's voice, asking my mum questions. We return home, and I'm put straight in bed. I get the sticky sweet medicine three times a day. I get fed up of staying in bed.

Fortunately, in time, I recover from this temporary blindness, and return to school. Miss, being very pleased to have me back in class, beckons me to her table at the front of the class, saying, "Betty Baker, you're my star. Work harder and succeed in your education." She looks directly into my eyes, making me feel uncomfortable.

"Yes, Mistress Barlow." I look down at my feet and smile, nodding in agreement.

"Spend your time searching for information. Sometimes this can't come to you. You've got to look for it." In her deep persuasive voice, she warns me.

"Education, Mistress! Do you mean this Bantu Education?" I ask her this question, not trying to be funny, but to show her that I've heard something about the standard of our education; I know it's not good enough.

"There's no other for you, Betty. Learn what you've got. You can improve on it later, when you're old enough to understand."

Her voice trails off before finishing the sentence, and she turns her back as she walks away from me. She returns and looks at my eyes. I see sadness in her eyes. As she swallows deeply, her lips tighten, stretching. And her left eye blinks – this talk seems to trouble her. What does she know, that makes her feel sad about me and my education?

Her words stick in my mind, and I keep remembering them every so often. I like her because of her concern about my future; she sees past my current status. Mistress always talks about my adult-life and not my present childhood. But I wish I could say to her, "Mistress, be happy because there's a great person in me. She is locked inside me. No one hears her talk. She never starts conversations, but responds well to instructions. She only does as told. She never cries loudly, when upset. You can see her sleeves or palms going across her face and her bloodshot eyes when someone provokes her or something has gone terribly wrong. During such moments, she only lifts up her glossy big eyes to hold back tears so that no one sees her cry. She is very strong and always strives for success, no matter the barriers in her way. Failure is her only enemy. Therefore, she always fights to succeed, and rarely complains. She normally grins or bites her inner lip, staring at people around her. She wishes somebody could listen to her own stories. Betty is always ready to make peace and settle for less. She even takes the blame to avoid conflicts, but lacks opportunities to demonstrate her potential. Some people call her names – the names she hates most, 'kaffir', coloured, coward, deaf, 'black', big-eyes and many more – and this makes her sad. However, there's one thing all these have in common – they are mean. But why can't she tolerate what others like? The answer to this question is simple – no one asked Betty what she wants to be called. Betty never agreed to be given other names other than Betty Baker; and this is unfair."

I've lived for many years, with hurt inside me, because of these names. "While I can't do much about this name-calling, I must stop moaning and tolerate them. The people calling these names have power and authority over me. I wish I could tell them to stop calling me these names. They sound bad in my ears.

Call me African; that's what I choose to be called. Do not use my skin colour when describing me because you often get this wrong. My skin colour is light brown, but you mistakenly think it's black. Call me bookworm because I like reading books. I'd be fine with this name and feel proud of it. I live hoping that one day I'll be free to say my wishes without fear of the government. When that day comes, it will be like a fairy tale."

Two months later

I'm at home for Easter holidays, about four o'clock in the afternoon. I lie on my bed resting, and think about the many things happening at Skoonfontein. Life at school is becoming monotonous. Visiting another town might make me feel better, so I pretend to be ill as an excuse to see Dr Berry. I don't mind getting the sticky green medicine, as long as I actually get to visit the town.

I wonder – what will I suffer from this time? I ask myself. Should it be a toothache, headache or stomach-ache? I'm not sure; but I must find something. It can't be the stomach-ache because Mum will just use blue soap and a syringe to clean up my tummy as she usually does. It hurts when she sticks the syringe into my backside. I've had enough of this. Toothache...Yes! I should say this. I can lose another tooth. So, I cover myself with blankets and start groaning until my Mama comes in.

"Betty! For goodness' sake, what's the matter with you?" my Mum asks, banging the door loudly before she walks into my bedroom. She is in a bad mood, I can tell. "Why are you in bed at this time of day?"

I remain quiet, thinking how best to respond so that she'll believe me.

"What's wrong with you?" she asks, shouting at me. My Mum can't stand sick people. "Get up!" she says, ripping off my blankets.

With the appearance of 'difficulty', I try to sit up and struggle to speak. "Toothache, Mummy," I say.

"Oh, which one is hurting this time?" The tone of Mum's voice was more sympathetic now. "You should have told me this. How did you expect me to know?"

"The back one, Mummy," I explain, feigning tears and opening my mouth to show her.

She looks for the tooth and then says, "Uh-huh, that one's rotten. There's no cure for toothache, Betty. You should have it removed immediately. I'll take you to the doctor tomorrow." Around Burgersdorp, doctors take care of all health issues, including dentists' work.

I feel like saying, "In town, yeah!" But I manage to control my excitement by biting my lower lip, and Mum covers me with blankets. "Please sleep earlier tonight. We've got a long way to go. We should aim to be at the bus-stop at half past ten in the morning," Mum says, slamming the door hard as she leaves my room.

"All right, Mum," I reply, happily.

I can tell she isn't impressed. The journey will cost her more than fifty shillings. My mum's reluctant to spend such money, and I can't blame her, knowing the effort that goes into earning it.

I cover my head with the blankets, deep in thought. Sometimes I have to lie to get things for myself. This is not good, but what else can I do? I know that Dr Berry will ask me with a big smile, "Betty Baker, what's troubling you this time?" He never tells anybody that I fake sickness. That's not his concern, I suppose. He gets his consultation fee and medication costs, and his private practice is successful, and full of patients.

I think about a lot of things, like the journey in an overflowing, stuffy, noisy bus that travels slowly on that bumpy dirt-road for ten miles. I'll be standing all the way, because normally children give up seats for older people, and that's always a bad journey. My parents aren't bothered about this. They've been doing it for many years.

"Cars are mostly driven by Europeans only, Betty," Dad usually says when I challenge him for not buying us a car. He doesn't intend to buy one because he can't afford it anyway. The greater part of my dad's income is paid in kind. We receive left-over food, and lovely used clothes from Baas and Missus, Baas Jimmie's wife. We live on their farm for free. Baas Jimmie always buys us paraffin for our primus stoves and lamps. He is certainly a good Baas!

I wish I could say, though, "No Dad, you should move on. That's your mind-set showing you the difficulty in owning a car. There are natives, who own cars in our days. Look at Miriam's dad; is he European? You need to change your way of thinking." Even so, I daren't speak to him like that. It would probably be humiliating, and very bad manners to tell an adult your views, especially your father.

We don't mind getting a lift on the back of Baas Lyndon's van (the farmer next to Baas Jimmie) and pay him the hiking fare. We often do this, even on dusty or rainy days. I'm happy using any transport available to get to town.

I soon fall asleep, to wake up hearing my mum's scream the following morning. "Betty, wake up! The warm water is ready for you to wash in the washing basin. Your breakfast is on the kitchen table. Hurry up, will you?"

"Okay, Mum," I say, yawning, wiping the sleep from my eyes. I jump out of my bed to get my flannel out of the dresser, and quickly wipe myself from head to toe. I put cream on my body, and brush my teeth. I put on my pink knickers which have frills at the back, and my matching dress. It's my favourite. I got them from Missus for Christmas. I try on my only black pumps, and my big toe sticks out, but they will do for now. I have no other shoes to wear.

Soon, I'm ready for the two mile-walk to the bus stop, still hoping to get a lift from one of the farmers. I wait in the living room for Mum. She comes out, and we walk slowly together towards the small gate. I realise I've forgotten my notepad on the bed, so I run back to get it. I run and catch up with Mum who's now heading towards the Big House – Baas and his family's residence.

We walk together to the bus stop, with me looking backwards every so often in case a van comes. We reach the bus stop, and there's no one else around.

Soon the bus arrives. My mum sticks out her hand, signalling it to stop. It does, and Eugene the bus conductor jumps out, giving us a warm welcome.

"Get in, Aunty. We're running late for the town," he says out loud. Unsurprisingly, I don't get a mention. It's common to overlook children here.

"We're going with those on the move, Aunty." He makes a joke, bouncing his right hand, and then laughs.

My mum struggles to get in: she's obese, and her knee hasn't completely recovered from Daisy's kick when she was milking her – that's Baas' cow. The step is too high for my Mum. Eugene comes around to help, and holds her hand as she steps into the bus. As she does this, she drops her handbag.

"Oh, I've dropped my handbag!" my mum yells hysterically.

"Don't worry about it," says Eugene, bending over to pick it up. "Here you are, Aunty," he says softly, handing Mum her bag. "Huh, it's heavy. Have you got loads of cash in here?" he asks, pointing at it.

"Thank you, son," Mum says, panting - as if she is running short of breath. Getting into the bus is always a big struggle for her. There's nothing that could be done about it. She says, "May God bless you, son," and continues chewing. She does this because her gums itch due to uncomfortable false teeth.

"May God bless me too, for all the hard work I do on this farm," I mumble to myself.

I push through behind my mum. She can't go any further because the bus is completely full. We can only stand by the driver. Poor Eugene stands on the lowest bus step, right by the door.

That's very kind of him, having to put up with this. I wonder what could happen if the door opens accidentally? No doubt he would be thrown out and perhaps break his legs, or even die. I can't believe that he has to put himself through this risky business for the sake of earning money. Suddenly, the bus pulls out of the bus stop. As it moves forward, Eugene shouts:

"Get your tickets everybody! Your tickets, please."

One and a half tickets," Mum says.

Eugene receives the coins, and checks them out. He puts the money in his satchel hanging from his neck before issuing a ticket. But my mum paid for both of us. Why does he give us one ticket? I wonder.

"Eugene, you've given me one ticket. Where's the other one?" Mum asks, appearing confused. She has been travelling on the buses, but without me.

"Sorry, Aunty, I issue tickets to adults only." I can see my mum's not pleased with this response.

"Don't worry, Mama - there seems to be little or no place for children in this world," I say, sadly.

"Oh well," says my mum, shrugging her shoulders. She gestures, 'No', shaking her head. The bus driver appears to ignore Eugene's conduct.

At the next bus stop, another passenger gets in, and then it can't hold any more. It drives past other bus stops. I see Eugene holding his left fist up, tapping his right palm into it signalling 'Bus Full' to those who might have been waiting there for hours. I wish I could give them my place and walk to town. I've done this several times before.

I see the tall trees on both sides of the road, and know we're nearly there. The main road is broad, with shops on both sides.

On the right-hand side, there is a petrol station and a restaurant called Dees á la Carte, written in big black letters on the wall behind the blue and white striped canopy.

The bus carries on up to the bus rank, and then stops. It's busy, as usual, with some traders rushing to the bus door to sell fruit to the passengers getting off the bus. All the traders are calling out loudly, trying to persuade us to buy their products.

"Peaches, reduced to three for ten cents now!"

"Sweet and juicy oranges to quench your thirst - only two cents each!"

Men and women, old and young, are all about their business selling their fruit. I look around this crowded and busy bus terminal, with more buses coming while others leave.

We get off the bus quickly, ignoring all the traders as they push through trying to sell to us. My mouth waters as my eye catches the ripe yellowish peaches and their wonderful smell. There's no chance of having any: my Mum has to ensure the money goes a long way for the essentials.

I look at other things of interest around me, but continue walking. After a little while, I hear Mum shout, "Betty, hurry up!" I'm not surprised - she always does this. I'm used to her going on and on.

Today's weather is brilliant – scorching sun, with a blue sky and no cloud. I'm excited about gathering facts for writing my composition – My town visit. So, I take note of everything I see. I hope that my teacher will be pleased. I'm excited, but I have to hide this from my mum, and continue pretending to be ill.

Cars pass, and sometimes hoot to people crossing the streets anywhere, as there are no pedestrian or pelican crossings. Would it be possible to have these road markings on a gravel road? Traffic lights could control the traffic, but there are none.

I walk a few steps forward, and then I stop to make some notes. I look around to find that my mum has left me behind. I run to catch up with her as she yells, again, "Betty, hurry up!"

Suddenly, my mum stops to greet Uncle Elvis and Aunty Lisa. They live on another farm far away from us. They haven't seen each other for a very long time and they start to talk, laugh and pat each other's shoulders for a lengthy time. I quickly become bored.

"Good, old friends," I say to myself, pleased to turn around and see what really happens in town, and make notes. I won't see everything, of course but I should see enough to write about when I return home.

Aunty and Uncle join us as we walk towards the Dees á la Carte Restaurant. I see many people walking about, but I'm more interested in the lighter-skinned ones - the Europeans and Coloureds, like me. We continue walking. I can't keep up with them, so I'm often left a bit behind. My mum notices this, and turns around, shouting impatiently.

"Come on, Betty, hurry up!" She grabs me hard by my hand. "We should be at the doctors by now!" Mum says, hoping to get me moving.

"Yes, Mum," I say, increasing my speed. I'm so attracted to what I see, I start dragging my feet again. Two younger European girls, around the same age as me, walk past. They are wearing flip-flops, blue t-shirts with straps and shorts, eating ice-cream which dribbles down the side of their mouths as they lick their lips. I look at them and my mouth begins to water. "You can't have it, Betty," I whisper to myself.

I can't even taste it: it's a luxury. I must stop being greedy, I tell myself. I continue walking, but I can't take my eyes off them. Mum seems to have a problem. She grabs me by my hand again, a bit rougher this time, and walks very fast, especially considering her sore knee. She holds my hand tightly, stopping me from admiring this beautiful town and lovely community.

We reach the Surgery on time; I can tell by seeing the very long queue. It is impossible to arrange appointments in advance, and the doctor can't send away people who just turn up. We have to live with this, so we join the slow queue until our turn comes.

When we enter the Surgery, I sit on the chair by my mum. The tall, bald European doctor who is wearing a white coat comes around. He asks the usual questions and Mum explains, "Betty is suffering from toothache, Doctor." The doctor looks at me, saying, "Let's have a look." He looks at my teeth and says, "Say, 'Ah'." I do, and then he repeats, "Open your mouth widely, and say, 'Ah!'"

"Ah," I say, opening my mouth until it's about to tear. "Aha, well, we can't save this one. It should come out," he mutters, looking at Mum for agreement. I hear my mum saying confidently, "Yes, Doctor." I wish she knew that I'm frightened of this process. I hate the pain that comes with it.

I'm happy that no one will ever discover my trick. The doctor leads me through to another consultation room where the nurse is already waiting. I sit on the dentist chair, and the nurse holds my head. I feel very uncomfortable and start breathing heavily, due to fear of the injection. I close my eyes as the needle goes into my gum. A tears rolls down my cheek. The friendly nurse says, "You're very brave - well done!" just to cheer me up. I return to the waiting room until I'm recalled. After a short while, the nurse appears from the door.

"Betty Baker, could you come through, please!" the nurse says, in her friendly, high-pitched voice. Immediately, I feel like I need the toilet – that's how nervous I am. I'm very glad that they call me by my name, though. I follow the nurse through to the consultation room, take off my jacket and sit on the huge dentist-chair. She puts a big bib around me and holds my head in position while the doctor extracts my tooth. The nurse gives me salty water to gargle before putting cotton wool into my bleeding gum. Both my mouth and cheek feel numb. Mummy pays the fee and collects the green medicine. My excitement vanishes as we leave the Surgery.

We go back the same way, passing the Dees á la Carte

Restaurant. This time we walk closer to the restaurant. It is full of people: I see families with children of my age and younger, sitting at the tables outside. I notice the difference between them and myself - they have a good life. I smell the delicious food coming from the restaurant and, knowing that I can't have it, I just stand there looking at them. My lips and throat feel dry. I swallow my saliva every so often, finding it difficult to walk past. In my mind, I wish to be like a European child. Could my mum have sensed my feelings? She grabs my hand, swinging it slightly up and down, counting "one and two" as we move on. This distracts my attention, and I pick up my pace. I say, "Mama, I'm thirsty."

"Okay, Betty, I'll get you something to drink," she says.

"I don't want water," I protest.

"I'll get you a cool drink," Mum says.

We come to the Las Vegas Café, and I see two doors facing us, not far away from each other. Above each door, there is a sign and white writing on a black board. On my left, the writing says, 'Non-Europeans.' On my right, it says, 'Europeans only'. The latter is the side with the tables.

The *Reservation of Separate Amenities Act of 1953* requires the display of the signs, to ensure errors don't occur. People from all racial groups must use their allocated facilities. There is no exception to this law, even in an emergency. These laws make provision for different races to receive unequal treatment and opportunities. Being classified a native, despite my appearance of having mixed genes, including that of the Europeans, forces me to have to accept the places reserved for the natives in the restaurant.

I know I must obey the laws at all times. The police arrest the law-breakers, and make them work hard on the streets and sometimes on Baas Jimmie's farm; so my mum and I walk into the door with the sign, 'Non-Europeans'. We wait for a long time to be served in this strictly takeaway part of the café. While waiting,

I look on the other side; this café is actually one building divided with a room-divider made of reeds. Europeans are having meals at the tables with their children. All servers have darker or brown skins; they wear blue dresses with white aprons, and their heads are covered with cream caps. They are moving in and out of this café serving food, drinks, collecting empty plates and glasses. I can hear loud cheerful laughter from the people on the other side.

It's my mum's turn to be served. "Could I have cold coca cola, please," she says. This coloured woman brings a bottle of coke, opens it and stretches her hand over the counter to receive the money first, before giving my mum the bottle. She takes it, and we go outside, stand by the wall and share the drink. Fortunately, the weather is bright and sunny. Had it been windy, rainy or snowy, we would still have been standing outside. My mouth feels numb. I take a sip of the coke but, no, I can't taste it, so I give it back to my mum.

Next to the Las Vegas Café is a Boland bank. It also has two signs displayed above the entrances reading 'Europeans only' and 'Non-Europeans'. The side for Non-Europeans has a very long queue that extends outside the bank. People are lining up against the wall on the pavement, and the tired ones are sitting down on the dusty ground.

A young European woman walks into the bank through her door. Perhaps there are a few customers or more cashiers on that side, and that's why she walks out quickly. Mum needs to buy a stamp from the Post Office in the town centre so we walk to there. It has two entrances with similar signs to those at the restaurant, café and the bank. We pass the 'Europeans Only' door to go into our side. We wait for a long time in the queue to be served. My note pad is almost full with my writing and sketches. I'm desperate for the toilet so, I tell my mum and quickly run out through my exit to the toilets across the road.

As I approach the toilets, I feel the bad smell. The toilets for the non-Europeans are the 'bucket-system' kind that gets emptied by 'uncles,' as everyone calls them. These are male toilet cleaners who operate tractors with a big tank at night only, emptying the toilet buckets. As I come closer, I notice urine flowing from the entrance down to the streets, and know they're 'our' toilets. I'm not surprised, as this is a busy time of the day. I go in, and there's hardly any space to stand on the floor due to the mess and filth. The buckets are almost overflowing, and the whole place has flies buzzing about.

I use this facility effectively, but have a problem there after. There's no toilet paper or newspaper to use. So I slip off my favourite pink underwear, that Missus gave me. Tears flood my eyes immediately, and I can't hold them back. Slowly, they flow down my cheeks and over my lips. I lick them; they taste salty and then dry my cheeks with my best underwear before using it as a wipe. At least, I'm happy to be clean, and no one will notice that I don't have them on. I manage well without them, until I reach home. I don't even tell my mum. 'My special birthday present - did I have to abandon them there?' I think to myself, my heart feeling torn apart. 'I was unprepared for this...'

* * *

The holiday is over. Early in the morning, I get up, have a wash, dress and walk to the road, to get a bus to Burgersdorp where I will get my connection to Butterworth High School. I decide now to share my holiday experience with my classmates and friends. When writing about 'my holidays', I don't mention the visit to town, I write about the farm experiences instead. Days go by quickly and soon, I'll be returning home for holidays.

I was one of Betty Baker's course tutors at St David's College when she started. She faced considerable difficulties in tackling the course. She showed determination and commitment in working to establish a foundation of knowledge and understanding of the British Education system. Once she had acquired good communication skills in English, she participated in the group discussions and showed that she could draw implications from education practice in this country that would be of value to her.

Matthew Bones
Lecturer
St David's College of Education
January 1977

Chapter 5

The Shooting

December, 1967

This afternoon I'll be boarding two buses to Baas Jimmie's farm to spend the Christmas holidays with my family. I'm not looking forward to it at all. Yawning, I undo my bed, empty the mattress, and pack all my belongings in my metal trunk. I think about everyone on the farm. I think I know a bit more about Baas now: perhaps he doesn't like the laws? How will this new knowledge influence me when I return there? I really don't know.

'Huh, Baas Jimmie, Small Baas Mark - are you really my boss as well?' I ask myself. Feeling agitated from the disturbing thoughts that this new knowledge has created in me, I bend over my thighs with both palms covering my face. I feel tearful, and struggle to release my anxiety. In a little while, I disown this dreadful feeling, letting my salty tears free onto the palm of my hands. I release my internal pain, crying out loudly. Was I better off not knowing anything?

I have no 'small baas' but Mark. Aah, he's a handsome, charming young man. I need to spend more time around him. Who knows, he might have different views about the laws. He is very quiet and I don't really know him.

Suddenly, another disturbing thought strikes me. I remember my mum, wearing my dad's old whitish underwear. She usually ties it with a string to hold it up due to its loose gusset. She wears it daily, and it gets a wash at night. My parents are very poor. My mum can't afford to buy herself underwear, not to mention clothes, yet she's worked on the farm since she married my dad. Dad has toiled here all his life. My parents care less about their status; they seem stuck here, and won't leave. Another pain grips my heart. *What's the point of worrying and complaining? Oh silly me.*

My parents genuinely adore the Douglas' family as if they were their own. They treat them as their son and daughter. They've known Jimmie from when he was a baby, and my mum was his nanny. Some days are better than others, though.

I pull my trunk into the middle of the dormitory ready to go out. In this process, I get distracted. Without realising it, I'm speaking to myself. "They are so devoted to them. Perhaps they know nothing, or very little," I say, not really bothered about Mandy passing by.

"What's that, sorry?" she asks, presuming I'm talking to her.

"No, don't worry, love. I'm thinking aloud, planning my holidays." She ignores me entirely, and carries on going out towards the clothes-line behind our dormitory.

I start humming my favourite chorus I learned at Sunday school, 'Yes, Jesus Loves Me' to distract the nerves. It doesn't work: my thoughts are too deep to ignore. "I should respect the farmers looking after us in their own terms, and stick to my original me," I continue to think aloud. "I should be closer to Mark; we might actually enjoy each other's company. He may learn from me, and perhaps I'll have a lot to learn from him. Hopefully, both our parents will be comfortable with our friendship. I wonder how my dad will react if I share with him what I now know. He always says, gesturing with his index finger, 'No political talk here. Those who want to discuss politics should do it away from me.' Perhaps one day he will change his mind."

I start feeling happy and excited at the thought of going home and interacting with Mark Douglas, and everybody I value the most. I know some good and popular things that are happening as a result of the current political climate, for example, the African National Congress (ANC) or the 'Viva Mandela, Viva!' in support of Nelson Mandela. Anyway, I have a lot to think about, but I have a duty to study any syllabus the government provides until I complete my education, and perhaps leave Skoonfontein.

On the farm, I'll speak to small Baas, Mark. He is studying at The University of Witwatersrand, one of the universities for European students instituted according to the 1959 University Education Law. He might help me out with my studies – who knows?

For some reason, today I'm thinking more about Mark than ever before. Is he his dad's favourite because he is his first-born son? Or perhaps it's because he is lovely, with good-looking features? Mark is two years older, and a bit taller than me – about five foot seven. His body often looks tanned, and he has dark-brown, thick, long hair cascading over his shoulders. He has a low voice, protruding lips, and greyish eyes. He always puts on casual clothes – jeans, t-shirts and trainers – except on Sundays. He wears suits and ties for church – The Dutch Reformed Fellowship. Lately, he has made an effort to talk to me, and isn't discouraged that I've always ignored him completely. I remember the olden days when he used to pass by me without saying, "Hello." *Ah, forget this, Betty, you were just a kid. Now you're a teenager.*

I believe I can engage him in a real conversation. How will I do this? My parents tell me to keep a 'reasonable distance' from

Baas Jimmie's children, and I am careful to observe this. Could they have been told the same by their parents? I doubt it because they are all friendly to me, especially since I moved to secondary school.

Always, I've shortened the conversation whenever they try talking to me, and I quickly walk away from them. I feel uncomfortable. I refuse to play with them or say anything to them. They are persistent though – small Baas Mark always stares and smiles at me. I've never smiled back. Does he know anything about these Apartheid Laws? If so, how much does he know? I go to Lottie's dormitory to say good-bye.

"Hey, Lottie, I'm leaving now. Have a good journey and I hope to see you next year, unless my application for a teacher training course is successful," I say, standing by the door.

"Enjoy your Christmas and New Year too. I'm leaving about 4.00 p.m. to catch the train from Queenstown to Johannesburg. I hope to be very busy this holiday, gathering more information about South Africa," Lottie replies, giving me a wink.

"Bring anything you can find, but be careful," I say.

"Betty, don't worry - I know. We need it, though, don't we?" Lottie answers, and I am slightly mollified.

"Well, I can't stay any longer to keep you company while you pack your stuff. Please stay in touch over the holidays. Will you remember that?"

"I'll be fine," Lottie says, forcing her overflowing suitcase to close. I give her a comforting hug. Feeling heartbroken from this separation, I turn my back towards her, and leave.

This time around, I will change my approach, and welcome Baas Jimmie's children. I'll accept their invitation into their Big House. I will be like a family friend and narrow the distance between us. As Mark is only two years older than I am, we should have a lot to talk about, especially secondary school life, and our ambitions.

"I hope his parents will go away, and that they invite me into the Big House. I'm looking forward to this," I say, lifting up my two clenched fists in excitement. I may borrow some interesting books from their bookshelves. I can also read the latest newspapers.

Eventually, I go to the telephone-booth to call a taxi. I pick up the receiver, and wind the handle to connect to the exchange.

"Exchange-number, please!" a man's voice says.

"Hello, hello," I say, surprised with this quick response. "34444 for taxis, please." I speak loudly. Immediately, I'm connected to the taxi operator.

"Hello, Tez Taxis."

"Could I have a taxi, please?"

"Where are you, and where to?"

"I'm at Butterworth High Hostel main entrance, and I'm going to the bus station."

"The taxi will be there in a few minutes," he says.

"Thank you."

The taxi arrives, and the driver helps me to put my trunk in the boot. Then the taxi pulls off, leaving a cloud of dust behind it. In about fifteen minutes, we are at the bus stop. I wait for half an hour before boarding the bus to Burgersdorp, my connection to Skoonfontein Farm.

The bus to Jimmie's farm is packed with farm labourers. Sadly, I don't know any of them. I remain quiet until I get off at my bus stop. I struggle to lift my trunk onto my head, and carry my bag with my right hand, slowly staggering home. As I leave the main road, I hear a car approaching from behind. I throw my luggage down to look, hoping it will be Baas Jimmie, and I'm right – it's him.

With great difficulty, I manage to load my luggage, and jump onto the back of the open van. I'm used to this. Baas always forgets to invite any of my family to sit in the front next to him, even on miserable rainy or snowy days. Soon, we arrive on the farm. He parks the van in front of the Big House on the drive way.

Bobby, one of his favourite dogs, welcomes him, wiggling his tail, perhaps hoping he is to be taken for a drive. He loves sticking his tongue out looking through the window of the van's front seat. That's enough to occupy Jimmie's mind, I suppose. He forgets about everything, and gives full attention to Bobby.

I drag my trunk home. It's no use leaving it for my mum to help, as she may be in the Big House preparing supper, and getting Theodora's baby into bed. I get home and make myself a cup of tea. Later, my mum returns, and the rest of the family is back. We all have supper from the left-over food mum has brought from the Big House.

"Mum, I'm old enough now to help you with your jobs in the Big House. Could you ask the missus if that's all right?" I ask Mum as she is about to shut the door, rushing off to work.

"Betty, I can try, but I don't think she will be happy to have both of us inside. I'll ask them, and suggest that two hands are better than one anyway. You get a lot done within a short time. When they see this benefit, they may agree."

"Try, Mum, please," I beg her. "Missus may appreciate having more work done at no extra cost."

Early in the morning the next day, my mum goes to the Big House to work as usual. After lunch, she returns to inform me, "Missus is very happy to have you helping me, Betty. However, she warned me, saying, 'Watch Betty. She should stick to the jobs you give her. She shouldn't be all over the house. Girls of her age are curious, and she could get you in trouble if you're not careful. Watch her, do you understand me, Gladys?'" Mum uses Missus' exact words to make sure I understand the importance of what she's saying.

"Okay, Mum, I understand," I assure her. Mum seems happier, too, and I see her off to work for her afternoon shift.

I have got what I wanted. Tomorrow, I'll be with my mum in the Big House. I start jumping up and down, in excitement. I look at the mirror, admiring myself, and feeling really inspired.

The day passes by speedily.

My mum comes home in the evening with good news for me again.

"Betty, Missus really needs you there. She has added more jobs for us to do tomorrow. Remember what we talked about earlier. You should be very careful."

"Oh Mum, c'mon, trust me. You know I'm responsible. How would she know if I touch anything?"

"Easily, Betty - she knows the order of everything. If you start moving things about where you were not asked to be, she will know. That would get me in trouble."

"Ahuh, here come 'limitations' again," I say to my mum, giggling.

Nevertheless, the next morning I prepare myself on time to join mum. She instructs me, and I happily obey her orders. I sweep the bedrooms, scrub and polish the wooden floors until they sparkle. I wash the curtains and hang them back. I iron all the washing. I arrange fresh flowers in the big vases and brighten the dark corridors, leaving the entire place tidy, with a scent. 'I'm a faithful helper,' I say to myself, walking slowly home, leaving my mum behind. I feel so tired that I fall asleep immediately. Mum comes back, and wakes me up with better news for me:

"Betty, Missus is very pleased with you," she says, walking about without looking at me. She continues, "She couldn't believe her eyes when she checked the vacant bedrooms. I've never managed to shine the veranda like you. Baas slipped and nearly fell down!"

"That's great news, Mum. I'll do it again," I respond.

"Yes, she wants you back."

My heart leaps joyfully. "That's wonderful, Mum."

From then on, I go to work in the Big House regularly with Mum. I speak to Mark Douglas every now and then, and find that we do have a lot in common. He is reading Political Science and History. When our eyes meet, my heart skips a beat. This is my secret, and I keep it to myself. I think I'm beginning to like him.

This particular Saturday afternoon, I've finished my work but Mum is still busy, so I wait for her in the back garden. It's beautiful, with green lawns and flowers. I sit on the bench admiring my surroundings and enjoying the sunshine. Suddenly, small Baas Mark comes along and stands by me.

"Hello, Betty," he says, staring at my face with what seems like admiration.

"Hello, Small Baas," I say, making eye contact with him for the very first time.

"You don't have to call me that, you know?" he says with a beaming smile on his face. I'm pleased by this.

"Oh well, I'm sorry. What should I call you then?"

"My name is Mark," he says. "I'll be very pleased if you use it."

"Will your parents be okay with that?" I feel very concerned.

"Yes, of course. I'm an adult now. I can do and say what pleases me."

"I have no problem with that, but I'll have to call you 'Small Baas' when other people are around – just to make things easier for me."

"Okay," he agrees, shaking his head in disapproval. We chat a bit. "Excuse me Betty," he says. "I'll be back soon." Mark goes inside. After a little while he brings with him a glass of orange squash and biscuits, and gives them to me.

"Thank you, Small Baas," I say, not really meaning it. My aim is just to embarrass him this time. He looks at me and laughs.

"You know I don't like you to call me that, Betty."

"Pardon me, then," I say. We talk about education. I tell him that I'm going into teacher training, and he encourages me to learn. "Knowledge and its application is the key to a successful life," he says.

I'm getting used to Mark, and I feel happy when we are together. He asks me to go for a walk around the farm with him some days. I'm uncomfortable about this at the start. I ask him to walk towards the back of our house and whistle a signal to get me out. I need to be safe lest Missus and Baas Jimmie see us, and disapprove of the friendship - something I anticipate will happen. They would then blame their son, not me, for coming around our house.

As we walk behind our house, towards the old rusty car that has been abandoned for ages, I feel my heart beat faster. I keep looking around in all directions. We walk towards it. Mark opens the door; it looks good inside. He sits in the back seat, and I stand holding the door.

"Betty," Mark calls to me. "Come closer to me, will you?" he continues, beckoning his hand towards himself. "You're beautiful," he says lowering his eyes for a moment before meeting my gaze with a strange intensity.

"Thanks, you too," I say, giving him a romantic look.

I'm a bit confused, though. Looking at his eyes, I see a handsome, confident young man. I listen to him speak: his voice triggers a sweet feeling inside me. He is wonderful, I conclude. I think about Lottie, Nancy, and our political discussion, but I see love in Mark. He seems to like me, too: I decide to see how things go. "You're gorgeous as well," I reply, surrendering myself to him.

He puts his arms around my shoulders, staring deeply into my eyes. I can hear his heart beating loudly as he presses himself onto my chest.

"I'd like to know you better, darling," he says, in his kind of soft, resonant voice. He moves his face closer to mine. Our lips touch. His deep breath accelerates. He kisses me, and I close my eyes tightly, enjoying the warmth within Mark's arms. "I love you, Betty. I love you very much," he says. "We must meet here again tomorrow, in the afternoon – don't you think so?"

I agree. Mark pulls me to himself again, and kisses me deeply, the 'passionate' kind this time around. Allowing my eyes to close,

I kiss him passionately too.

The old rusty Mercedes Benz car becomes our meeting spot. We meet up regularly. Whenever I hear his whistling, I go outside and head towards the old car. Our bond is natural, and we continue to spend a lot of time together.

Mark's version:

Betty, I've always found her attractive. I like the colour of her skin, her figure, hair, and height. She has everything a young man would wish for in a young woman. She is bright and can engage in a conversation. What more do I want? Nothing really. But, I have one problem; I don't think my parents will want me to love her. In that case, what will I do? Challenge them to give me reasonable reasons? Of course it's the laws. I don't think I care any more of what might happen to me. I'm in it now, and I love her – I love Betty.

January, the following year

I return from the Big House, after helping my mum serve morning coffee and breakfast. Feeling rather tired, I drag myself into the bedroom I share with Rita. Surprisingly, her bed is stripped – no blankets, no sheets. I look into our wardrobe, and her clothes aren't there. I look for her pair of shoes – they are missing. I search my parents' bedroom, and pass through the dining room to the kitchen, looking for clues – but nothing. Where is Rita?

No one said anything about Rita going away. I've lived with her most of my life. My parents fostered her, and that's all I know. I walked the long journeys to school with her most days. She defended me when I faced criticism from grown-ups and teasing from my schoolmates. She stopped my friends from hitting me. She lent me her clothes, and even carried me on her back, saving me from being pricked by thorns, when I had no shoes to wear.

Could she have decided to run away? But why would she? How could she not tell me? Perhaps, she's gone to another farm to find work. *That's not like her though*, I console myself. She hardly does any housework, rarely cooks dinner and supper or washes up, never chops firewood or drives the cattle to the river to drink. She's always in bed claiming to be ill, but not ill enough to see the doctor. I sit down feeling hurt.

The knock on the door distracts me. It's Theodora, Mark's mum. She gives me a letter in a big brown envelope. Eager to see what's inside, I open it immediately, and continue walking towards my bedroom.

"Great! I'm accepted at Benson Vale Teacher Training College! I'm going to train as a primary school teacher!" This is a two year course, but it's a long haul. So I'm not overly excited about this because I know this qualification is for working in specific areas, teaching the native children only. This gives me little pleasure, but I can't do anything about it for now. It's still an opportunity to help others succeed. Just then, my mum comes into my bedroom.

"Mummy, where's Rita?" I ask, my voice trembling, trying to hide my true feelings.

She replies moodily, "This is not the right time to ask me, Betty. Have you fed the chickens, and is everything all right?"

I pretend not to hear what she says, and rush to the kitchen to make her a cup of tea. My mum will never open her bag and give me anything until she has drunk 'tea from my own house', she always says.

While I'm serving her hot tea, I hear a whistle, and I recognise the tune. I know this song, *Goei nag, Goei nag, slaap my kleindjie* – Good night, Good night, sleep my young one. "It's my dad," I say happily. "Maybe, he's popping in for a short break from work." Joyfully, I run back into the corridor to the kitchen situated towards the back of our house to fetch an empty cup to pour him tea while it's hot. I don't want to be sent back to reheat it. I get the cup, and put the saucer beneath to take to my dad, the man I love. As I rush through the kitchen door, trying to get there before the tea gets cold, the cup flies over the saucer. Fearfully, I stretch my knee forward to prevent it from dropping on the floor. I can't drop it – my parents will be mad. I try to stop it from falling but it's too late to save it. It breaks, scattering into pieces everywhere. I quickly put down the saucer and pick up the broken china pieces before anyone sees this disaster.

I open the back door quietly, and walk a few steps to the back garden. I hold the bigger piece of china in my right hand, and aim to throw it, so that it lands far away, where no one will ever find it. As it leaves my hand, it cuts my index finger deeply.

The blood spurts out, triggering a severe pain. I stand still, pressing the cut hard to stop the bleeding and to suppress the pain, looking around to see if anyone sees me. I can't make a big fuss out of this; otherwise I'll get myself in trouble with my mum. So, I quickly go back inside, put a plaster on the deep bleeding cut, pretending nothing has happened.

I serve them both the tea, and then sit down. I tell them that I've got a place to train as a teacher, and that my course starts in two days. My mum shouts, "Oh, thank you, thank you, Lord!" She goes on and on, not realising I'm in pain.

"Well done, Betty," says my dad. Feeling the intensity of the pain from the cut, I quickly disappear into my bedroom. Later, I begin to prepare for my journey to the Teachers' College.

The next morning, I carry my belongings to the bus stop. Rita isn't there to help me, and kiss me good-bye. I'm sad about this, and anxious about leaving home again, and not seeing Mark for some time. I guess Rita might have returned to her parents or found a better shelter for herself. I don't have a long time to wait – the bus soon arrives. I buy my ticket, board the bus and find a vacant seat. The engine revs loudly as the bus pulls off gently. I look out through the window as we vanish into the winding dirt roads, leaving a cloud of dust behind.

Sitting quietly on the bus, I think about being a teacher. I have mixed feelings – why do I have to learn this Bantu education syllabus that I know is specific for those teaching the natives? What else could I do if I refuse it? Nothing – I'll end up doing menial work, or having no job to go to at all. In spite of all this, I will do my course.

I arrive at the college, and soon settle down well. The classes start, and I establish myself into the college routines. Days, weeks and months pass without hearing from Mark. I miss him so much that it hurts. My expectation for a letter from him never fades. I wish to receive a letter from him to relieve my emptiness. Refusing to allow this situation to distress me, I choose to believe and trust him. It's amazing what the mind is capable of doing. As the amount of work I have to do increases, and we have tests to prepare for, I have less time to think about Mark. I hope the Law will be more understanding, and allow us to engage in a fulfilling relationship. But where will this lead to? Will he marry me? I just don't know.

It's been announced that we are due to go out to local primary schools for teaching practice. I'm excited to be a teacher for the first time. I prepare my twenty lessons for the week, and Mrs Liver, my tutor, approves of them. By the end of the week, I'm ready to teach. Will I beat them, like other teachers do? No, trainees aren't allowed to use corporal punishment. I should make my lessons interesting, to inspire them to learn, rather than beat them.

On Monday morning, the school bus arrives to take us to our allocated schools. I go in, take the front seat, and read a novel entitled *I am David*. This is a story about a boy who could not smile. A prison guard helps him to escape from a concentration camp in Eastern Europe through Italy and Greece to Denmark. Whenever I have spare time, I love to read books. I need to know more about the world, and I hope that one day I'll be able to share my exact feelings with someone, here, or perhaps even abroad.

The bus pulls out of the driveway onto the main dirt road. We head towards the town, passing over the bridge with the river flowing gently beneath. It's a long way before we get to my school. I try to concentrate on my book, finding it interesting, and I'm drawn in. I feel a tear escape my eye. I cry discreetly, covering my eyes with a handkerchief, and gently rubbing my cheeks to avoid removing my makeup. I distract myself by looking at the roadside. The bus slows to drop off the first lot, and then it's my turn. Feeling low from the story I've just read, I gather my stuff and wait for my stop.

I get off the bus and walk to the school: it's a reasonable distance from the town. I report to the principal's office. He takes me to a Standard One class to meet the teacher, and introduces me to the children. After the Assembly, I teach Mathematics and English, and the morning goes on very well.

At lunchtime, I go down town to buy myself more reading materials. It's a lovely hot afternoon: the sky is blue, with birds flapping their wings in the air, and I can hear them singing on the trees. I enter the supermarket that sells books and newspapers, and buy *The Daily Dispatch*, and a grammar book. On my way back, I take a different route, passing by the Sparrow Laer Primere Skool, meaning Lower Primary School, which is for Europeans only. It's a shortcut, and will give me more time to rest before the afternoon session starts.

As I walk past, I see children in the playground. I stand and watch them through the five foot tall barbed-wire fence with razor blade trimming that surrounds the school. It's very well secured indeed.

Some children are playing on the swings; others are sliding down slides; another small group is going up and down the seesaw. The rest are playing tennis, netball, hula-hoops, volley ball, cricket and other ball games. Opposite the playgrounds are outdoor swimming pools. Some boys jump in and disappear under the water for a while. I see their heads above the water, and then they disappear again, and come out at the other end. I shouldn't hang on the fence for too long. An adult, perhaps one of their teachers appears, gesturing at me from a distance to go away. I don't move. She takes a few steps towards me. I resist and she shouts, "Hey, 'kaffir'!" (meaning 'unbeliever', or 'a derogatory name for the native'), then gives a signal again for me to 'go away'.

She speaks to one of the children, who beckon to another, and they both run into the building. I'm afraid she might be sending a child to their principal to call the police and cause trouble for me. I rush away then turn and look at her as she walks towards the school buildings. I wish I was a European child, just so I was able to enjoy their privileges.

I walk along the roadside to my school. It's still lunch-time and some children are sitting in the shade under the trees narrating stories. I come closer to listen. The stories vary in length, but all have a moral. The story-teller ends by asking,

"What is the moral of this story? And what can you learn from it?" Story-telling is allocated time in the curriculum because of its benefit to the children. It precedes creative writing. It seems that the children like it so much that they continue sharing stories at playtime.

Other children are sitting on the ground playing the 'Puca' game. They have dug a round shallow pit on the ground and put twelve stones in. They take turns to throw a stone up and, while it's in the air, take all the small stones out of the pit, and then catch the falling stone. The stone goes up once more and then they push the rest back into the pit keeping one. They then continue until all the stones are out of this pit. When they fail to get the right number in, they're out and the next child takes over. The children seem to be enjoying this game as they talk and laugh.

Another group of children are playing a game called 'Round-us'. There are two teams, the Fielding Team and the Playing Team, and four goal posts with a circle in the middle. Two girls are throwing an improvised ball made of old stockings and fabric over to each other, while the rest of the opponents run into the goal posts. The two girls try to throw the ball at those who run between the goal posts. Those who are touched have to go out, but if one of the players scores twenty-four, they all shout, "Twenty-four!" and run into the circle and the game starts again. However, if they are all touched, the game is over and they swap sides. I stand there watching them for a while.

They play happily, enjoying school life.

Some boys and girls are playing 'Touch'. A child chases and touches someone. That one does the same to the others, and the game goes on. Another game I find fascinating is the 'ball' game. Children are in two teams, A and B, separated by a line drawn on the ground. A child from team B rolls the ball and calls a name of the child from team A. The named child runs, kicks the ball as far away as possible, runs and touches the line, and then goes back to the starting point. While running, they throw a ball at them; if they are hit, they're out; if not, they score a goal.

In the classrooms, other children are playing with their homemade skipping ropes which are made from grass. They sing the song 'Cat Chases a Mouse'; they hop three times, and then go out. The cat mews. They hop once and go out.

Other children are playing a game in pairs. I move closer to see them keeping a rhythm with clapping hands and patting knees. They all speak in a chorus, "1, 2, 3 – 4, 3 - 4 up, up, 3-4, 3-4 down, down, 3-4, 3-4 left side 3-4, 3-4, right side, hurray!" The games are beautiful, with children playing together all by themselves with no teachers or adults around.

I carry on up to my classroom and sit down to reflect on what I've seen. The bell rings, the children walk in, and I continue to teach, appreciating the creativeness which I've just observed. This part of the country is similar to Skoonfontein. I remember my childhood days. The school finishes, and I board the bus back to the hostel. It's noisier this time and we all chat together, sharing and laughing about our first teaching experience. The rest of the week goes well, and we later find that we've all got good grades for our teaching practice.

December 1967

I'm home for the Christmas holidays. I'm looking forward to spending time with my boyfriend, Mark.

"Mum, would you like some help in the Big House tomorrow?"

"Of course, Betty. It makes my life easier when you're there. Be ready for 8 o'clock, then."

At 7.30 a.m., I'm ready, and having porridge for breakfast. After drinking coffee, I wait in the living room for my mum. We walk together to the Big House and she knocks on the door. Missus takes her time to welcome us in. She goes through a long list of today's jobs – "Washing the windows, scrubbing and polishing the floors until they shine. You know what I mean Gladys, don't you?"

"Yes, Missus, you want everything spotless."

I stand there, looking at her, smiling and nodding frequently, wondering how she expects my mum to complete all that hard work. It's good that I came along to help her.

I start cleaning all the bedrooms, including Mark's, while he's outside taking the dog for a walk and deliberately ignoring me. I am thinking. Baas Jimmie is having visitors for barbecue today. The whole family will be sitting outside together, so I'm unlikely to see Mark. I really miss him.

My love for him has grown stronger over the year. He is definitely opposed to the Apartheid Laws, and is a genuine socialist. But he can't show this because this would 'disgrace' his entire family; his dad warned him, he told me this. I also know that Baas Jimmie would never cope with that kind of life. He is one of the respected European Farmers, expected to uphold the South African laws. I hope they never find out. I work between the house and the garden preparing salads, collecting and replacing clean utensils. I hear loud talking, and ignore them.

I return to our house, leaving my mum to finish the last of the day's chores. Through our front window, I can see the visitors' cars pulling out gradually one by one. I'm contented, suppressing my feelings of love. At least, Mark has seen me around.

It's summertime, and light outside. *Perhaps Mark will go for a walk past our house, and I can see him?* I feel my tummy rumble as I think of him. I miss him loads. I keep looking through the window until I see the last car drive off.

Suddenly, Mark comes out and walks towards the sheds. He returns shortly and walks towards the back of our house. I conclude he's out to meet me in the old car. Usually, he whistles loudly as he walks past our house. I wait for a while and then sneak out discreetly.

I hear the whistle, and believe that Mark is calling me. My heart leaps with joy. I feel fulfilled and confident. I'm wearing my black trousers and white top which I got from Mark's mum. I walk out quietly behind our house passing the stables and the kraal towards the fields, where the old cars are. I can't see Mark from the distance, but I know he is waiting for me inside the ancient rusty car, our usual meeting spot.

* * *

We should be all right tonight. Baas Jimmie and Missus should be in bed earlier after the heavy alcohol drinking with their guests. They won't notice that Mark is still out. And he's a grown man, for goodness' sake: they should leave him to follow his own mind.

I reach the old car, and Mark is lying on his back waiting for me, with the car door slightly open. As he hears my footsteps, he sits up.

"Betty!" he shouts, opening his arms to cuddle me.

"Mark!" I say, throwing myself into his opened arms, satisfied. We hold each other tightly for a while before we begin to kiss and talk. He gives me a good kiss – the type of kiss I enjoy most. I later stare into his eyes, making sense of every word he says. *I still love him,* I think to myself: *he's amazing!*

He tells me about their visitors – his family friends and his uncle. We talk about life generally and I ask him many questions about the European culture. What happens if his family discovers our affair? Should I fall pregnant, what will he do? What if we decide to live together permanently and, therefore, have to marry? What do we do if I'm put in prison for breaking the *Mixed Marriages Law, Act 55 of 1949* which prohibits us from marrying?

Mark is mature and independent in his thinking. He allays all my fears, and commands me not to worry because he doesn't.

"Betty, be courageous for your beliefs," he says. I regain my courage and assure myself; I'm in love with my small Baas Mark. He is such good company.

I touch his soft, silky hair, moving my hand gradually around his head. We hold each other, and kiss, cheeks, lips, and everywhere. He confesses how much he loves me. There's less talk and more action, groaning out of pleasure. Mark becomes so ready that I want to make him happy. As he is about to go further, I hear a shout, "Mark!" and recognise his father's loud aggressive voice.

"Mark, please listen," I say softly, trembling in fear. Our bodies are so entwined together that Mark feels I'm engulfed in terrible fright. I cling onto him tightly anticipating the end of my precious life. Mark ignores me and continues with kisses.

"Betty!" I recognise my mum's voice.

"Mark, we're in trouble. They're looking for us. What shall we do?" I ask, panicking. I clasp my arms around him. I could hear his heart beating as he breathes heavily.

"Nothing, Betty, we're fine. Don't be afraid. Just relax please, darling. Stay quiet, please," says Mark, sticking his head out of the back window, listening carefully.

Feeling a bit weak, and sweating, I sit up and look at our home. As the sun has set, the atmosphere is darker, making it almost impossible to see clearly at a distance. All I can see are three figures coming towards us. Without doubt, I am assured that we're caught – that's Mark's mum and dad, and my mum.

After a moment of excruciating silence, Mark says, "Betty, let's go." I remain still. "C'mon, get up!" he says firmly, pulling my hand.

Bravely, we both get out of the old rusty car and walk straight towards them, hand in hand. We get closer to them, about one hundred metres. Mark is about to branch into the direction of the Big House, so he changes his position to hug and kiss me, "Goodnight, my Betty."

Then, I hear, *Bang! Bang!*

"Betty!" Mark cries out loudly in anguish. "Betty, hold me," he repeats, his body pushing me backwards. I grab him trying to hold his heavy body upright without success. He slides sideways, drops on the ground and the blood spurts out from his forehead where the bullet penetrated him. His eyes roll over involuntarily, and I realise Mark could die.

"No, Mark, don't leave me!" I wail hysterically in shock and frustration. I look at his chest. He is alive, and seems to be struggling to breathe. His eyes close and open again. "I love you, Betty." Those words were clear.

I hear my mum screaming, "No, Baas" and then cries in despair, "My God, oh my God!" Whether his mum screamed or not, I can't tell. At that moment, there was only fast movement and commotion.

"He's killed him!"

Jimmie, holding his shotgun in his hand, comes running to the scene. The whisky effect might have vanished as he realises what he has done. He drops his shot gun on the ground, calling in distress, "Mark, Mark!" He shakes his body. There is no response. "Wake up!" He kneels down over Mark.

I feel a harsh grip on my hand; it's my mum. "Go!" she says, whispering. As I turn around to walk away, my mum following behind me, I hear Jimmie wailing terribly, "Mark, my only son! It's me, your dad... No, my son; you will live...Jesus!"

I think my mum realises I'm not walking fast enough; I'm weak, shocked and confused. So, she grabs my hand more firmly, as she overtakes me whispering, "Betty, we've got to leave this farm, now! We can't stay here for another night. Hurry up!" Mum appears to be in her worst state of mind. Still confused, attempting to make sense of what has happened, I reduce my speed and ultimately drag myself behind my mother. She gets annoyed. Looking back at me, she says,

"Hurry up, Betty! Snatch whatever you can! The police might be here soon. Baas may follow us to take out his anger and grief. He might want revenge. Quick!" We get home and alert dad.

"Benjamin, wake up! We must leave now!"

My dad opens his eyes, still drowsy from sleep. "Don't be silly, where should we go?" he says, sitting up. "Gladys, sit down, what's the matter?"

My dad tries to understand what's happening; my mum is not giving the full explanation. She's rushing around saying, "We'll talk on the way. Baas had a lot of whisky. He was very drunk. He couldn't have done that."

"Done what? Speak to me – I need to know." But my dad still follows us to the main road.

With extreme difficulty, Mum tries to explain the details of what happened. "I loved him, like my own son. I brought him up!" she screams.

Dad cannot come to terms with what has happened. There's just chaos. "What is it?" he keeps asking, as if he has lost his mind.

"Baas Jimmie pulled the trigger, pointing at the kids," says Mum. "They were in the wrong place together – Betty and Mark."

"Where is Mark now?"

"I doubt if he'll survive. I don't know. We had to rush away out of fear that he would want revenge on us."

"I don't think he knew what he was doing – too much alcohol. I know Baas Jimmie; he is the good Baas."

"Mum, we left Mark breathing," I confirm.

"No, no, no!" In his shock, that's all my dad can say. "We must go away now!" he grabs some bags and leads the way. The tension gets worse, as each one of us grieves in our own way.

My dad makes repeated groaning noises, and murmurs, "Why? Why did you allow it, Lord?" My mum cries openly, constantly wiping off tears with the apron she's wearing. My head is throbbing, and my eyes are blinded with tears, making it hard for me to keep up the pace. I feel a deep pain in my heart – a pain of loss and regret – and the internal ache in me increases with every second. I feel the emptiness that accompanies the thought that Mark Douglas will probably be gone forever. I'll never see him again, or feel his gentle touch. I will miss him. My eyes flood with tears, and I bottle them up by squeezing my eyes and lips tightly together. *No, Mark will not die,* I console myself.

I walk between my parents for a little while, carrying my suitcase on my head. My dad's long legs allow him to stride, leaving both my mum and me behind. He realises this, and looks back shouting, "Hurry up!"

I keep up with him for a little while, and then the distance between us starts to increase, gradually. Feeling exhausted, I run a bit. I can't keep the pace; I drag my feet, panting heavily. My heart thumps loudly. I think I am going to faint. I put my right hand on my chest to suppress the pain coming from within. I look back to see how far my mama is behind me. The atmosphere is dark, with a cold breeze cutting through; I can see a figure following, and I know it's her. I put my suitcase down, sit on it, waiting for her.

As she arrives, she can hardly breathe. Her body weight contributes to her struggling to rush, and worse of all the shock and hurt. My dad waits for us. I hope we shall all rest, to allow both my mum and I to regain strength, for this journey seems to be long and draining.

"We must hurry up. Our lives are in danger," he says, carrying on.

"Dad, please, let us wait a bit; Mum is out of breath." He slows down; we walk together, but not for long.

For a time, I walk deliberately slowly, hoping Jimmie will catch up with us, enact his revenge and kill me. I don't care anymore. This seems a better option than having to face guilt and loneliness all my life. It's hard fumbling in the dark on such a bad road with deep potholes. The grass is so tall in some areas that we are unable to walk faster. I take a few steps forward and peep backwards.

I try to reason all this. *Will Baas and his wife follow us or try to save Mark, by rushing him to the hospital? Is Mark dead? If not, how will he be in the future? Will he still be the man he was?* Finally, I think, *whether Mark lives or dies, I'll never know.*

We have a long walk until we reach the main road towards Burgersdorp. We get to the T-junction and turn right. The road is quiet at this time of the night. Walking between my mum and dad in such a pitch-black night with no street light to bring a glimpse of light is hard indeed. I wonder where we're going but no one tells me. My mum talks to herself, muttering "you've got us into this trouble."

"They're following us," says Dad. Mum turns and looks backward at the same time as me. I see the moving lights from a distance. As we approach a small bridge, Dad shouts, "Get in under here!" I go in first with Mum following. We're all panting and no one talks. I hear the sound of the cars driving above us on the road.

They have not discovered us; at least, we're safe for the night. We all fall asleep and the sound of cars wakes me up early the next day. With no water to wash or drink, and food to eat, we continue our journey to nowhere. We pass many farms on route until we come to a side road with a bridge. We go in to hide again.

Dad leaves us for hours while he tries to trace his cousin who lives at Kanevlak village nearby. He returns to collect us with Uncle Ben who is limping because of a gold mining accident in Johannesburg which took place many years ago. He got trapped underground for a week when his mine collapsed. We go to his house and he welcomes us in, making us feel at home.

Over time, we settle well again. Dad starts making red bricks to sell and his business develops gradually, until he has orders waiting. He employs Ruben and Stutterheim to help him meet the demand. They work long hours daily, just like at Skoonfontein farm.

I mourn the loss of my boyfriend, Mark, for months with outbursts in between. One day I think he died from the bullet shot and other times, I doubt myself and think he could have survived. Perhaps the help he needed came on time and he's in the hospital. Whatever happened that evening doesn't matter to me anymore; the fact is, I've been so deeply hurt ever since I heard that bullet shot, Mark calling my name and I couldn't help him, the pool of blood and Baas Jimmie's wailing.

Having nobody to comfort me, I cry until I am dried out of tears to shed. These are my darkest moments which only I could feel. I couldn't say, "Goodbye" to the boy I love. If he died and is buried, I may never lay a wreath, put a rose or stone on his grave. If he died, his headstone will be engraved, *Mark Douglas, born on*

21 June 1948 and died on the 20th December 1967 and a scripture. Perhaps, I'd visit him one day in their family cemetery – his last resting place.

I dream about him so often. Sometimes he just disappears, leaving me in deep sorrow. I wake up screaming or chasing him. I dream of those affectionate moments – when he assured me that he would live with me forever, anywhere in the world. I miss him so much.

Some thoughts I couldn't dismiss from my distressed mind: when Mark took me in his arms, his voice, declaring hope for our future – these echo through me every so often; his assurance of loving me, when I doubted it, which made me carry on in our relationship. I wish to be with him very much and I mostly remember our last tragic night together. He was so loving and he wouldn't let me go. My heart aches terribly. I feel a sharp pain on my left, just beneath my breast. I put my right hand over it and press very hard to suppress the pain but it doesn't go away.

The loud bang, his body-weight as he leaned against me, the gasp, and his words, "Betty, I love you." The sight of Mark's pooled blood traumatises me the most. The horrific cry from Jimmie in despair echoes in my ears. I hardly sleep.

* * *

The world is wonderful, and full of surprises. No one can comprehend these, unless he or she has experienced them. I'm glad this happened after Rita, my cousin, had left. It could have been worse if they were around, and had to go through such a misery by night. I can't imagine not seeing Mark again.

I certify that Betty Baker has been one of the best teachers at this school. She teaches English and History in Standards Three, Four and Five. She shows enthusiasm in imparting her knowledge to the learners. Her teaching and learning approaches take place with ease, and she gets teacher-learner rapport going excellently in her classes. Her empathy towards learners' problems and needs is such that she extends extra help by counselling them and encouraging peer-support.

Betty Baker initiated extra-mural activities in this school, such as supporting programmes for children with communication and emotional difficulties. Due to this programme, learners are able to open up and communicate their problems, which stem from either home or school. I asked her to conduct teacher- development workshops, which have been successful.

She also coaches netball and conducts the school-choir. Her scripture reading during school's assembly is brought down to the level of learners for better understanding. Her long association with this school provides her with a breadth of experience in dealing with her colleagues and learners from various ethnic backgrounds, as well as the opportunity to apply her specialised skills in a real situation.

I wish her success in her future endeavours and that this certification receives the merit it deserves.

Mrs Penny Groves
Headmistress,
Mount View Primary School
10th July, 1971

The day before the shooting disaster

I'm in bed at uncle Ben's home alone thinking. I remember the Douglas family having barbecues, fun all afternoon, playing board games, swimming, and drinking all sorts of drinks – alcoholic, hot drinks and non-alcoholic ones, and Jimmie getting over the limit. I see him driving around the barns in his jeep, while heavily drunk. There are no traffic officers to stop and check on him. The nearest police station is in Burgersdorp. In fact, that's where many public services are based - quite a long way from Skoonfontein.

As I'm working, helping my mum in the Big House, I hear the high revs of the jeep, before it goes quiet. I look through the kitchen window, and see Baas Jimmie stepping out of the van, shutting the door very hard, rushing towards the back where the visitors and Theodora are sitting. He opens a folding chair and sits down facing the swimming pool, with his back towards the barbecue stand.

I take my eyes off him for a little while, to wash up the empty glasses. There's a row outside, where the Douglases are entertaining their visitors. I'm curious to know what this is all about. I decide to go out to collect firewood, as it is closer to where the family is gathered. I hear the disagreement between Mark and his dad. Listening carefully, Jimmie is opposing Mark's intention of becoming a human rights solicitor in South Africa.

"I don't believe in this human rights thing. We do have rights, so who are you going to defend?" Jimmie challenges Mark. Marie and her husband are opposing him, arguing that Mark should be allowed to decide his future.

"Not while living under my roof," says Jimmie. As the alcohol intake begins to work, his agitation increases. He walks about, stretching his thin lips, making faces, demonstrating the power he holds.

Jimmie continues nagging Mark, refusing to discuss other

issues. He just wants to talk about South Africa and its successful governance. He is fond of the government, "because the natives have some authority, and are running their affairs in their homelands." Mark speaks against the South African practice of discriminating against certain racial groups, and walks away in a rage in the end.

I take the firewood into the kitchen, and ask Theodora if it is okay for me to leave.

"Of course you can; you've finished your chores for now."

I quickly walk back to our house, hoping to connect with Mark.

After a short while, I hear his whistle. I look out of the window, and see him pass our house, heading towards the old car, our usual meeting place. A few moments later, things go wrong. What caused Baas Jimmie to pull the trigger at us? No one knows; only Jimmie Douglas can tell.

Jimmie rushes towards us. Missus Theodora, after seeing Jimmie pointing the gun at us and hearing the gun shots, hurries behind Jimmie to get to where Mark and I are. She finds her husband kneeling over Mark, who is lying down on the pool of his blood, gasping for breath. Immediately, she rushes back to the house, probably to call the ambulance, while Jimmie is doing all he can - applying First Aid to save his son.

Some months later

I have not given up loving Mark, nor ruled out being with him again. I don't know where he is, whether dead or alive. Nevertheless, I'm hopeful that I'll see him again some day. I can't dismiss the idea that he might have a special need, that requires him to be looked after by his parents, day and night, or he may be cared for in a government hospital. Perhaps he has recovered already and is a human rights lawyer, something he desperately wanted to do, especially after having an intimate, secret relationship with me. I don't allow this situation to distress me. I think positively.

I could travel to Burgersdorp, and visit the library to search the archives for the news from the month Baas Jimmie shot Mark. There may be some articles about that incident. I may be able to establish what actually happened to Mark after all.

I decide: *I'll visit the family graveyard first, to find out if Mark's grave is there. If he is dead, I can have closure, and if he is alive, we can continue our relationship. He can visit me now in my home without being afraid of Jimmie, Theodora, my parents or anybody else.*

However, I'd still have other problems here – the headman, and the villagers. They know I'm unmarried, and this act is 'immoral'. Therefore, they will never approve seeing a man in my home, especially a European. The place would be in total havoc. I'll have no reason to give them for having him in. He could come at night, and if anybody is inquisitive, and they knock at my door, he can go into hiding under my bed. It's high enough; there will be sufficient room for him underneath. I'll quickly lead them outside to finish the talk, just in case Mark becomes uncomfortable, or needs to cough or use the toilet – the pit latrine outside.

My thoughts drift from the present. I recall life at Skoonfontein. I miss Mark Douglas very much. *Where is he? Will we continue our love affair, if we can find each other? Yes, maybe he still loves me too. He kissed me, after all?*

My thoughts trigger my tears. I rush to my bed, bury myself under the pillow, and cry out loudly. I speak to myself, 'Mark - we parted too early. You were very kind to me. I'd like to be with you. I miss you… I love you.'

I must have fallen asleep. I wake up from my dream, hearing Mark calling, "Betty!" I missed the opportunity to say 'Goodbye', or 'Rest in peace'. I must do this. I must go to Skoonfontein Farm to look for Mark, or his grave, and lay a stone. I must have him, or release him from my heart for good, and move on. I stay in, awake, finding it hard to sleep. I reach the conclusion in the early morning to visit Skoonfontein the next Saturday. This is the risk I'm prepared to take, just as I did that last night at Skoonfontein.

Early on Saturday, I get up, and prepare myself to return to the farm, to look for my boyfriend Mark, or his headstone, and pay him my last respects. I flag down the van passing by. It stops, and I jump in. I'm not in the mood for a talk, but this driver continues asking me questions to which I respond, "Yes," or "No," noncommittally, hoping he will leave me alone.

He doesn't give up: he wants to know where exactly I'm off to, and why I should be visiting the Boer farm. I surely cannot be 'sexually messing about' with them, says this driver, perhaps wondering why on earth somebody looking good like me, would be visiting a farm. I don't dare to tell him the true story regarding my visit. Instead, I make up a story:

"My aunt used to work for Baas Jimmie in Skoonfontein. She died after a short illness, and was buried on his farm. On her anniversary, I make it my priority to visit her grave, to clean it up," I say.

"Oh, that's very kind of you to do that. Few young ladies are like you. They usually forget and move on," this man says.

Great - my story has stopped the driver from digging into my life. He starts apologising.

"I'm very sorry to hear this, young lady. Will it help if I drop you closer to the farm, and then you can find your way back?"

"Yes, thank you. That's very kind of you."

He drives as close as he can to the farm, and drops me. He accepts the hiking fee, and drives off. I wait by the roadside for a while. I walk across the fields towards the family cemetery. The grass is tall. This is to my advantage. I should be concealed from a distance. My brown pair of trousers with a matching jacket helps me to be invisible from afar as well.

As I approach the cemetery entrance, I notice that it looks

bigger than when we left. I see many more headstones. My heart beating very fast, I open the gate, walk a few steps forward on the overgrown grass and start reading the names from the graves. The headstone of the first grave is almost covered in sand and tilting to the right. I take my handkerchief out of my hand bag, and brush off the sand. It says, 'James Douglas, Senior, died on 12 August 1927 aged 63' and the one next to it appears fresher, with clear writing, hidden behind the long grass. It says, 'Theodora Douglas, born in 1918, died in 1968 aged 50'.

"Oh, Theodora - That's Missus, has she died?" Thinking, *I got this wrong,* I bend over, saying, "died - Theodora – that's Mark's mum! How did she die? Oh no!"

I blurt out a cry before carrying on. The cemetery has overgrown weeds, and knocked-over headstones. It could do with cleaning, I think. This was one of my parents' jobs to clean it up, water the flowers, and then plant new ones if necessary. It is a respected place, where the Douglas' ancestors are buried.

I look in the direction of the farm houses, ensuring my safety. My heart sinks as I approach the next headstone. On it, the writing is 'Mark Douglas'... I look at it; the dates of birth and death aren't clear. This grave is run down too, with grass all over it. I feel a lump dropping into my throat. It hurts. I swallow my saliva to remove it. This lump won't go. I bend over to pull out the grass out of the way. I disturb a snake; it slithers away. I stand motionless for a while.

And then, I open my mouth to speak, "Mark. You were never annoyed with me." Tears flood my eyes, as I continue expressing myself. "I can't believe you're lying here." My voice vanishes. I whisper, "I love you loads. May your soul rest in peace." I take out the bottle of coke from my bag to have a sip. It removes the lump. I feel it disappear. I had the stone I picked up from the road in my hand. I put it down beside me, and pull out the grass to read the dates below his name. It reads, 'Born in 1930, and died in 1945 – Rest in peace, and rise in glory. We'll meet up with you again.' I release the tears I have been holding for a long time. I pull the weeds off, and tidy it up a bit, feeling relieved - this is not my boyfriend's grave. I turn around, walking towards my right-hand side, passing other graves with broken headstones. I search the whole place, and can't find my Mark Douglas, who was born in 1948.

As I turn around on my way back, I see a van driving towards the fields and the cemetery. I sense trouble. Fear grips me. I hurry towards the direction of the road. The van drives towards me. *I'm dead. That's it. Baas Jimmie won't spare me.* I carry on walking, determined to face the worst. The van stops. A youngish European man flings the door open, and jumps out.

"Hey, woman, what are you doing here?"

"I'm sorry, Baas; I'm visiting my Aunty's grave. She was buried here. She worked for Baas Jimmie and Theodora Douglas for many years, before she died."

"Okay, I own this farm now. I don't like people trespassing on my land."

"I'm so sorry, Baas; I came to pay my last respects. I do this yearly on her death anniversary – to remember her. She loved me."

"This is private land. Do you understand me, and what that implies?"

"Yes, Baas," I reply with my fragile voice, hoping to gain sympathy. In my mind, I'm wondering what happened to Mark and Baas Jimmie; if they had passed away, their graves would be in this cemetery, perhaps next to Theodora's.

"This is my farm. So go away now!" As I turn my back to walk aside, he speaks to me again.

"Have you finished your business?" I keep quiet wondering, *what business? I didn't come to run a business here. After all, I spent my money on this journey.* But he explains himself:

"I mean to say, have you worked on your Aunty's grave? Are you happy now?"

"Yes, thank you," I reply, with a nervous giggle, pretending to be satisfied. I'm unhappy, and confused. I need to solve a mystery – Mark and Jimmie's whereabouts. So, I ask him, "Where is Baas Jimmie, who previously owned this farm?"

"I do not wish to discuss anything with you. Go now, and do not visit your dead aunt ever again."

I'm free. I walk all the way, hoping to stop the first car to pass by. I wonder what happened to Missus. People die of various causes. I wonder what happened to Jimmie and Mark.

I'll discover one day – or perhaps I'll never know. I have no connections with the Europeans here. This may complicate this matter.

I walk for a long distance without a car passing by. My legs ache; my eyes are in floods of tears, because this breaks my heart. I feel dizzy as if my head is spinning around. In my mind, I'm asking one question, *where are they, then?* I know now about Theodora, and not about Mark and Jimmie Douglas. If they are dead, and I can find their graves, my heart can rest.

Suddenly, I hear the car sound from behind me. It's dark; only the lights shine on me. I stick my hand out to stop it.

"What are you doing here this time, woman?"

"I have visited my family. Now I'm returning to my home," I respond to shut him up.

"Get in, and let's go," he says. "You're beautiful. Who do you resemble?"

"Thank you. People say, I'm my dad's spitting image," I say, and then keep quiet, hoping he will leave me alone to ponder over the day's key issues.

The driver wants to drop me in town. As it is very late, I ask for a lift to the township where natives live; I know where I belong. The first house I go into takes me in for the night, and I proceed home the next day. I feel relieved that I've visited the farm to look for Mark. I don't give up hope that I might bump into him one day.

6th June 1974

Dear Betty,

Sometimes, when I'm alone, your voice echoes faintly across the broad sea. When the touch and feel of your beautiful body are out of reach, I wonder...where will we meet again?

Will it be down a long country lane, with hedges of sweet-smelling hawthorn, wild raspberry bushes and honeysuckle?

Or with dry stonewalls of limestone, winding as a viper to the lofty heights of an English hill?

When will we meet again? Might it even be in another life?

As maybe our physical bodies are destined never to reside together on this earth?

One thing's for sure, our souls are intertwined.

We may need to retire to bed together, drifting into a sleep. Or in that place, speak, share thoughts, hopes and ambitions. Furthermore, in that place, we may hold hands until the raw light of dawn pulls us apart.

So, for us...my Sweetheart, the night would hold no terror or fright. However, just a blissful walk together!

Love from
Greg x

Poem sent from Great Britain

Chapter 6

The Hearing

July 1968

It's a misty morning, with a cool breeze, in Aliwal North. Visibility is poor, with cars having their fog lights turned on, driving slowly, avoiding running over the pedestrians, crossing the streets randomly. Some drivers are blowing their horns, frustrated with the traffic jams on the road by the Magistrates' Court. The streets are busy with many farm-workers, who have come to see justice for Mark Douglas, who the Bakers love. Some men are sitting by the Magistrates' Court, smoking their long pipes and chatting across among themselves as early as seven o'clock, ensuring they get a place inside the tiny courtroom.

The paperboys are doing their rounds, delivering newspapers to the shops. The headline on the front page of today's 'The Daily News' reads, 'JIMMIE DOUGLAS IN COURT', attracting people's attention. This seems to be the most read article this morning, especially by the natives, who have come from the farms around Burgersdorp, Aliwal North, Lady Grey and Bethulie. Newspapers in native languages have covered the story also.

As the courtroom on the natives' side is not big enough to accommodate everyone, so some people are listening to the deliberations through the loud speaker system, and an interpreter from outside. My dad, mama, uncle and aunt are among the people, who have come to see Baas Jimmie on trial.

They have arrived on time, and secured a good view in the second row from the front. I'm happy to be seated with them.

The court is summoned to stand up as the judge and court messengers walk in. There is a remarkable silence, with no one talking, moving about or shuffling – you could hear a penny drop. The back door opens, and two police officers accompanying Baas Jimmie walk in, with him in the middle. Today, he is dressed in a grey suit, his hair and beard well groomed. He has lost a lot of weight.

"Where is Missus?" whispers my dad, appearing sad. He stands up to have a better view on the other side, perhaps hoping to see Theodora. Sitting down, he whispers again, "It's strange for Theodora not to be here to support him." My dad still loves the Douglas' family like his own.

Aunty shrugs her shoulders in response, as if to imply, 'I don't know', but she scans the courtroom until she actually stands up, ensuring a clear view. "No, Theodora is not here," she whispers. I think, *should I tell them? How will they react?*

I tap my aunt on the shoulder, whispering in her ear, "Aunty, Missus passed away. I saw her grave in their cemetery." My aunt looks at me for a moment, in disbelief, before turning around, whispering to my parents.

Marie and her husband, the neighbours of the Douglases, are sitting in the front row, on the European side of the court. Jimmie is sitting closer to his solicitor on the dock situated on the right-hand side of the courtroom.

The prosecutor stands up and calls the court to order, before reading the charges, and concluding with, "Jimmie Douglas, do you plead guilty, or innocent?"

Jimmie stands up and responds, "I reserve my right to remain silent."

The prosecutor then says, "The defendant is exercising his right; therefore, the case number SA&P Douglas V State is adjourned for trial on Tuesday 22 October 1968, and that's in three months' time. The defendant will be remanded in custody. Bail is refused. You can take him back to the cells."

The officers take him through the back door into the cells, where he has been locked up, in preparation for the trial. The court is commanded to stand, and then dismissed.

There is a lot of murmuring from the natives' side, as they walk out to join others outside. Their views vary, but they are all sympathetic to the tragedy in the Douglas' family. Some say Jimmie deserves punishment, if he is found guilty. Others are just shaking their heads, hiding their internal grief. Some have only heard that Theodora is late. I listen hoping to hear them mention Mark, and perhaps what has happened to him. Sadly, no one actually says anything about him. What I sense from most of them is shock, and disappointment. Some refer to 'the dark cloud' in Skoonfontein.

I have known Betty Baker on a professional basis for a period of three years, and worked alongside her, and as a teacher supporting children learning English as an additional language. Betty was aware of the needs of the children in her class, and always asked for and acted upon advice, providing appropriate support. An example of this was her constant concern about a boy who spoke very little English when he was admitted to her class. Betty supported both his language and learning needs, and ensured he had access to the curriculum by providing one- to-one support where possible, checking that he understood during the introduction of a lesson and during the activity. He made excellent progress with his spoken and written English, and progressed from being a beginner, working towards Level One to Level Two, during the academic year. Betty has the highest expectations for all her pupils, and a broad knowledge of their needs.

Mrs Patsy Farmer
English Specialist
Ben Schoeman Primere Skool
July 1974

Chapter 7

The Trial

October 1968

Three months seems to be over soon since attending a pre-hearing of Baas' case, I think. On Tuesday morning the 22nd October we all travel from Kanevlak village in my uncle's minibus to Baas Jimmie's trial in Burgersdorp. Every seat is filled with our family members and the farm labourers we picked up around Skoonfontein on our way to court. Being the key witness, it is imperative that I attend, and I also desperately need closure with Mark. *Is he alive or not? We promised to love each other for ever, and he suffered for my sake. How could I pay him back for that? Perhaps I'll meet him again in court; who knows what might happen?*

The moment everybody has been waiting for comes; at 10.30am, the door from the cells flings opens, suddenly.

Baas Jimmie Douglas enters the courtroom through this back door, looking down, appearing frustrated and more miserable than before with his shoulders sagging, tense lines about his mouth and wispy unkempt hair. Two police officers are accompanying him, one on each side. His hands are handcuffed. I look at him, feeling sad about how a good man could be in this situation. How his life could turn into such a misery is unbelievable. I then realise he is just as much a victim of the Law as the natives have been. Looking at him above other people's heads, I remember his kindness, giving me a lift in his van when I had a heavy metal trunk to carry home from school. Unable to stop tears rolling down my cheeks, I look up at the ceiling for a little while to gather my strength. I dismiss the thoughts of the nasty things he's done to us in the past. I know it's his weaknesses, but today I choose to focus on his strengths, and feel the pain and the shame he must be going through.

They are walking very slowly towards the dock. I expect him to have his usual walk, with his feet apart. But his feet appear restricted; walking is a struggle for him. I know Baas Jimmie; he always makes giant strides, but strangely, not today. I rise up from my seat until I'm on tiptoes to have a clear view of his feet. Unaware of my actions, I shout loudly in surprise, "Huh, Baas!"

His feet are in chains. Could it be he attempted to escape from his cell? I remember the night I spent in the stables with Rita, and the man who cried constantly throughout the night, with his hands in chains and the corn sheaves left beside him to exhibit theft evidence. He must have been uncomfortable to be in handcuffs all night long, waiting for the day, to be handed over to the police authorities for the alleged theft.

Jimmie, in a pinstriped navy blue suit and a creased blue shirt and a blue tie with black stripes sits on a wooden bench closer to his solicitor, who has a file opened in front of himself, and a pen in his hand. The two police officers remain standing behind him. The solicitor is here to offer him professional advice throughout the proceedings. He has been warned previously that the crimes he is accused of carry a sentence of life imprisonment. Jimmie, as I know him, would not expect to get this kind of penalty in South Africa. All the people rise when the judges walk in, dressed in their dignified robes. I am fortunate to be inside. Crowds are gathered outside, and there are scuffles as people are pushing to get a better view among the reporters, who are raising their cameras, obstructing other people. The atmosphere is chaotic. I dart my eyes all around the room. I look across to the side for the Europeans, hoping to see Mark.

The trial starts with the Prosecutor reading the accusations. Baas Jimmie is charged with attempted murder of his son, Mark Douglas, and murdering his own wife, Theodora.

"Are you guilty or not guilty, Mr Douglas?"

He rises up saying, "Innocent, Sir." There is uproar and shuffling in the court, until the usher shouts, "Silence!"

Everyone on both sides of the court room becomes quiet instantly. Staring at Baas, with my head throbbing from stress, I find it hard to believe the crimes he is accused of, yet I was there the night he shot Mark. I heard the bullet sound, and felt Mark's weight on me before he dropped down. I find it difficult to comprehend that this 'loving dad', as Mark called him, is today accused of murdering his own family. This hurts me the most because I know all of these people very well, and love them as my own.

Jimmie's solicitor rises to speak in his defence.

"Your honour, my clients is known to be a kind and helpful man. He is very sorry for his actions. He had not intentions to hurt anyone."

He describes him as a responsible man, who upheld the laws. When the Prosecutor asks Jimmie some questions, his response shows remorse. Jimmie's voice sounds hoarse; he looks across to our side, as if he remembers the good olden days at Skoonfontein. His voice fades completely, and he reaches for a glass of water. He takes a sip and puts the glass down. He unblocks his throat ready to talk, tries to speak, but upon mentioning Mark and Theodora's names, he breaks down into uncontrollable tears. The court is dismissed for a short break, and then resumes.

"Mark Douglas!" the prosecutor calls, and the usher leads him to the witness box, on their side. "Huh!" I whisper, and then take a deep breath, followed by a sharp sting in my heart. My face heats up from blushing. Clenching my jaws, and holding my hands together, I look down, and then up to the dock, listening to Mark, feeling some energy has just left me. He narrates the events surrounding the attempted murder, as he recalls them. Finally, he says, "After hearing the second shot, I remember no more." Mark, rubbing his eyes gently, looks at his dad and then speaks with a slurred voice, "Daddy, I love you." And then Mark looks down; his tears drip and disappear beneath his chin. He puts his hand into his pocket, takes out a handkerchief and presses it onto his face with both hands, sobbing. This confession must have triggered the 'daddy-and-son' affection, and perhaps brought up the memories of what was once a happy, rich family.

As he recalls that evening, Mark's voice is faint, and he pauses a lot. He is constantly looking at Baas Jimmie. He makes a clear point about what he wants to study in the future, and become in later life. "It is right to stand up for my beliefs. I have a right to defend the people of all races that I believe to be innocent. I do not have to apologise because some of these people are 'natives'. They also need protection. That's why I wanted to be a lawyer. My dad told me to drop law. Betty's family committed themselves to us. It was right for me to love her." Mark stops talking for a moment, closes his eyes, and after that looks up at Jimmie saying, "Dad, you hurt me." Then Mark returns to his seat.

A state witness, Maureen, one of their neighbours, then gives evidence:

"Jimmie's life changed for the worse ever since he shot his son, Mark. He drank heavily, driving his van recklessly all day and shooting randomly. He has been terrorising almost everybody in and around Skoonfontein. I have been in their home several times, witnessing rows between him and his wife, Theodora." Maureen reaches for her handkerchief, and covers her eyes. "What I saw him do to his wife was horrible. Surely, Theo didn't want to die. She didn't deserve it either. She ran for her life, and was close to me when the last bullet penetrated her heart from the back, sending her flying to the ground, face down. I turned her over to lie on her back, applying First Aid. Her eyes rolled over, and she died on the spot."

As this woman explains her side of the story, I wonder how painful her account is to Mark's ears. For me, it was good to hear what actually sent Missus to the grave. For Mark, could it be like spraying a wound with salt?

I start wondering if he knew anything himself. The court adjourns for lunch.

This is the most horrible day for me and my parents. Should Jimmie go to prison, we will be losing two 'family members': Theodora in such a dreadful manner, and Jimmie, who will be put away for a long time, and probably die in jail. I stand up to locate Mark, but he isn't there. This matter is unbearable for all of us. My dad's holding my mum, her head covered with a black shawl, and they walk out of the court room. I see them wiping their faces: they are crying. My mum can hardly control herself. As soon as they are outside, she throws herself in my dad's arms, screaming, "The Douglas' family - my God, why have you allowed this?" Their friends go to comfort them.

They walk across the road to the shops to buy loaves of brown bread and sour milk, which they share among themselves, sitting on the green lawn by the road side. My eyes are fixed on the European people milling outside the court; I wish to have Mark by my side. There are quite a number of Europeans in court today, yet there is no sight of Mark. I don't dare to ask any of them. I hope he will be back in court after lunch.

The court resumes in the afternoon, with the Prosecutor

pronouncing further charges against Jimmie, including possessing unlicensed fire arms, and reckless shooting, endangering the farm-workers. I feel tears dripping slowly down my face, and I wipe them off discreetly with the back of my hand, careful not to smudge my mascara.

I'm called to the witness box on the side of the natives. As I walk to take my stand, I look across the room by the door. Mark is now sitting at the end of the last row there dressed in a navy blue suit, and a striped tie. Words vanish from my mind. I stand still for a while, looking at him, more handsome, than ever before. Tearfully, I give the details of the events that occurred that night, and then sit down.

Koos Van Tonder takes the witness stand on the European side.

Koos, a constable off duty on that day and the Douglases' friend, who was at the barbecue earlier on and had returned to collect his board game he left behind, gives his moving testimony, saying: "As I walked towards the door from my car, I heard and saw Theodora saying repeatedly 'Oh my God!' and pushing in the kitchen back door to open it. Hurriedly, she got to the corridor, reaching out for the telephone by the window. She turned the handle very fast and picked it up, screaming, 'Hello, come to Skoonfontein – now! Quickly, Mark is alive!'

"Unaware of what had happened after I had left, and as part of my work, I rushed to the sitting room to listen from another receiver, trying to figure out what the problem was, exactly. A voice said, 'This is the Burgersdorp exchange; could I have the number please? Do you want the ambulance or the police?' The operator, trying to get more information about the service Theodora needed, was becoming desperate with her hysterical utterances at the other end of the line. He required clear directions, in order to dispatch the emergency vehicle.

"'Hello! What's happening?' the telephone operator asked again. I reached out for my notebook and started taking notes, looking across the room to the corridor where Theodora was standing.

"Theodora sobbed, 'My son, Mark, is dying. Help! Hurry up!'

"'Okay, Skoonfontein, right... I can see it on the map.'

"'It's my husband. He shot him. Please, hurry!'

"Theodora hung up, and wound the telephone again. She got through to a different operator. Coincidentally, it was Jakobus, their family friend, who was not at the barbecue.

"'Number, please?' he asked.

"'Ambulance! Please be quick! My son Mark, has been shot. I'm Theodora Douglas, from Skoonfontein.'

"'Okay, Theo - it's me, Jako; I'm sending the ambulance now.' Theodora could hardly speak; she just cried, pleading, 'Please help! Come over straight away after sending the ambulance.'

"Jako called Theodora, asking, what had happened and about where Jimmie was. 'It's him! He shot them,' that was Theodora's reply.

"'Shot who?' asked Jako.

"'Mark.'

"'Mark? ...Sorry, Theo... Okay, the ambulance is on its way,' Jakobus reassured her, and hung up. I did not want to disturb her, so, I remained in the sitting room, shocked with this news. Theodora rang again, asking the exchange for number 70239. I could hear Marie, one of the friends who had visited the Douglas family earlier, answering the phone saying, *'Hello, Marie, wat praat, kan ek help?'* meaning in English, 'Marie speaking, can I help?' Theodora, still screaming, explained. 'Jimmie shot them; the bullets hit Mark; he's badly hurt, bleeding and struggling to breathe.'

"Marie cut her short, saying, 'Theo, okay; I'm coming now.'

"Having heard what had happened, and also in shock and desperation, this time around I walked to the corridor to meet Theodora. I heard the revs of Marie's van arriving at Jimmie's farm. Theodora rushed out, and I followed her into Marie's van.

Marie drove off to the fields. As we arrived at the scene of the shooting, the ambulance was pulling away, with Jimmie sitting at the back with Mark. The sirens went off, and the blue lights flickering all the way, in this speedily-driven ambulance. I sat in this van without saying a word.

"Marie drove frantically behind the ambulance to the Blanke Hospitaal, meaning the European Hospital. 'I've never driven a car over 120 kilometres per hour,' she confided later.

"Theodora, Marie and I sat in the waiting-room, while Mark, carried on a stretcher, was rushed into theatre for emergency treatment. Jimmie, who was probably now sobered up, followed the stretcher and waited outside the theatre. He returned to join us after about six hours, following Mark's admission to the Intensive Care Unit. Theodora's voice was faint, and her face swollen, from crying.

"'It's okay, Theo,' I heard Marie say, patting her shoulders, giving her a hug for comfort. 'Mark should recover. The doctors are looking after him now.'

"'What if…?' Maybe she wanted to say, '…if Mark survives, but never recovers fully?' Hurt overcame her speech; she continued crying. However, later she summoned up the strength to complete her sentence.

"'There's no need to think about that now, Marie,' I said encouraging her. 'Life is the most important thing, regardless.' Jimmie returned at this point.

"'Let's go home!' he said, joining us, appearing dreadful with his bloody eyes. We all went to the car park and squeezed in front of this three-seater van and left the hospital, with Jimmie being upset for not receiving sympathy from all the nurses and doctors. According to him, he was stopping his son from committing crime.

"'What Mark was doing with that Betty, I really don't understand. He returned from the university with these funny thoughts - the United Nations' declarations of democracy, equal opportunities, human rights, and so on,' Jimmie kept going on and on.

"'What was this all about, Jim?' Marie asked inquisitively.

"Jimmie explained, 'Mark changed his career from being a medical doctor to a Human Rights lawyer.'

"'Okay, whose right was he concerned about, then?' Marie asked him.

"Jimmie, shrugging his shoulders, replied, 'I don't know; as you know, our race has all the rights.'

"'Hmmh,' Marie responded, nodding her head, and trying to stay awake, at that time of the day.

"'Mark was always around Betty lately; that's where I suspect he got all these lunatic ideas from – I think,' Jimmie said. Jimmie continued talking to Marie, who was struggling to keep her eyes open behind the wheel, sometimes blaming Theodora for the mess he found himself in. 'Don't worry, I'll get that Betty. She must pay for the damage she's caused,' Jimmie said in conclusion, as the van stopped in front of their Big House.

"Theodora invited us in for coffee, but Marie refused this offer saying, 'Thanks love; that's very kind of you. You have a lot to get on with. However, please call me again when you need support. Tarra,' That's all Marie could say as she turned on the engine ready to drive off.

"'How can I pay you back?' Theodora asked with her voice raised.

"'Don't worry, Theo, just be a good neighbour. I hope Mark recovers. Give my love to him.'

"And Marie drove off, as Jimmie, Theodora and myself walked towards the house. Strangely Jimmie and Theodora were not hand in hand as they usually did. Certainly, this incident had affected both of them. I remained with them, and was prepared to do so, as long as they needed me. They are my friends. Jimmie went into their bedroom and came out carrying a shotgun, and headed towards the Baker's house. Perhaps he hoped to find them asleep. I followed him. In his anger and frustration, he kicked the door open, and went in, searching all the bedrooms. To his surprise, there was no one in. 'Betty, where are you!' he cried out loudly, dropping his shotgun. After a while, he must have come to terms with the reality: the Bakers were gone and probably for good. He had to deal with this incident - more importantly, with the police.

"Sobbing, he picked up his gun, maybe having many thoughts in his mind, as he dragged his feet back home. 'What's this life all about?' he repeatedly asked himself. 'The Bakers have left me, with no one else to do the farm work. Mark is in the hospital; he may die. If he lives, he may require constant care – that's what the surgeon advised. Who will provide that? He may never be a graduate, have a wife and children.'

"Jimmie went into the kitchen, made a pot of coffee for himself and took it to the sitting room. He poured it into the mug until it overflowed onto the table covered with a cream table-cloth. To me he appeared to be not concentrating. He drank it slowly, perhaps thinking about the police, who had to be after him. I don't know. Tears kept flowing down his cheeks, like rain, and he wiped them off with his blue handkerchief. He slept right there on the sofa, for the first time in their marriage. He told me he always slept in the bedroom, next to his wife. I slept on the other sofa.

"The next morning, we all visited Mark in the hospital. The news wasn't hopeful, although the doctors were doing their very best. He needed some time in the hospital for recovery. The sister responsible told us about the police visit, asking for professional statements and a medical report.

"'Surely they will want to speak to all of you?' she said, and refused to answer our questions, and just kept saying, 'that's all I can tell you for now.'

"This news disturbed Jimmie again; he started sobbing, as we walked to the car park.

"Nevertheless, he had to face the consequence of his actions. In his view, the crimes he committed were not intentional and were, therefore, justifiable. 'I did my best to stop mixed racial relationships in my own home,' I overheard him saying this.

"So often he blamed alcoholic drinks and not himself. We all returned to the farm; Jimmie driving their 4x4 truck this time. The latest news caused more tension between them. As soon as they got in, Jimmie went to the kitchen, poured himself gin and tonic, and drank it down. He must have hoped to forget about the latest events at Skoonfontein Farm. Heavy drinking became his habit, here after.

"I returned to my home briefly, and stayed with the Douglases most of the time, supporting them emotionally and in every way possible. The next visitors to knock at the Douglases' doors were the investigation officers. They took statements from both, first starting with Theodora. This was too much for her. During the questioning, she broke down in tears. She became the state witness against her husband. Will Jimmie like this? His turn came. He didn't deny going out with a shotgun to protect 'themselves' against the natives.

"He admitted having had too much alcohol, and worrying that Mark wasn't home, following the row they had had. He insisted that he was a good citizen, had obeyed the laws – keeping the natives on his farm, and using just 'reasonable force', where necessary. However, he denied attempted murder, due to immoderate use of alcohol. Jimmie accepted, seeing his son with Betty, could have provoked him into taking the action, and he could have acted without thinking. He couldn't remember well what he did that evening. I volunteered an interview, and was able to have my version from when I returned to Jimmie's house recorded. I became the second state witness. The police, after receiving sufficient answers to their questions, were satisfied there was enough evidence to press charges against Jimmie, and then they arrested him. Jimmie spent that night in the cells."

After this long speech, Koos then sits down. The court plays the recording from the ambulance service up to the end; Koos' account is so accurate. Judge Retief asks, "Do you want to say anything, Mr Douglas?"

Baas Jimmie remains quiet for about a second. "No, your honour," he replies, looking up at him while sitting down.

The judge allows a short break, while summing up all the deliberations. The court resumes, and he then says:

"Jimmie Douglas, you have let yourself down. You have let your family down. You have let your community down. You are an extremely dangerous person to the community, and yourself. If you couldn't spare your own innocent family; you don't deserve a life within your community. You must stay in prison indefinitely, and you will not be considered for parole until you have served at least forty years."

The court is dismissed, and Mark walks out of the courtroom, through 'their door' with his relatives and friends. Baas Jimmie is escorted to a cell, I imagine similar to the one the man in the stable was sent to, with a low brick stand, a mattress, a water tap and a toilet bucket, where he is going to spend his term in isolation, unless his condition is reviewed.

I push through the natives from around Skoonfontein Farm, who are walking towards 'our door'; I want to speak to Mark outside, and comfort him. The people are moving slowly, as some try to speak to each other – expressing their sadness, and getting their sorrows off their chests...

"Hey, this is the hardest sentence Judge Retief has passed to a non-native in my life time!" exclaims an elderly farmworker sympathetically, taking out his pipe from the sachet. He fills it with tobacco before sitting on a big stone to smoke, coughing constantly. He is trying to come to terms with the latest news from Skoonfontein Farm.

"I've never slept well since I heard about this incident," says another woman, wrapping a shawl around her shoulder.

"I've known Jimmie, since he was a young man; I can't believe he could turn out to be so dangerous."

"Seeing him on the dock breaks my heart," says another woman wiping off her tears with a white handkerchief, before burying her face into it crying like a baby.

"I miss them. Skoonfontein has never been the same without the Douglas family," says another man called Stuurman, sobbing, wiping tears off his blood-red, swollen eyes.

Hoping to draw Mark's attention to me, I push forward to get myself outside quickly; the lingering crowd is blocking my way. Fortunately, I manage to squeeze through and reach the door. From a distance, I can see Mark, walking among other Europeans towards a car parked by the road side. "Mark," I shout. He doesn't respond to my call. My heart sinks as I continue to shout, "Mark, Mark!" but he shows no sign of hearing me.

There is a heavy police presence, and many reporters around. I manage to squeeze through this crowd, pushing my way past all the natives, until I reach the police line. The police stand almost directly between me and the European people there, making it difficult to walk past them to where Mark is standing by his car. I force my way between the police, slipping through and running towards the car. The reporters are holding up their cameras taking photos for their story coverage. There is some commotion as the police are blocking my way. I call him even more loudly, hoping to get his attention this time, "Mark!" It doesn't work. I push forward harder to break the police line.

"Arrest her!" another police officer shouts.

"Mark Douglas!" I scream harder again, waving my arm, but in vain. Knowing Mark's tender heart, I know he is worried about his dad, and thinking about his mum, and perhaps me too. He can't have forgotten me, I know for sure. His heart must be torn apart – the ache from the loss of his mum, his dad in prison, and torn apart from me. What a disaster!

He must be crying, unable to notice me. My eyes are right on him.

"Let me speak to Mark, please!" I plead with the police once more. One officer completely ignores me. Mark gradually opens the back door of his car while speaking to another man next to him.

"Mark, please wait for me!" My voice is blunt from screaming; I'm panting heavily from struggling to break through one more time.

"Mark, it's me, Betty Baker!"

Mark puts his foot in the car, slides his body gently inside, and shuts the door. I'm now just five metres away from him.

"No, Mark, please wait!" I scream, drawing the attention of the Press. I cry out loudly from the top of my voice, with my back bent and my face buried in my hands. A police officer holds my right hand, leading me to the police van in the car park. The back door is flung open.

"Get in!" the officer says. Anyone watching me might think I am losing my mind. No one can ever understand the pain I am feeling at that moment, except those who have had a similar experience. The van stops at the police station. An officer, who was sitting in the passenger seat, opens the door, and says:

"Get out!" I comply. He says, "Go home now. Do not cause any trouble again."

I enjoyed team-teaching with Betty when she joined us at Summer Hill Primary School. I can confirm that she has fitted in easily into our school life, worked well with all pupils, staff and support staff. She could take full responsibility for all professional tasks. She recognised and responded effectively to equal opportunity issues as they arise in the classroom, including challenging stereotyped views and inappropriate behaviour, following our behavioural policy and procedure. Betty responded to pupils' learning needs. Her planning was well founded in good subject knowledge, showing clear progression for all children. Children found her lessons interesting because she used various stimuli. She had good communication skills, and always took my advice. She demonstrated a sound knowledge and understanding of teachers' legal liabilities, and assisted with the organisation of out-of-school learning activities. She demonstrated the skills of a more than competent teacher.

Mrs M. Brent
Headmistress
Summer Hill Primary School

Chapter 8

Illegal Love

January 1970

I return to Benson Vale Teacher Training College to complete my course. Being a teacher would certainly make my parents proud; I'll be the first in our family to go beyond Standard Six and hold a profession. Skoonfontein Farm has never produced a school teacher: so, I'll be leading the way. It is renowned for having 'out-of-school-children', or school drop-outs. I hope the farm labourers' community will one day know about my achievements. This thought comforts and encourages me.

I work very hard, getting the best grades in all my subjects. Music is my favourite. Is it because the music tutor is friendly? The music period is on Friday before lunch. I sing first soprano in the college-choir. I like 'The Hallelujah Chorus' from the Messiah; we also sing 'The Goslings'.

My worst subject is cursive handwriting. Oh my God, I struggle with this! My letters are uneven. I just can't get the right letter size. On this day, I watch Mrs Stone through the corner of my left eye, walking between the rows checking on every trainee's chalkboard, ensuring the correct handwriting movement. Suddenly, Mollie gets a smack on her head. I turn around as she drops the white chalk and duster to shield herself with her hands.

Mrs Stone places each foot with delicate precision; therefore, it's impossible to hear her footsteps. I'm aware she's moving closer to me. I haven't written much. I write a sentence, glance to see how far she is, and then erase it. My heart is pounding loudly, and my hands are sweating profusely. I'm afraid of this woman.

Conscious of her presence behind me, I smell her perfume. My right hand shivers slightly - I stop writing. As the vibration of my hand increases, the piece of chalk slips through my fingers onto the floor. I quickly bend over to pick it up, expecting the beating on the back of my head. I start writing another word. I quickly erase it again, because it just doesn't look right. I pause, until I feel a relatively slight tap on my shoulder.

"Betty, come here," says Mrs Stone softly, beckoning me to follow her towards the back of the classroom. I guess I'm in trouble. Looking at her face, I gauge her moods. I shiver from fright, the palm of my hand still sweating. I pretend to be brushing off fluff from my uniform, but actually dry my hands. It's impossible to anticipate her next move. Just in case she flicks, something common with her, I take one step backwards, leaving a reasonable gap between us - should I have to run away.

She picks up her handbag, puts her hand in it, searching. I wonder what all this is about. I don't dare to ask. She takes out a bunch of keys. Handing them to me, she says, "It's better for you to go and clean my house. Empty all the bins, and in my bedroom you'll find my washing basket of dirty clothes: wash them all."

"Yes, Mrs Stone," I say, receiving the keys, beaming with a smile. My tutor is doing me a big favour, sending me to clean her house during this period. I don't only miss learning the chalkboard writing skill, but the smacking that comes with it. She returns to her home after school, and finds her house spotless.

"You've done a great job, Betty, thank you. You're better off as a cleaner," she says, sitting down on a sofa, ready to have a cup of tea.

Cleaner? I ask myself in my mind, but with my eyes wider open than usual, looking at her and smiling. I hope she won't read my mind or notice my surprised look; I can't dare disagree with a teacher and get myself in trouble.

Anyway, the school term draws closer. We've covered most of the syllabus. I take my final external examinations, but it's impossible to predict the results, as marking will be done in Pretoria. Shortly, after that, I return to Uncle Ben's house, my new home. I wait patiently for the results to arrive. I integrate well with this family. Recognising and respecting that it's not my home, I make an effort to do all the chores to impress them.

My Aunty Lisa is really pleased with me. "Betty never rests," she says. "She is constantly up and about."

"Betty!" I hear Aunty calling me.

"Yes, Aunty. Is everything all right with you? Would you like a cup of tea, or anything?"

"No, dear," she replies calmly. "I'm just wondering what you are doing. What are you up to? Take a break, will you?"

"Okay, Aunty, I'll rest a bit - if you say so."

Straightaway, I drag my feet into my bedroom, feeling extremely exhausted: I'm so grateful to my aunt. I can't complain - this is not my home. We desperately need their shelter at the moment. I wonder if Aunty would ever discover my true feelings. I am drowsy, and doze off to sleep.

* * *

Two weeks later, my uncle calls me from the doorway, carrying a brown, officially-stamped envelope. Immediately, I sense that it contains my results. Unsure of how best to react, I force a cold smile, hoping my uncle will give me the envelope and leave. This doesn't happen. He is curious, and wants me to open the envelope in front of him. Instead of putting it down, he holds onto it saying, "This is yours, Betty. Open it, and let's have the good news."

"No, go away!" I command, holding tightly onto the envelope, drawing it towards my chest. I suspect it's my results. "Please, leave me alone, Uncle," I plead once more. Reluctantly, he lets go before dragging his feet, slowly moving away. However, he stops, looks back, and then carries on.

I wait for him to disappear, before opening it, in case it's bad news. He returns and refuses to move this time around. "Let's hear the good news, Betty," he says. I can't get away with holding onto it any longer. I'm inquisitive too. So, I open my letter, ready to face whatever I find.

I scream loudly, "Yes, Jesus!" and start jumping up and down; a beam of a smile covers my face. Uncle Ben grabs the letter in my hands, and reads it aloud. "Overall – passed. Good, Betty!" he says, walking out towards their house. I follow him.

"She's made it, Lisa! Gladys and Benjamin have given birth to a teacher!" He passes on my results to my dad.

After looking at the report, he says, nodding vigorously, "Yes, she's through." That's all my dad could say, expressing his joy and appreciation.

"Excuse me, Papa, what's the matter?" my mum asks, looking at him in dismay. She pauses, kneading the bread-dough, and then stands up. This is becoming serious.

"Betty has finished training – that's what I'm saying, Gladys."

"Betty is really a qualified teacher now? Thank you, Lord!" my mama shouts, waving her hands above her head. I stand silently, wondering if she's aware of her actions.

"Mama, yes this is true. I've qualified. Calm down now." I bend over to pick up my letter from the floor, and read it again.

Opening it with excitement, I receive the long-awaited good news. I've definitely passed, and have been appointed to teach at Mount View Primary School – named after this remote village far away from home, in this way *serving my natives according to the 1953 Bantu Education Act 47'*. I sigh with great relief.

Finally, I'm leaving this home, to spend my independent adult life away from my family. On the following days, I start preparing my stuff, thrilled about the unknown I'm embarking on.

My heart pounding joyously, I pack my clothes in my metal trunk. I choose a single bed and blankets to take. Aunty Lisa cooks chicken, bakes cakes, scones and bread. She's charitable, offering me curtains, pots, cutlery, plates and dishes. Have I taken everything I need? Standing by the door, I wonder. "Oh, I need a bucket." I remember, and then rush to the kitchen to get one.

Starting a new career and life where I'd never been, where nobody knows me, is extremely interesting. I'll soon be called 'Mistress' or 'Miss'. I'll live in my own home by myself. I am going to be the 'Baas,' doing what pleases me, whenever I choose. That's the best of all.

I wouldn't be reprimanded for returning home late after seeing my friends. I sense my maximum freedom. "Yes, it's here!" I can't get over it. I'm very excited because I'm stepping into my destiny, with my mind flooded with future prospects of success. However, I still wonder if I can accomplish my goals in this country.

"Betty!" my dad shouts impatiently, banging my bedroom door.

"Dad," I reply, wondering what might have upset him this evening.

"Come here, Betty!" I take some time putting on my cardigan and shoes. He becomes irritable, having to wait longer. "Hurry up, will you?" he says aggressively, in his usual rough voice.

That's his character, I know it. Dad speaks that way. He might have acquired this attitude unknowingly from Baas Jimmie. That's how he addressed my dad, sometimes even calling him, 'Boy'.

I've not finished packing yet. However, I leave everything for a while, to hear what my dad has in mind. I go into their bedroom, lean on the wall by the door, just in case things go wrong, and I have to run out. This happens often, when Dad gets into a rage. He doesn't argue with children.

"I've hired Mr Hurst to take us to Mount View tomorrow morning," he says. "We leave very early - about five o'clock. Put all your stuff by the door, so that we can get it out easily, without disturbing everybody."

"Okay, Dad," I reply cheerfully, leaving him behind in peace. 'Good heavens! Did he have to be so rough, while disclosing such pleasurable news?' I grumble, but ensuring no one hears me.

I move my stuff close to the door as Dad advises. I go to sleep, feeling very tired. I can hardly sleep. Eventually, I hear the cockerels crow, and realise it's morning. It's too early to prepare the morning coffee for the grown-ups. After about an hour of lying down thinking, I get up and have a bath outside behind the house. I then serve the morning coffee. Within a short period of time, I get dressed, ready to go off to Mount View. Just then, I hear the car park outside, and I peep through the window.

I hurry to my parents' room, and knock at the door saying, "Dad, Mr Hurst is here." Surprisingly, my dad is also almost ready. "All right, tell him I'll be there in a second. Open the door; let him in, and make him comfortable."

I open the door. "Good morning, Sir," I say, gently stretching my hand towards him.

"Hello, Betty, are you all ready? We've got a very long way to go," he says, hastily. My dad, dressed in his pin-striped, navy blue suit with a matching shirt and tie, joins us. He excitedly shakes his hand, giving him a hug to his left and right. My dad offers him a cup of tea.

He's desperate to get on the road, and refuses to have it. Through my dad's persuasion, he accepts the offer in the end. They both load the van, quickly. I go back in for a final check. I nearly bump into my mum. She is waiting at the door entrance.

I can't tell whether she is coming out or remaining there to wave us good-bye.

I turn around to see if she is following me. At that moment, her hand is pressing hard on the handkerchief, covering her eyes. My mum's crying. I return to the house, opening my arms widely to embrace her. With tears rushing down my cheeks, removing my face powder, I say, "Mama, don't cry." I feel her grip behind my back.

"Look after yourself, Betty," she sobs. "God will be with you."

I walk forward, wiping the tears off my face, resisting looking back until I get into the van. I sit in front between my dad and Mr Hurst. He puts in the ignition key, turning it to start the engine. He engages the first gear, revs the engine, and the van slowly pulls off. My glassy eyes, overflowing with tears, are on my mum. Her left hand is on her eyes, and the right hand is waving goodbye.

Feeling sorry for my mum, I bow my head down, crying like a baby, as Mr Hurst drives up the hill joining the dirt road. After a while, I wipe off my face until I am completely dry. They both restrain themselves from interfering between mother and daughter, leaving it to me to sort out. I gasp as if I'm choking for a while.

The scenery distracts my attention. I keep looking at the road side, measuring the distance between the telephone poles, by counting, one, two, three…, before passing the next one.

The journey starts in silence, and then my dad and Mr Hurst talk about the importance of having cars. They discuss life in the olden days, when South Africa was under British rule in the 1900s. They are quiet for a while. My dad remarks on the picturesque landscape. My thoughts are still with my mum. Seeing her crying is difficult for me to bear. She is a strong woman, and I know she will be fine. My heart sinks, and my eyes fill with tears, as I suppress sadness, having to leave my mum in that state.

The journey is long and tiring - all day and all night. We stop to refuel at the petrol stations, and to stretch our legs. Some of the main roads are made up with tarmac, and the minor gravel roads are winding around the high mountains. I'm frightened of what can happen, should Mr Hurst make a driving mistake: there will be little chance for us to survive, if the car crashes.

We get onto the long dirt winding road, and there are no buildings in sight. The road soon narrows, so that only one car can pass at a time. We wait for the speeding oncoming car. "This road is very dangerous." I make this comment, to ensure Mr Hurst is awake and aware.

"Of course, people drive at their own risk here," he says.

"The state of this road has always been appalling – for decades," my dad adds, appearing angry.

"No one really cares, I suppose," says Mr Hurst, seemingly irritated.

Eventually, the darkness begins to turn into greyish white, leaving the atmosphere clearer and lighter. A thick rolling mist swirls around the main road. I can hardly see ahead. Mr Hurst is doing his very best, ensuring our safety. It's dawn. I feel a sense of relief as we reach our destination – Mount View village where my independent, adult life journey begins. Mr Hurst, utterly exhausted, stops his van, winding his window down.

My dad jumps out and knocks at the house by the roadside to ask for the home of the village headman.

"Knock, knock, is there anyone here?" he asks, gently tapping the door. There is no response. He knocks again. "Hello!" he shouts louder, trying to wake up the people.

A man's voice, in a strange accent, asks from inside, "Who are you, this time of the day?"

"I'm Mr Baker. I've brought you a teacher from far away. Her name is Betty Baker. She is my daughter." The door shuts in my dad's face. He bangs it repeatedly again.

The top part of the door opens slightly. The man speaks to my dad for a long time. Covered in a blanket, he comes with my dad, who's wearing a big smile by now, to give Mr Hurst directions to the teachers' quarters. He seems relieved, now that he knows exactly where to take me. Mr Hurst yawns, puts the key into the ignition, and starts the van. We drive for about three more miles to the teachers' quarters.

I take a deep breath, easing stress. At last, we've reached my destination. The van stops in front of the studio flat reserved for me. We offload my belongings. My dad and Mr Hurst, yawning, say 'good-bye' before driving off, waving until the van disappears onto the winding dirt road between the bushes. They have a long, unsafe journey back home.

I soon settle down, and embark on my teaching career. I write my weekly lesson plans at the weekends, and do any marking during the week. I've got lots of work to do. My colleagues are all friendly. Some Saturday afternoons we get together for barbecues. I learn the regional dialect, and soon communicate effectively with the local people and parents of the children in my school.

* * *

It's Friday, at lunch-break; I've just received a note from my colleague, Martha, inviting me to her home. She's throwing a party the next night. I'm not excited about this: I feel something is missing in my life. At first, I don't know what this is. I feel lonely, yet I'm among friendly and happy people. There's a strong emptiness within me. I'm tearful, yet I have no specific reason for this. Am I homesick, I wonder? No, I can't miss living in my uncle's home. I have no home. I am missing Mark Douglas.

I do my planning for the next week as usual. The days pass faster, and I am busy the whole week. Friday, I finish earlier and go home. My colleagues visit me for a cup of tea. We sit outside talking and laughing at the week's events. They tell me about the culture in this area, and invite me to visit the local shop to open an account.

About ten o'clock one Saturday morning, I walk to the shop with Ralph Waters, one of my colleagues. He tells me briefly about the shopkeeper, Mr Arthur Davies, a European man in his sixties, who settled in this village after the Second World War. He refuses to leave, because, "This is my home," he says. It's about two miles away from our residence.

As we approach this big old building with high walls, I can see the villagers going towards the entrance, and others coming out of the shop. We continue and enter this busy shop, with customers talking loudly to each other. We stand at the end of the counter, waiting to be served. Teachers are respected here. The shopkeeper comes around to get an item for a customer.

"Hello, Baas Davies," Ralph says, with great respect. Baas Davies looks up, and replies, "Hello, Ralph," but ignores me, as if I don't exist. He continues serving his customers. I stand there feeling very bad. I occupy my thoughts by looking around this dark shop, with lots of things hanging on the wall and ceiling, almost obstructing the light. I look at the unpolished wooden floor and high counter. It's impossible for me to rest my hands on it, for a bit of comfort.

Baas Davies is a giant of about six foot tall, bald, with a few thin greyish hairs remaining, clean-shaven with a moustache, and a massive hanging belly. He's wearing brown shorts, and a cream shirt rolled up to his elbows. Due to his body weight, the buttons seem to be about to tear. His breathing is very loud, as if he's running short of breath.

His assistant, perhaps his wife, is sitting on the chair behind the cash machine on the other side of this counter. I can only see clearly her brunette hair tied up in the middle of her head. I tiptoe to have a better view of her. She's of European origin. Her face is slightly wrinkled, with long eyelashes, and she wears red lipstick; her make-up suits her face. She appears lovely for her age.

Baas Davies is occupied, serving the customers, bringing the goods to the machine for payment, before passing them over to his customers – all natives. Noisy customers continue to walk in and out of the shop.

"It is a very busy day," I say to Ralph, trying to hint that we've been waiting for a long time, and I can't accept this.

"Sorry Betty, this shop's always busy. It is the only shop available to serve all the villages around here."

"Uhuh."

"People travel from far to come here to do their shopping," says Ralph. "Don't worry; he will come to serve us. I'm one of his best customers. I can take anything I need on account, and pay at the end of the month. He trusts me."

"He also trusts you not to go away, isn't it? And he continues serving people, who have just come in after us," I say, sadly.

"Shush," says Ralph, looking extremely disappointed. "I'm sorry. He should consider the customers who came first."

We stand there waiting for about twenty more minutes. At last, Baas Davies comes over to our side as it gets quieter.

"Yes, Ralph, my friend, what can I do for you today?" he asks, frankly, packing goods on the shelves.

"Baas, please meet Miss Betty Baker, a new teacher at my school. She comes from the west. She's just finished college."

"What have you brought us, young lady?" Baas asks, without paying too much attention to me.

"Nothing, Baas," I reply, smiling.

"Betty may want to open an account, and pay you at the end of the month, like us, if that's all right Baas?"

"Yes, of course - I'm here to make money." He turns and looks at me, and says, "Let me know when you're ready to open an account, young Betty. Come and meet my wife, Annie, also." So, we walk towards the cashier.

"Love, we have a new customer, a teacher in Ralph's school. Apparently she comes from the west. I've agreed to give her an account." And then he walks away.

Missus Davies smiles, with nothing to say. I guess she's shy. Ralph makes his shopping on account. I pay cash for mine. On the way back home, Ralph defends Baas for keeping us waiting. He manages to convince me, saying, "Be patient Betty; they are nice people. You'll soon get used to them, and crack jokes, just like me."

I continue coming to the shop on my own for my groceries, but I don't open an account. I pay cash for all my shopping. This doesn't bother Baas. He still gets his money, and his business is booming with no competition.

On Thursday after work, I walk into the shop to buy some milk. I wait for my turn to be served. Baas Davies comes over to me. "Yes, young Betty, what can I do for you today?" he asks politely, looking at me.

"Could I have fresh milk, butter, bread and simba crisps please?" I place my order respectfully. He takes my items to the cash machine.

There's a young European man today serving. I give him the money. He takes it and stares at me. "It's my first time to see you here. Where are you from?" he says, in a fluent English accent.

"I'm Betty Baker, the new teacher from the west."

"How do you find it here? Are you having a good time?" he asks politely, and with great enthusiasm.

"It's all right," I reply, feeling a bit uncomfortable.

"You've got a lovely voice," he says. Before I can say something in reply, Baas comes around, and perhaps tells him off for holding other customers up. At that moment, I collect my change and walk out of the shop.

After walking for about half a mile, I hear the running footsteps behind me. I turn around and realise it's the small Baas that served me. I check my shopping bag, thinking I might have left something behind. I notice my butter isn't there. He's got it in his hand. By the time he meets me, he is panting, as if he is about to pass out. I stop.

"Hi, young Betty," he says, still panting heavily.

"Good afternoon," I reply. "Oh, did I leave my butter behind?"

"Yes, I saw it after you had gone. We had to get my mum on the cash machine, while I tried to get it back to you."

"Thanks, that's very kind of you," I say feeling rather shy. We've been standing together for some time, talking. But what can I do? He is chatting to me, and holding onto my butter. I start walking slowly, hoping that he will realise, I'm feeling rather awkward - *give me my butter and go away*. I'm wrong. He is so relaxed; instead, he tries to engage me in a boring conversation.

"Young Betty - I hope you don't mind me calling you 'young'?"

"Not at all," I reply.

He stares at me, saying nothing.

"I've got to go," I say, trying to appear to be in a hurry, just to get him off my back.

"Come on, love! Could you please wait a bit? I'd like to talk to you. I've not met someone like you here."

"I'm sorry. I can't stop for long; we are breaking the law."

"What law are we breaking? Bloody hell!" he explodes.

"What's your name?" I ask him, taking more steps forward, trembling in fear.

"I'm Gregory Davies. I live in England. I'm visiting my dad, and his second wife, Annie."

"All right, it's nice meeting you. Could I have my butter, please? And I'd better go, before we get into trouble." He passes it to me, but continues to walk by my side.

"I'll come to the shop again. Please go back now - your dad might be worried."

"Promise me, you'll come to the shop again," he says.

"Yes, I will," I say, trying to get rid of him swiftly.

Gregory looks at me. He seems to be more interested, but how can that be? Doesn't he know the laws here in South Africa? I dismiss my thoughts about Gregory, and walk back to my home. I don't tell my colleagues I had a chat with Baas Davies' son. I hope no one will ever know. I occupy my mind remembering my happy days with Mark.

I go to the shop again after two weeks to get myself some groceries. As I walk into the shop entrance, I look at the cash machine to see if Gregory is there, and I quickly join the queue. I catch his eyes looking at me. Today, Missus is serving the customers.

I look at her pale skin, with red lipstick. She has blue eyes, with her slinky hair tied in a pony-tail today. She is moving swiftly. Baas Davies is also in the shop, unpacking goods from cardboard boxes, as well as serving the customers.

By the time I get to the machine, Gregory has vanished. I'm not bothered about him. I come out of the shop carrying my groceries in my bag. I look up and see him sitting on an old tractor plough by the road side. As I walk past him, he gets up.

"Hi, young Betty - it's nice to see you again. Thank you for coming."

"Hello, Gregory," I say, stretching my right hand towards him. He grabs it, and doesn't let it go.

"How do you do, Sir?" I ask hoping to impress him with my well-spoken English.

"You can call me 'Greg' from this day forwards. That's how I'm known."

"Known where?"

"Right here in South Africa, and in England, my home."

"Oh."

"That's where most of my family and friends live."

"Greg – okay - this sounds better." I rehearse calling him by his name. "You'd better call me 'Betty', or 'Bet' - whatever."

"Betty, Bet, whatever." He bounces his right hand; presumably hoping to make sense of what he heard me say. "I've got something to tell you," he continues, looking straight at me. "The first day we met, I didn't want to take my eyes off you. This is unusual for me. I'm a traveller, meeting lots of people. You are special. I'm attracted to you. I love you or shall I say I fancy you." He pulls me towards himself. "This is true! I love you."

"No, you can't love me," I say, remembering Mark's incident, slightly pushing him away from me. "We're not allowed, I'm sorry."

Fear grips me. Is this real? Doesn't he know that Europeans are restricted to loving within their own race and no other? I don't dismiss he might be sincere like Mark Douglas, my boyfriend.

I try to gauge Greg's emotions, wondering if he's just attracted to me sexually, or is he considering a long-term relationship, leading to marriage? I can't tell. I ask him many questions, hoping to discover the motive behind his proposal of love. I'm unsuccessful. No, I can't be in love with him; if I am, I'll be hurting myself, because he cannot marry me – it's illegal. Moreover, I wouldn't cope with a similar relationship like the one with Mark. I still have room for Mark in my heart.

I stand still in front of him, looking at his gorgeous eyes.

He lifts his hand up, and pats my face. "Betty. You're pretty. I love your eyes, I love the colour of your skin, I love everything about you, I love you, believe me," he says.

I find myself drawn towards Greg, and believing him, but I ask him to 'go away', to save both of us from trouble.

"Baby, don't be afraid - trust me," he says, and then bends over and kisses me on my forehead. I push him away.

"I'm better off trusting stones than people!" I exclaim. He stops. I pick up my shopping bag and walk slowly towards my home, concerned lest someone has seen us. I may get in trouble for breaking the Immorality Act.

Gregory's Version

Wow, I like this girl. She's the kind of person I'd like to be with. She smiles every so often. Mmh, oh well let's see. Gosh, my dad – what will he say? And Annie? Do I care? Do I have to? This is my life, and what I do is for my future. Yes, I want Betty. *I love her.*

* * *

Weeks pass without my going to the shop. Instead I send children to buy my groceries. I'm avoiding meeting Greg. I remember the episode with Mark every so often. This still disturbs me. I have constant outbursts of emotion, whenever I recall the events of that bloody night. Months pass.

Suddenly, I begin to think about Greg all the time. He says he loves me. So, why don't I tell him that I love him too? I know about the *Immorality Law Act 21 of 1950* that was amended in 1957. Greg and I can't be in love. This law is enforced; we can't get away with it. Greg will have to understand and dismiss his feelings. Can I suppress my feelings for him?

No, no, I'm attracted to him as well, now. I love his muscular, athletically-built body, his blonde hair, hazel eyes, well- proportioned lips, and all – yes, everything about him. His casual dressing style and cool walk are something I just can't get over. I want to see him so often. Even a glance of him from a distance satisfies me.

I go to the shop. As soon as I walk in, I get Greg's eye contact, and then he walks out. We stand outside the shop for a very long time talking.

"Bet, I can't help it. I'm really in love with you, from my heart," he says.

"Will you marry me, then?" I ask him, testing his motives. "Promise me, please," I suggest hoping to hear more assertions from him. Greg looks at me. I wonder what he is thinking.

"Betty, could you ask my dad, to give you a part-time Saturday job, please?"

"Why should I? I'm happy with my job."

"So that you can come to our house, and we will have a good time together without causing suspicion. People will think you're at home because you work for us. No one will know, not even my dad and step-mother."

"This is not convincing, Greg, a teacher doing housework on Saturdays. Who will believe this?"

"Can you say you want to top up your earnings, or something along those lines?"

"I think people will be suspicious of me getting this part-time job, in your father's shop."

I need time to think carefully about this. I must be convinced first, before I make others believe me. I can't deceive myself: I love him. However, I have a duty to uphold the laws - Dad told me. If I don't obey the laws, I might go to prison. And I don't want that.

Anyway, I go to the shop and discuss weekend employment opportunities with Baas Davies.

"Come to meet 'Missus', (meaning his wife), next Saturday," he suggests.

I go to the shop to finalise the work arrangement for Saturdays. I know this will give Greg and me an opportunity to be together privately, to build our relationship. Missus agrees to have me in, thus giving Getty, the support worker, a day off.

"Come to me in the shop at eight o'clock in the morning. I'll tell you everything that needs doing."

"Yes, Missus." My heart leaps with joy.

The first Saturday, Missus leaves Greg and her husband in the shop and takes me around, showing me the house and the jobs that I'll do most Saturdays. We go into the kitchen; I have to wash up the dishes, scrub the floors and cook them supper. In the laundry, I have to check the washing baskets, hand-wash the clothes, linen, and underwear. I must ensure clothes are ironed and returned to the wardrobes. I must change the sheets on all the beds.

"Greg will also be around to show you things until you're familiar with the routines," she says.

"Yes, Missus," I agree, confidently.

I get on with the jobs straightaway. By midday, I am running out of breath from tiredness. I keep going anyway, to avoid being proven incapable, and lose my golden time with Gregory. I finish after five o'clock, and pass by the shop to let them know I'm leaving, and hand over the keys. The shop closes at half past five, so they usually count the money, balancing their books, ready to close until the next Monday. Sunday is a holy day. The shop stays closed.

The following Saturdays are easier, because Greg comes around to help me, so that we have plenty of quality time, 'messing about' together.

"Betty!" I hear Greg calling me from outside. I go out to him, sitting in the veranda, with a bottle of coke and two glasses on the table. "Will you join me, please?" he says, pulling the chair next to him.

I sit down with my hands clasped on the table, and my eyes constantly looking at the small gate, imagining Baas or Missus coming through. He can't see my thoughts, so he nibbles on my lips. We can't be there for as long as we wish, I'm aware. So, after finishing my drink I get up saying, "I better do all the jobs, so that this opportunity remains open for us, Greg." Giving me another kiss, and a squeeze, he says, "Okay, I see you next week." Our secret friendship grows stronger, but most importantly the 'chemistry' between us is unbearable, considering the fear we have of being caught committing the crime. It becomes sad to both of us to see the day ending. We can only see each other the next Saturday. Annie leaves many jobs. This impinges on our special time.

News spreads quickly; someone might have reported us. On Tuesday afternoon, Harold, one of my colleagues, pops into my door, saying, "Hi Betty – just a warning – stop long talks with Baas's son at the shop; there is a rumour going around about you and him." And then walks away. I think to myself, *so the police are aware of us. We are targets of their observation.* The security forces are suspicious, and need to gather more evidence for us to be charged in court.

I go to the shop as usual. This particular Saturday, we work quickly; there is less to be done. In the afternoon, instead of chilling in the garden, we go to the garage. It seems reasonable to be anywhere after finishing the jobs.

We talk, laugh, touch and kiss, just like lovers do. Greg pulls down his trousers. Panting heavily, he pulls me towards him, holding me tightly. I can feel him. Just as I'm about to give in, my God, I hear a row outside. Through the window, I see a police officer in uniform running towards the garage door, shouting, "Police, open the door!" A bang follows, probably a kick. I hear dogs barking. I'm not sure whether it's the family dogs, or police dogs.

Immediately, I jump up, shoving myself between the car and the rough concrete wall of the garage to reach the door. I sustain some bruises on my left arm, and I'm bleeding. Ignoring the pain in my arm, concerned about my predicament, I peep through the tiny opening of the garage door. There is no need for me to be scared, I remind myself. I rush back to Greg, who appears cool, leaning over the car bonnet still holding onto his pants.

"Here they are; we're in trouble," I whisper to Greg firmly, but careful not to blame him. "Gregory, please jump out of that window!" I am panicking. My tummy rumbles, but I ignore it. My heart thumping loudly, and my body shaking, struggling to breathe, I call him again, "Greg!"

"Hmm!" he replies. He is very sluggish to move. God knows which stage he is at!

"Greg, please jump out. Hurry!" I whisper again, but this time pointing to the opposite window. I open it widely, grab his hand, and help him out and down. I watch him landing safely on the ground with both feet.

The garage door rattles, opening to the outside, just on time. Mr Davies and one of the police officers appear, asking, "Betty! Where's Gregory?" They scream almost at the same time.

"He may be in his bedroom, or in the kitchen. I don't know. Have you called him?" I reply, stuttering nervously. I feel my heart beating faster. I worry. They might arrest me. I look above his head, trying to hide guilt.

"What are you doing here, Betty? Tell me the truth," the police officer says. My arm throbbing with pain, I stand still, ignoring the burning sensation, staring at them.

"I'm cleaning the car, Sir. I've finished my normal jobs, and I have spare time left, so, I thought it is right for me to come over here, and clean the car, to make up for my hours," I say with my trembling voice, expecting anything.

As they all squeeze through to reach where I'm standing, I feel uncomfortable and start walking around the car, to avoid colliding with them, until I come out of the garage. They search for clues, but find none as they disturbed us before we got too far. Greg, with his eyes wide open, comes around towards me, with the police officer following him. Did he remember to do the zip of his trousers? Oh well, he should be fine. His white t-shirt, with England writing across his chest, is hanging over his crotch.

"Mr Davies," says the police officer, taking a document out of his car. "By law, Betty and Gregory aren't allowed to be together privately. Our intelligence is accurate. They are accused of having a sexual relationship. Do you know anything about this?"

"No," Mr Davies replies reluctantly, shaking his head sideways. There is a silence before Mr Davies speaks again.

"You know very well, sergeant; I can't allow that to happen here. No, not in my home, not anywhere - over my dead body! We don't mix, absolutely," confirms Mr Davies, raising his voice, gesturing with his right hand.

"Well, I'm giving both of them a written caution. Should we catch them in compromising circumstances, we will have enough court evidence for a prosecution. Be aware, we will be gathering this. Gregory, read here," he passes on the notes. Greg grabs them, and moves his eyes from left to right, reading silently. "When you are happy with the content, sign it," says the police officer. Then he turns around saying, "Betty, read this warning aloud, making sense of every word you are uttering. You will be judged by it."

I read aloud:

21st June 1970
POLICE FINAL WRITTEN CAUTION

I, Betty Baker, have been caught by the police with Gregory Davies, committing immorality in breach of the Immorality Act of 1950, amended in 1957. I declare that I fully understand the consequence thereof, should I do the same thing again.
Signed: B Baker on 21st June 1970
Witnessed: Paul Van Wyk and James Petro

"Do you both understand the implication of this caution?" Constable Petro asks, staring at me with a menacing look.

"Yes, Sir," we both say, in a chorus.

"*Jamie, dis genoeg. Laat ons weg gaan,*" says Paul, in Afrikaans, meaning 'Jamie, it's enough. Let's go.' As James walks past me, he makes a comment, '*Vuilig*' meaning 'Dirty'. I look at Greg, who doesn't understand Afrikaans, as I turn and walk away. 'This is South Africa.' I say this in my mind. Perhaps he saw or touched an unclean surface – that's the reason for his comment, I assure myself.

I can't take this harassment any more. I must decide what to do next. Should I stay here, and get in trouble for being in love with the man I choose? Or leave this country and my entire family behind, perhaps never to see them again? It's a difficult choice to make.

Gregory's own version

I'm fast asleep in my bedroom. I wake up hearing our dogs barking. I listen. I hear running footsteps. I get up and move the curtain slightly to one side, to see who is outside. I see the torchlight around the garages and garden, to my left and right. I see armed police officers. There's a loud bang at the door, followed by shouts.

"Police, Mr Davies. Open the door!" I put on my trousers, open my door, and as I head towards the main entrance, I meet my dad in the corridor. He appears disgusted.

"Stay behind, son!" he commands.

I take a step backwards, allowing my dad to pass me; and then I stand between him and Annie, my stepmother. My dad opens the door.

"Yes, can I help you?"

"We have a warrant to search your property, Mr Davies. Do you want to make a declaration of something you have illegally in your house?"

"No," says my dad, shaking his head.

"We advise you to stand aside as we do the search, and do not interfere with the officers, do you all understand?"

"Yes," we all respond.

We stand by the mirror in the corridor together, as three

officers go into our house. They search everywhere for about an hour. We then sit in the living room with an officer guarding us. They return. "You can go back and sleep," their commander says. We all go to the dining room. Annie goes to the kitchen to make us cups of tea.

Dad says, "This is becoming unbearable. I can't have this harassment for the rest of my life." I keep quiet, look down and not knowing what to say.

"Gregory," says my dad, looking at my face.

"You must return to England. You don't understand life here. It's illegal for us to have a relationship with non-Europeans. Haven't you noticed the signs in all public buildings?" Clearing his throat, he continues, "Boy, we don't mix with them."

"But, Dad, that's wrong. You can't discriminate against other people on racial grounds."

"That's the English law; it doesn't apply here. Tomorrow, go to the travel agency, and book yourself the next available seat."

Annie, with a cloak covering her shoulders, soon returns with a tray. She pours the tea, and then sits down. She seems to be in deep thought.

"We would like to have you here, Gregory. We can organise a party for you, and invite girls from our community so that you can find yourself a European companion. Should we do that?" Annie asks, trying to help me.

"No thanks. I'm in love with Betty," I reply, fervently.

"But she is a native," says Dad, bluntly. "You will never marry her here, son. Why waste your time in a relationship that has no future? If you break the laws, you will be put in prison, and be deported with a criminal record. Do you want that to happen to you? I'll not accept these kinds of raids, and I don't want other Europeans to isolate me, just because we 'hang about with the natives'."

"Just for loving the woman I choose, Dad?" I ask, with exasperation. Gradually, my heart begins to break. I keep my emotions under control. I don't want to cry. I remind myself that I made a choice to love Betty, and I'm not going to backtrack it. I take a deep breath of relief.

This is ridiculous. I whisper to myself. "Okay, Dad, I'll return to England, and will take Betty with me."

* * *

I'm back in my bed, thinking about what has just happened tonight. I find it hard to believe and accept that I can't love Betty by law, because our skins aren't the same colour. I love her - the typical kind of 'love at first sight'. Perhaps another young man should convince me that my views are wrong, and the law is right. I must speak to someone younger, someone likely to understand how it feels to have strong feelings of love for a woman. Carlos Gilianno, an Italian man, runs a restaurant in town. I'll have my lunch there tomorrow and have a chat with him about this. I must arrive just after twelve o'clock, before many people get there for lunch an hour later. We can discuss my relationship freely, and then I can return to Britain in the next few weeks, having decided what I'll do about Betty.

* * *

At eleven o'clock, I get into my dad's van and drive to town. I'm fortunate to find a parking space in front of the restaurant. The tables are bare, as I anticipated. Carlos notices me. He comes over to take my order.

"Hi, Gregory," he says.

"Hi, my friend," I say, hoping he won't notice that I feel bad. "Could I have two bottles of coke with ice cubes please? One is yours. Please join me at the table for a while before it gets busy; are you expecting many customers today?"

"Hopefully - that's what I like."

Carlos walks away, and Fanny, one of the waitresses, brings a tray with drinks. There's also a bottle of wine. She pours a drop of wine for both of us to taste, and we give the signal, "It's nice - please fill up the glasses." She does so, with great respect, and then quickly disappears into the kitchen.

Carlos pours more drink into the glass, and looks across thoughtfully.

"What's the news today, mate?"

"Nothing I can think of, my friend." I organise my thoughts in my mind. I want to make the best approach. So I ask Carlos, "What are your views about natives socialising with the Europeans, getting into firm relationships and marrying?"

Looking up into the ceiling, Carlos replies, "Oh dear, that's impossible. It's going against the laws of nature."

"What do you mean?" I ask inquisitively, feeling hot all over my body, with my right hand shivering, but not letting him know the background of my question.

"Their bodies are completely different to ours."

"Mh, in what way?" Now I really stare at him.

"The skin feels and responds differently from ours. It's not nice for them to make children – a European and a native. It's like being out in the bush. A buck can't mate with a lion."

I look at his face, and he seems certain of what he says. I listen controlling my feeling. I realise it was all up to education. It is unbelievable how people can be indoctrinated. Here, I have the most beautiful woman in the world, Betty. Why would anybody query our feelings for each other?

"Carlos, where's your wife?"

"Back home."

"So? Don't you miss her, mate?"

"Of course, I do. We actually do spend lots of time together, when possible. She has a good job – managing one of our companies in Italy. She can't move over to live with me here."

"Do you really love her?"

"What do you think? Of course I do."

"Why aren't you together then? Why choose to satisfy financial needs before the physical?" I ask Carlos to provoke his feelings.

I have heard Carlos' viewpoint. I just have to accept that my time to see Betty has come to an end. I have to return to England. This thought triggers an intensive sense of the pain of loss within me. I feel my tears about to rush out. Resting on my elbows on the table, with my eyes buried behind the palms of my hands, I manage to hold them back at first, and then let them go freely down my cheeks, before I wipe them off.

"Gregory, there's no need for this. Just accept that's how things are here."

"Okay, mate, I better go," I say, getting up from my chair and shoving it forward. Trying to smile, I say, "Take care of yourself," as I leave Carlos.

Instead of going straight to my dad's van, I go into the café by the railway station. As I'm standing waiting to be seated, a tall fair-haired man walks in, and sits at the table. I realise he speaks Afrikaans well. This is another right person to speak to, I think, as I move myself slowly towards his table.

He has a large suitcase by himself, obviously about to embark on a substantial journey. I ask him, "Where are you off to mate?" I can tell, he is an Afrikaner.

"England."

"Really, why now?"

"I've decided to leave South Africa."

"Tell me more about it."

"I know, the climate isn't that great, but I appreciate their way of thinking."

"Hmm," I think this conversation is taking an exciting turn.

I ask him, "Do you see the natives as lesser beings here?"

"No way," he says, raising his eyebrows. "From a very early age, I thought what we were taught was wrong." He pauses, and qualifies his statement, "My parents have similar views as me. They brought me up to assess situations before I find an opinion. That's why I'm going to England; to be away from this way of thinking. I've been told that in England, everybody has the freedom to attain their potential, and there are no apartheid laws there."

I am struck by the stark contrast; encouraged that there are some people whose thoughts are not entrenched through the government's indoctrination of the masses into believing in unfairness. I see now why some people want to go to England. I am absolutely convinced, and more determined than ever, to take Betty back to England with me.

At Betty's home

The time is 9.30 p.m., and it's dark outside. The wind is blowing and there's a chill in the air. I hear a knock at my door. I turn the lights out and peep through the window. I see a man with a dark balaclava, a hat, gloves and a three-quarter length coat – all in grey. From his body structure, I can tell it's my Greg. In our planning, we agreed to him disguising himself. What is he doing here? Everybody will know he's been. Oh my God, I'm in trouble again.

"Bet, darling, open the door quickly! It's me, Greg!" I sense the urgency in his voice. I'm concerned someone will notice him, and get the police around. I open my door quickly, and let him in. Standing by the door, I say, "Greg, I'm very sorry - you can't stay here for long. I'll get into more trouble. Are you all right?"

"No," he says, shaking his head. "It's very bad out there. Bet, darling, I want you to know that I love you very much." Looking at Greg, I'm certain that his fear of losing me is great. I can't bear the thought of living without him too.

"I know Greg, but it's impossible to continue like this."

"Betty, let's get out of here, I'm taking you away with me."

"Where shall we go?"

"Let's go to England. There is no racism there. I've got my booking sorted. When I get home, I'll arrange for you to join me."

"Mmmm." I stare at Greg, saying nothing. I can't entertain the thoughts of having Greg away from me, for any length of time. I feel like screaming; my love for him is so deep. I can't envisage us parting. I look at Greg, pull him towards me, and give him a long, deep kiss; the one to leave in his memory. I could feel the wetness from my eyes dropping onto Greg's cheeks. I close my eyes, so that I can cry. I feel my head pounding. I look at him one more time, before speaking.

"I'm very sorry, darling. I can't leave South Africa. I don't have a valid passport to travel abroad. Look, I only have a travel document endorsed to be used to travel around the homelands of Transkei, Ciskei, Botswana, Swaziland, Lesotho, Bophutatswana and Venda. I can't even go to live in certain parts of South Africa – the laws won't allow me."

Greg appears confused. He takes my travel document, looks at it and shakes his head.

"Are you a South African citizen?"

"No, I'm not. I could have been, and the government introduced new laws later, thus removing my citizenship."

"What's your nationality then?"

"I'm not a citizen of any country at the moment. According to the law, I'm just called a 'Homeland Citizen'."

"So, what passport do you hold?"

"None at the moment, I'm afraid."

"How can you travel beyond South Africa? What kind of law is this that prevents you from travelling freely? This is crazy." There is a remarkable silence. Both Greg and I are confused about this legal system.

"I'd like to go away with you, but without a valid passport and a visa, it is impossible," Greg says.

I look at him, thinking, "What are my options now?" The

thought of Greg leaving me behind tears me; a part of me is about to be taken away.

"That's one of the problems I have to face as a native. In addition, my money is limited. I earn just enough to sustain me to the end of the month – that's about one hundred and forty rand."

"I'm sorry to hear this. There are strict passport checks at the airport. You need a valid and recognised passport, and a visa to go to Europe," Greg advises me. "You can't apply for a visa with this 'rubbish' document. It's not recognised." Greg pulls a face, shaking his head sideways, before throwing my green travel document of the floor.

This talk triggers my emotions. I sob. Tears start flowing down my cheeks again, and heavily this time. I feel bitter. My sadness becomes intolerable. I see my bleak life clearly, embedded in pain and suffering, and I yearn for a more fulfilling future.

"Bet, I have a friend, Thomas Kruger. He lives in South West Africa. I met him at the United Nations Conference in London. I'll bring his address next time; perhaps you can visit him, for a start. He may be able to help us, because in his work as a solicitor, they handle human rights issues. You may apply for a South African passport through his help. I'm going back to dad's home. I'll see you soon," says Greg, leaving my home in haste. I watch him take a few steps forward, and turn to look at me. I sense his feeling of hurt.

"Remember to come and say good-bye before you return to England, Greg," I say affectionately.

"Bet, I promise you I will come around to say good-bye." I look up at him and smile.

Greg grabs my hand gently saying, "Betty, I'm sorry - I've got to go." Holding back an ocean of tears, I cling on him.

"Promise, Greg, you'll return to say good-bye - then I'll let you go." Tears start pouring down my cheek, and Greg's cheeks.

We wipe them off.

"I promise you'll see me soon again; that's a deal," Greg says and smiles, before kissing me goodnight. He puts on his coat, gloves and balaclava, opens the door, looks back, and hugs me, before disappearing into the dark village.

I start thinking about my journey. I need a free lift to Queenstown. From there, I can spend my money to buy a train ticket, perhaps just to get to De Aar or so. I'll connect trains from there and stay in hiding behind luggage in the compartment, where no one can take notice of me. I'll reach South West Africa. However, I have to wait for the right time, when trains are busy and everybody is excited about Christmas. With staff shortages, there should be the minimum of checks.

* * *

Greg visits me again, to say good-bye, as promised. He gives me two pieces of paper with addresses written on them. The first one says:

Thomas Kruger
26 Post Street, Swakopmund
South West Africa
Tel. 064 20713

And the second reads:

Gregory Davies
50 Powland Street, Skipton, North Yorkshire
Great Britain
Tel 01756 850699

I hold on to them, for safekeeping, and to put them in my handbag later. I look at Greg. He's gorgeous. We come close, hug and kiss each other. I feel the wetness on his cheeks, and notice he is crying. His cheeks are so red; I am crying too. We hold each other tightly as we kiss the very last good-bye. It's a very difficult moment for both of us. My hope is that we shall meet again in England, because I believe there's no racism there.

"Betty…" Greg calls looking at me expressionlessly.

"Mmmm…" I answer.

Rolling his eyes, and blinking every so often he says, "Rejoice, I love you." Gradually, I tell my heart, 'Let him go.'

* * *

I feel terribly alone. I miss Greg. I want to hear the sound of his voice, and talk to him for ever. I decide to go on that risky journey, following my heart and leaving the country. I write my letter of resignation:

To the School Committee
Firstly, I thank you for giving me the opportunity to teach at Mount View Primary School. I've enjoyed serving my fellow natives here, providing their children with the skills and education they require to be successful in life. I did my work to the best of my ability.

However, the time for me has come to move on, in search of the greener pastures elsewhere, for my children and I to graze on. This letter serves as my official document for immediate resignation from the teaching post I hold.
Yours faithfully,
Betty Baker

I can't wait for the next day to submit my letter to the principal. Of course, this will be a surprise to everyone in the school. I knock at her door.

"Come in," Mrs Grove says, immediately. I walk in, and pull the chair to sit opposite her. She puts down her spectacles, grins, looking straight at my eyes. Feeling innocent, I look at her face, saying, "Hello, Mrs Grove."

"Yes, Betty," she says. She is wearing her usual navy blue jacket, that over a white shirt. Her pearl necklace matches her stud earrings. These blend in nicely with her bright red lipstick. Her grey hair is curled into a bun at the back of her head. She holds onto the frame of her spectacles with her left hand. "What can I do for you? Are you all right, Miss Baker?" she asks, as she continues fiddling with the books on top of her table. It's my first time to visit her office out of my own initiative. She seems to sense something is wrong with me.

I lay my letter in front of her, saying, "I've now decided to resign and move on with my life. Please read the letter, and thank you for all your help. Could you write a reference for me please? I may not be able to collect it. So push it under my door, if I'm out." I look at her as I get up, saying, "I've got lots to do, so I'd better leave you with this." I look at her face, smile to the point where my eyelids crease saying, "Good bye, principal," before shutting the door behind me.

I return to my flat, pack my few necessities in a small suitcase, ready to leave the next day. I get up very early; have a wash, put on my jeans and t-shirt. I wear my jewellery and make-up. I carry my coat and my handbag, and walk to the road. I stand by the roadside to hitchhike.

After a little while a car approaches. I stick out my hand and point my thumb down. The car stops. I go to the driver, who winds down his window.

"I'm going to Queenstown, please!" I say loudly, still holding onto the handle of my suitcase.

"I'm sorry. I'm going to Aliwal North, lady," he says.

"That's fine with me. I'll continue hitch-hiking from there."

"Okay, let's go."

He puts my suitcase in the boot, while I open the front passenger door, and make myself comfortable on the seat. I shut the door, and he drives off.

"Mhmm, I'm 'smelling' a lady," the driver makes this comment while looking at me with romantic eyes. "Are you running away from your husband?"

I wish he knows how I feel, and just shut up. Before I respond he asks again, "Where are you from and what are you doing in Queenstown?"

"I live in this village, and I'm going away for a break."

He tries to engage me in a conversation, but I don't feel like saying much.

"Okay, I'd better give you your space. I think you need some."

Great! He's got the message. I'm worried about being in Aliwal North. This is one of the areas reserved for Europeans, although there are some natives living in the townships. I've been here before.

Soon, we arrive in Aliwal North. He takes me up to the junction to Queenstown.

"That's very kind of you, thank you very much," I say, fumbling with my handbag as if reaching out for a fee.

"Not to worry about money - just take care of yourself, and have a good journey," he says, getting into his car, blowing his horn before speeding off. I grab the handle of my suitcase, carrying it to the strategic position for the next lift.

I wait for a while, before the next car passes. I stick my hand out again, not realising it's a European driver. Even if he wanted to, he wouldn't stop anyway, for fear of breaching the *1953 Reservation of Separate Amenity Law.* They shouldn't get themselves in trouble for kindness.

It's difficult to tell the skin colours of the people in speeding cars until they drive past. However, I continue to stop every passing car. Many of them don't stop. I regret hiking from this end. There may be fewer native cars passing this way. I start worrying, as I don't want to miss the evening train to De Aar. I have no choice now, but to keep trying, stopping every car driving past, hoping for the best.

A white Toyota van without canopy approaches. I stick my arm out, giving a stop signal. It slows down until it stops further away from me. Two passengers are sitting in front. I speak to the driver – a native.

"I'm going to Queenstown."

"Sorry, lady, I'm full in front. Will you go on the back?"

"Yes, I don't mind," I reply. I swing my luggage over and then jump on the back of this van, sit in the middle facing backwards, to avoid crosswinds.

I'm in fact pleased, because no one will try chatting with me. Before he pulls off, I ask him to drop me off at the railway station. He agrees, and drives off. Sitting alone at the back of this van, my mind drifts into deep thoughts. *Will I ever see my parents again? Did I really try enough to find Mark?* My determination to leave South Africa is stronger than the losses I have to endure. Crosswinds blow strongly. I'm uncomfortable, and feel cold. To pass the time, I think more about Greg, and my hope for our future.

We arrive in Queenstown on time. The van stops at this busy railway station. The driver helps me out, and hands me my luggage.

"Have a good journey!" he says, without asking for money.

"Thank you. Bye-bye," I say rushing to the ticket office to buy my ticket – third class. I go to the station shop to buy brown bread and some apples. I wait on the platform for the train to arrive. It's on time.

I walk to the third class carriage, and get on board. The first class is reserved for Europeans only, second class for the natives, who can afford it. The poorer natives travel in third class compartments. I don't mind this, because the arrival time is the same. I have a long journey to travel, and a risky one too.

After an overnight trip, we finally arrive in De Aar, for my connection to South West Africa. I go straight to the platform to board my next train.

The train is full, just as I hoped for. On each side of the compartment there are three beds. I go up to the top bed, to sleep behind the passengers' luggage. The train travels all day. I get up when I need the toilet at the end of the carriage. I stretch my legs a bit, looking through the train windows in the corridor. I can't hang around for too long here. I don't want the train-guard to see me. He might want to inspect my ticket that I don't have. I read a book and my reference letter from Mrs Groves.

This is not bad; it should impress my future employers. It's self-explanatory. I fold the letter, and put it safely in the side pocket of my suitcase. The temperatures are high; it's scorching hot on the train. The train stops for a while.

Some passengers get off the train at Upington railway station, and new passengers join us. Among them, there is a young man, who is keen to talk to me. I quickly excuse myself, giving a good reason for wanting to sleep. He leaves me alone. I hear the ticket inspector calling for tickets. He opens our compartment, looks around saying in Afrikaans, "You all have your tickets here?"

"Ja, Baas," someone responds, before he shuts the door, walking down the tiny corridor to another compartment.

The train finally arrives at Windhoek station about 7.00 a.m., and I have one more connection to Swakopmund. I get off the train, but stay on the platform with other passengers in transit. I wish I didn't have to wait here. Fortunately, my next train is also on time. So, I board my train, arriving at my destination in the afternoon.

I get off and go straight to the telephone booth to call Thomas Kruger. I dial the number. Before I even insert the coins, I get a recorded message saying, "This number is out of order, try again later."

Hopelessly, I put my suitcase down and sit on it, watching the people passing by. Some young women hurry past me, and I recognise their accent to be that of South African natives. I go to them.

"Hi, I'm Betty. I was wondering if you could help me."

"What's the matter with you?"

"I need to get to 175, Ludwig Straat, Pioneerspark. I'm visiting Thomas Kruger," I say, showing them the address.

"Thomas Kruger, huh, my goodness – this sounds more like a 'Boer'! Why do you want him?"

Before I respond, she interrupts me saying, "Come and stop with us if you want."

I'm relieved, but tired. I stay positive. Gloria and Caroline help me carry my suitcase to the taxi rank. We drive out of the city for some time, reaching the native township. The houses are all small bungalows with two bedrooms, a kitchen, bathroom and a living room. The conditions seem bleak here, and some of the properties are run down. As we approach, I look with enthusiasm at the buildings, and there are many people outside. We get out of the taxi, and I follow them to their apartment.

Drains are bubbling, stinking sewerage is running everywhere above the ground. It is scorching hot. We jump over the filthy puddles, pushing between the people to get to our door. Some traders are selling different things, including meat and fish. The heat attracts flies, and they are buzzing everywhere.

"*Donkey-gxanike!*" some traders are shouting in their native language.

I understand the first bit - *donkey*, so it's easy to guess the other, as I could see the meat. Anyway, the girls confirm: it is donkey-meat. In her kindness, a certain lady offers me a piece of meat. I accept it, ignoring the unusual smell, and have a go at it. The taste is fine, though it could have done with thorough washing, as I can chew grains of sand in it.

People coming from the villages to work in the city live here. Some are homeless immigrants from other countries. Residents need an identification document to be allowed in – a similar situation like the South African townships. The natives here are required to carry identification at all times to adhere to the *Natives Act Pass Laws.* Failure to show the pass when demanded by the police is deemed a criminal offence.

I can't live here, I think to myself. So, I stay with these women for about a week, and then I look around for proper accommodation. Soon, the girls introduce me to a man, who owns houses for rent. He is pleased to share the house that he lives in, sparing me the tiny bedroom situated by the main entrance, for a reasonable rent.

I'm so pleased with this excellent news. I hire a taxi to move my belongings - a suitcase and some carrier bags. I pay the full amount of rent in advance, to ensure that I secure the room. I ask Caroline and Gloria to stop over with me for the night. It's been a very hot day, and I'm extremely exhausted. We stay outside, having some drinks. Again, I remind my friends saying, "Please don't go away tonight. I don't know this man yet."

"Okay, don't worry, love," Caroline reassures me. "We'll keep an eye on you." I leave them outside chatting, and go straight to sleep.

I have no reason to be suspicious of my landlord. He appears old, obese, and uninterested. So, I go into my bedroom, quickly put on my blue, short summer nightdress, made of two layers of net. As I'm drained, I soon fall asleep.

I wake up hearing a key unlock the main door. I open my eyes, still lying in my bed, to see the landlord returning from work. He is a security guard, and in full uniform. I realise then that I'm alone in the house. Both Gloria and Caroline have left. Sleep and tiredness disappear at that very moment. I lie still, pretending to be in deep sleep. With my head covered, I can hear my heart beat loudly. I can hardly breathe. I watch this man's movement through a small hole in my blanket. He puts on the lights, and then says in a horrid voice, "So, you are here!"

From where he is standing by the door opening of my room, he should have noticed I'm alone. "Come and sleep with me here," he says. That's enough instruction to trigger next my drastic response.

Without a word, I jump up, forcing myself out of the small opening between him and the doorframe, hoping to escape. I'm wrong. He grabs me by his rough hands. Struggling to break loose, I fall face down onto the floor. He turns off the light in the living room.

"Get up!" he commands. I don't respond. He puts his foot on my body and then neck, shaking me. I feel the rubber sole pressing hard on my neck. Scared of rape, death or both, I lie down, not knowing what to do. His patience is running out. He says, "I don't have time to beg you. I mean what I say - hurry up." I do not respond. "Okay, stay there: I'll carry you."

He bends over, picks me up in his arms and carries me towards the dark corridor into his bedroom. I struggle to break loose. I knock the shot gun off his belt with my knee. He is too strong for me. He puts me down on his big bed, perhaps king size. The mattress is very soft in the middle. As soon as he drops me, I sink.

"I don't want trouble, do you understand?" he says slowly in a soft voice. He turns the light on. I look at his eyes – they are big and reddish. He is obese, breathing aloud, blowing out his breath and clean shaven. I notice this bedroom hasn't got a door also. I move myself over to the edge of this bed and gather courage before asking him firmly, "What are you doing?"

"I've asked you to come and sleep with me in my bedroom. You go on and on making this a big deal. Don't you realise that these walls are thin?"

Walls aren't thick, so neighbours will hear me if I scream, I repeat this in my mind.

"I will not hurt you if you cooperate. Make up your mind. I'll have a quick one, and that's all. That's your choice."

I start negotiating with him. "Look, you just came in, and you are horrible to me. What's your name?"

He doesn't answer me. He is wilfully, deliberately, undressing himself. He takes off his jacket, loosens his tie, and takes it off; he undoes his shirt buttons and takes it off; he takes off his vest. He sits on the bed, taking off his stinky boots and socks, making a lot of noises, yawning and groaning. He slips off his trousers, remaining in his big loose black boxer shorts. He leaves the gun in his trousers. Sitting next to me, he puts his right hand on my thigh, and starts moving it about gently. He is disturbed.

He gets up and rushes for the toilet, just opposite his bedroom. He is careful to leave the toilet door open, and looks back at me every so often. I hear the sound of his wee, and then it goes quiet. He turns around and sits on the pot. He holds his tummy with crossed arms, as if he is in pain. He appears stuck; all I can hear is lots of noises. He flushes the toilet, while sitting on the pot, and continues his business. He bends his head forward towards his thighs. It's hard for me to imagine what he hopes to do on his return.

The corridor is so narrow, that he would see me passing by, should I try to escape through to the main door. I guess he has locked it, and has not left the key there.

I can't surrender. I have one way if I can regain enough strength, and that's to escape through the window. The risk in jumping out, falling over, and hurting myself outside is minimal. It's a lot better than what might happen when this man returns. These thoughts are strong enough for me to act on, while he's in the middle of his business on the toilet.

I step on the bed, put my foot on the windowsill, while turning the handle. The window flings opens widely. I jump down, landing safely on my feet. I run away from his house into the dark, but not too far. I'm unfamiliar with the area. I can see the dim light of his bedroom. I watch his room go dark.

I assume the man is asleep. I'm safe to return just to sleep in front of his door. Frightened of the passers-by all night, I sit up, covering myself with the top thin and transparent layer of my nightdress. The fear and the cooler temperature of the night keep me awake, shivering.

The early-morning breeze brings a chill that cuts through my bones. I start to cry, but not loud enough for him to hear me. I watch people walking past, a few metres away from me, coming from parties.

I soon hear the man's footsteps moving about inside his house, perhaps preparing for work. I get up and move to one side from the door; I sit down hiding slightly from his door's view. I watch him pulling the door handle behind, walking away. Fortunately, he has left the door opened, probably for me to return.

I'm in a terrible state, longing for a shoulder to cry on, but there's no one to comfort me this time. I drag my feet back into the house, feeling very tired from lack of proper sleep. I start getting dressed. As I'm about to put on my last piece of garment, Caroline and Gloria return.

By then, I can hardly speak. I just look at them with my swollen, blotted bloodshot eyes, and suddenly burst into tears again.

"What did he do to you?" they ask appearing very concerned. "Tell us, Betty, we can sort him out."

They try to stop me from crying, so that I can speak – it's impossible for now. No word can soothe me. However, after a while, I stop crying. I have two thoughts in my mind - not another night in this house, and never to return to South Africa.

Later that day Gloria and Caroline help me move my suitcase to Kay. She kindly allows me to sleep in her living room, next to my luggage. She has less furniture, and not even a carpet on the floors, but has more love to accommodate a stranger like me in her home.

She's a lone parent, doing domestic work for a young European family. She brings left-over food to share with me and her children. This means so much to me. I can feel a wave of relief. At least, I am safer here.

I look for work, so that I can maintain myself. Every morning I call Employment Agencies. I read the newspapers, searching for work. I'm confident about selling my skills to impress all the employers.

I see a temporary teaching post advertised in Windhoek, at Ben Schoeman Primere Skool, and apply. The Principal invites me to visit the school to have a chat with him and the staff. I prepare for the journey by train to Windhoek the following morning. The train arrives at the station on time, enabling me to walk to the taxi rank, to hire a taxi to this school.

A child directs me to the Principal's office. I knock at the door. A tall man in his fifties sitting behind his desk lifts up his eyes, pushes his chair backwards, and gets up to meet me by the door. He shakes my hand, beckoning me to another chair opposite his.

"I'm Mr Beans. Please take a seat."

"I'm Betty Baker. I spoke to you on the phone. Thank you for the opportunity to meet you."

He is very polite, and offers to make me a drink.

"Tea with milk, and one spoon of sugar, please," I say, sitting upright on the chair. He walks out. I scan my eyes around the office, passing time. This is just a man's office, with blank walls. I notice English books on the bookshelves, and on his desk. He also speaks English fluently, although the official language here is Afrikaans. *This reveals to me a bit about him himself,* I say in my mind, thinking he must be supporting the freedom fighters.

Mr Beans returns with a cup of milky hot tea and sugar, all on the tray. "I'm looking for an English teacher on a temporary basis, to cover maternity for six months," he says. "I'm impressed with your standard of communication. How soon could you start?"

"Well, I'm available right now. Of course, I'll need a day to collect my stuff from Swakopmund. Will you provide me with accommodation?"

"Yes, I'll ask my friend about that." Mr Beans gives me the

application forms. After filling in the forms and showing him my original certificates and reference letter from Mount View, we agree on my start date.

"Your class will be waiting for you, Miss Baker," he says as he sees me off at the main entrance of the staff and administration building. I'm thrilled with my new job in a bigger school than the last one in South Africa.

Within a month of arriving in this country, I'm back to teaching again, the job I cherish mostly. Life is better here; there is legal racial integration. I'm now organised, teaching and living well. I give up searching for Thomas; however, I still have room for Mark in my heart. But, I write a letter to Gregory.

Pos bus 14467
Swakopmund
South West Africa
19 December, 1971

Dear Greg,
I hope you are well. Thank you for your unconditional love. I gave up searching for your friend, Thomas. I'm all right at this moment. Please reply and let me know how you're doing.
All my love,
Betty x

I go to the Post Office to buy a stamp, and then post my letter to Greg. Eight weeks later, I receive his reply.

Gregory Davies
50, Powland Street
Skipton, North Yorkshire, Great Britain
19 February 1972

Dear Betty,

It's great to hear from you again. I never lost hope that we will be together one day. I reckon you'll be able to join me soon; so, let me know when you're ready to come: I'll send you a ticket. Tell me more about your life there.

Love from

Greg x

I reply. This time, I write a bit more about the general style of life and culture.

People live in their own ways. They enjoy life, especially weekends from Friday until Sunday evening; they hold fund- raising activities called 'braaivleis'. This means barbecues in English. The DJ plays music, and those who wish to dance do so, while others chat over drinks, 'six to six', meaning from 6.00 p.m.to 6.00 a.m. I enjoy barbecues. I've also made friends, who have introduced me to their social lifestyle - discos. Weekends are all exciting. I can't help bubbling with the excitement inside me. However, in some moments, life becomes a struggle, with some excruciating pain.

There are times when I wish I wouldn't see the sun rises and sets again... these are 'the dark moments'. However, I try to enjoy my job, working extremely hard. In some way, it's like the same-old South Africa you know....I miss you.

Love, Betty x

After reading my letter, I seal it in an envelope. Deep in thought about the current state of my life, I walk down to the Post Office. I buy a stamp for forty cents, and get an airmail sticker. The cashier is very kind to accept it over the counter. Imagining Greg's excitement when receiving my letter, I return home.

I live a peaceful life with everyone, daily. I have experienced many of life's ups and downs. I'm determined to do whatever I can to improve the level of my education and knowledge, generally. In my spare time, I read my reference letter, to encourage myself. My eyes fill up with tears, making it impossible to see and read the text. I'm tired of wiping them off. I continue reading, until tears drop on the paper, smudging it.

In my imagination, Greg's face flashes before me. *Betty, what are you doing here?* I ask myself. *When will you follow your heart, and go to be with Greg in England?* Shaking my head, I remember the fact that this is impossible to do from South Africa.

I am thinking about many things: Skoonfontein, my family and my future. I may be separated from them, but my life goes on! I can feel such happiness within me.

from Betty's journal, 14th July 1973

Chapter 9

The Tribunal

December 1972

E arly in the morning, I open the front door to get out to the city for a job search, as my temporary job at Ben Schoeman has finished. I walk down the street towards the number 187 bus stop. Staggering, I struggle to stay balanced due to the strong wind. I trip on something hard and fall over; landing with both knees and hands on the ground. My handbag drops off my shoulder.

"Ouch!" I lie there for a while before getting up slowly, and collecting my handbag. Brushing my hands and bending over to look at the cut below my right knee, I get a tissue from my handbag to clean the wound dripping with blood. I bind my handkerchief around the wound to stop the blood-flow and turn around and look back, wondering what made me fall. I see a tied blue carrier bag, probably with concrete inside. I recognise the letters *OK*, the name of a big supermarket on the high street.

That's what I tripped on.

This is not surprising: litter is scattered everywhere, and fly-tipping seems to be the norm in this area. Rats run around in daylight feeling good after feeding from rotten, smelly food in overflowing rubbish bins. Some dry yellowish and brown leaves are cluttering the gullies. Others are scattered all over the streets and pavements.

I force my way forward, finding it difficult, and struggling to breathe. With cross winds blowing so strongly, it's hard for me to remain upright. I manage to balance, defying the wind blowing me sideways. At a distance, I see a cloud of dust appearing to be touching the sky. Blown papers are flying about, polluting the atmosphere. My eyes are sandy and reddish from constant rubbing and trying to remove the sand grains. 'Huh, this is Windhoek,' I moan to myself. The literal translation of Windhoek is 'windy corner'.

I arrive at the bus-stop and join the end of the long queue. It's rather noisy, with various people chatting among themselves in their vernacular. I can hardly understand a word they're saying. *Is it Damara, Khoisan, Portuguese or Tswana?* I wonder. Listening again, I still can't tell, but conclude it's definitely not Afrikaans.

After a short while, the pain from my knee subsides, but leaves me with a slight limp. The empty bus pulls into our stand for number 187. People rush in, but the queue is moving slowly. I keep my fingers crossed, hoping to get on even if I don't get a seat: I'd be happy to stand all the way. Now, there's only one other passenger in front of me. Just as he puts his foot on the lower step, the driver shouts, "The bus is full!" immediately slamming the bus door, and beginning to pull away.

"Please, I'm late for work!" shouts this man, banging the door. The driver ignores him completely, and drives off. I look at his face, feeling bad - as though it had happened to me. The bus soon disappears into the main road, and out of my sight.

"It's useless trying to plead with these drivers," I say,

comforting him.

"He's rude, and doesn't care about other people," replies this man, panting heavily. "He is disrespectful," he adds, waving his hand away from his body. Oh, shame, the door nearly trapped him! This could have been worse, I thought.

I wait patiently, listening to the many grumbling passengers left behind. They are concerned about getting to work late, and having to face their bosses. Others are worried about getting the sack. I appear to be the only person to be at least comfortable. If only they could know I was the worse off; but who could tell?

Soon another bus pulls into the stand. As the door flings open, a man appears from my right hand side, suddenly, and pushes himself through into the door.

"Stop!" someone shouts from the back. I hold onto the bus to stop myself from falling over. People start pushing to the front, trying to go in first. This behaviour annoys me; however I let them have their way.

"Hey, mate, go back to the end of the queue!" shouts the driver, in vain. This man completely ignores him, and walks straight to the backseat, takes out a cigarette and smokes.

I get in, and sit by the window, watch the passengers, as they walk in, filling the vacant seats. I'm very impressed by a woman, wearing an outfit looking like a bride's wedding gown, and a headscarf, shaped like horns. I discover later that she belongs to a Herero ethnic group. The passengers are quiet in comparison to South Africa - perhaps it's their culture, I think.

After travelling for about five miles, we arrive at the terminus. Feeling low and lacking enthusiasm, I drag my feet, walking out towards the main street. I continue to walk slowly, window-shopping until I reach the outskirts. Suddenly, I remember my teacher, Mr Parker saying, "People judge us by our appearance and character."

This thought pricks my conscience, helping me regain confidence. Walking elegantly, ignoring my bruised knees, I go into a café for a drink, hoping to find someone to talk to. I place my order for a cup of tea at the counter, before sitting at the back table facing the entrance.

One of the waitresses comes around to the table next to mine to collect the tray with used plates, cups and cutlery.

"Are you all right there, love?" she asks, wiping the table with a damp cloth.

"Yeah, I'm okay, thanks – just looking for work at the moment."

"What kind of work?" she asks with interest.

"Any work would do for now," I reply, not caring to hide my desperation.

"Well, perhaps you could help me?"

"Yes, please, that would be great," I reply frankly, taking another small sip of my tea to ensure it lasts.

The lady disappears into the back, and returns shortly with her manager, John De Klerk. A tall European man, about six foot two, with a very strong Afrikaans accent, pulls out the chair at my table to sit down directly opposite me.

"Hello," he says in Afrikaans, looking straight into my eyes.

"Good morning, Sir," I reply in English, looking straight back at him.

"So, you're an English-speaker; that's good for my business." He switches over to English. "Katie says you're looking for a job. Is that correct?"

"Yes, Sir, that's true."

"What job are you after, exactly?" asks Mr De Klerk. Before I respond he asks the next question. "What's your experience, or speciality?"

"I'm an experienced qualified primary school teacher."

"I can offer you a job as a cashier. How's that?"

"I'll take it, thank you."

"When can you start?" he asks, getting out of the chair, walking across to the counter to speak to the cashier. As he returns, I'm ready with the answer.

"Tomorrow, Sir," I respond hastily, grinning and looking to impress him.

"You should be able to pick up the nitty-gritty of the job pretty well. Everybody is helpful here; the key is looking after our customers, ensuring they return. Report at half past seven for an eight o'clock start, okay? I'll have your uniform ready by then," he says, before disappearing through the back door of the café into the kitchen.

Breathing gently with relief, I look outside through the big window, watching the people passing by. Despair grips me, as I think of the job I've just accepted. I must get on with it, regardless of the risk involved in defending the cash machine during robberies, and my lack of experience in this line of work. My cup is almost empty. I drink the last drop, get up and look across the tables, making eye-contact and giving a slight wave to my future colleagues, before leaving. They wave back, smiling.

I wander about in the city before returning to the bus terminus for my bus back home.

The terminus is quite crowded with shoppers and buses. My thoughts are flooded with my strong desire to continue working as an English teacher here in South West Africa until I get the opportunity to follow my heart and live with Greg, wherever possible. Even so, for now, teaching seems too difficult to accomplish – it's a dream, but one that I hope will come true, just like at Ben Schoeman. At the moment, I must hold on to my cashier job, and earn money to pay my basic living expenses.

I have exciting news at least. I get off the bus, and walk slowly this time towards my home. "It's a job," I say, convincing myself. I quickly do my little jobs and go to bed for an early night. I'm unable to sleep for most of the night due to anxiety about the job that I'm about to embark on. I must have drifted into sleep because I wake up from a strange dream, crying, and realise it's time to get ready for work.

I haven't got much time to ponder over the dream. I prepare myself and walk to the bus-stop. I'm the first passenger, ready to board the next bus that arrives. The bus is almost empty at this hour of the morning, so I manage to get myself a seat, and have a nice, comfortable journey. As the bus approaches the stop before the terminus, my heart starts to pound heavily. I sense discomfort as I rise up, ready to move towards the door. The bus stops, and I jump out. Stretching my body, I open my mouth, yawning. Tiredness due to lack of sleep engulfs my body, as I walk towards the café.

I push the door, assuming it's already open. Realising it is locked I knock on the glass-door behind the burglar bars. I don't get a response. I walk around to see if there's another entrance to the building, but the café is shut and I wait outside, leaning by the wall. The other workers soon arrive simultaneously. We converse until Mr De Klerk arrives in his grey Mercedes Benz.

"*Goeie more,*" he says, or 'Good morning,' in English, opening the burglar bars and the door to let us all in. We respond in chorus, "Good morning, Sir."

"Betty Baker, it's nice to see you again."

"Thank you, Sir."

"Will you come over to the office to collect your uniform?"

"Yes, Sir."

I follow him through a long and dark corridor, until outside the building. We squeeze through a narrow passage into another building. His office is here. He puts his key in to open it and then, with his knee gives a little push, to release the jammed door. "Go in," he says. I do as told, but stand by the door, leaning on the wall. He turns on the light, and walk straight towards his desk, humming. He beckons me to, "come around".

I do, until I stand in front of his desk. He opens another door of the storeroom, and comes back to his desk. When he walks past me this time, he pats my shoulders. "Don't worry, you'll be fine," he says.

I hold my breath in fear, not knowing how to respond on this occasion. He gives me a new brown skirt, a similarly- coloured cap, and a cream shirt in a transparent plastic bag.

"You can try them on," he says.

Not in your presence, I think to myself. I stand still for a while, holding my uniform in my hand, indicating that he should go out.

He gets my non-verbal message, and quickly walks out. I put them on, and they are the right fit. I then make my way out to the kitchen to work alongside Marta, our supervisor, who trains me on the cash machine. We do all the jobs, mopping the floors, cleaning the windows, and preparing the teas and meals, before the customers begin to arrive. My first day goes well, and I gladly continue working for Mr De Klerk.

Some days are worse than others, though. One day, Mr Beans, the principal of the Ben Schoeman Primere Skool where I taught temporarily, walks in. He comes straight to the counter to place his order and recognises me. Amazed, he says, "Betty Baker, is this you? What are you doing here?"

"I'm working temporarily, until I hear whether there's a vacancy at your school." We engage in a friendly conversation for some time.

When no one is looking, I give him a piece of paper confirming my contact details. He promises to be in touch with me as soon as possible. I don't know what he's thinking as he leaves the café.

A few weeks pass, and I do not hear from him.

'Oh well, that's just one of those things I have to accept and put up with,' I say to myself, pondering about teaching in comparison to the cashier job. Some people do fail to keep to their promises, don't they? That's normal. It's not because of ignorance, but because of unforeseen circumstances. I eventually forget about Mr Beans.

Six months later, John hands me a telephone message to

contact Mr Beans urgently. I guess what this is all about, and I'm right. He has offered me a teaching opportunity at Ben Schoeman Primere Skool again, because the country is going through a tremendous teacher shortage. Perhaps within a year I can upgrade my qualification issued by the Department of Bantu Education in South Africa.

Now, I have the teaching job I aspired to. From Monday to Friday, I leave my rented home at 7.00 a.m. for school, and return around 2.30 p.m. I work very hard to impress my management team, parents and children. All appears well.

Suddenly, one Friday afternoon, Mr Beans summons me to his office, handing me a letter terminating my service at the school. The letter refers to a recent change of the law regarding teachers trained out of the country. So, in total shock, I receive this letter, and bid farewell to my colleagues, wondering what's going to happen to me next.

A few months later

I pick up a newspaper from the Library, and Arthur Benson Infant School has advertised a temporary post for six months. Not deterred by my previous experience, I apply for it. Surprisingly, I'm called for an interview in the following week. After explaining the circumstances regarding the South African teachers' qualification, I'm accepted on condition that I enrol on the upgrading programme administered by the Star Academy.

Mrs Magdalene Arno is assigned to mentor and then assess me, to determine my suitability for a permanent licence to teach in any administration in this country.

I've almost reached the end of my assessment period, although several things have gone wrong. Mrs Arno has not been talking to me; she writes comments and hands me the sheet. I feel she is unpleasant towards me. I put up with this treatment as it is not my usual nature to complain. I'm easy-going, and accept positive criticism willingly.

Nevertheless, at this point I've submitted my concerns regarding how she handled my assessment as outlined by the Academy's policies. I've done this, knowing my dad would have said, "Leave it, Betty, and just move on."

I can vividly remember the incident my dad referred to, when we lived in Skoonfontein. Baas Jimmie's friend's son hurt my finger. The Baas was unable to help me, and then I later told my dad.

Here, I am in a similar situation, using the Star Academy's Complaints' Procedure against their own representative. It comforts me to know these democratic policies exist.

Mrs Arno says that she needs to re-assess me constantly, together with her colleague. Once I've passed all re-assessments, I can then be assessed further to meet the requirements of the country's Board of Education before I can be granted a licence to teach.

I prepare my last Year One Dance lesson thoroughly for observation - adapting the activities from the lessons the school already use from their 'Dance Scheme'. As dance is my favourite subject, and I have done special training in Physical Education, I am relaxed.

Mrs Arno walks in carrying her clip-board as usual, and sits at the desk I reserved for her, where she has a good view of all the thirty children in the hall. My folder with the lesson plan, in three parts, warm-up, play three tracks, and do movements, and cool-down, is on this desk, open for her.

After changing into their PE kits, the children walk on all fours into the field with multi-coloured rubber mats scattered all over the floor. Each child stands on their mat, waiting for my instructions:

"Stand up with a straight back, and listen to my story about 'the toy shop'." I play the tape. "The toys are sad, because the shop is dusty and clumsy. Show me a sad face. The toys are asleep on the shelf. Curl up on the floor. Now, stretch and march, like a toy soldier. When the music changes, show me a happy face. Copy me as I show you the movements the toys can make. Gallop, like a horse, into space and changing your direction."

I notice Belinda sitting down, and not participating. As I get next to her, she starts vomiting. I get everybody to sit down, while I deal with this emergency. I send one of the children to the office with a message that I need someone to come to the playground immediately, because Belinda is sick.

That disturbs the progression of my lesson, as some children appear unstable. The secretary collects her, leaving me to continue with the lesson:

"When the music starts, I want you to jump like a frog. Walk like an elephant. When the music changes, greet your friend, and clean the toy-shop together. Reach out to the top shelf, bottom shelf and the middle shelf. When the music stops, freeze in an interesting position. Change positions."

To cool down, the children stretch their arms and legs gently, for a count of five, and then relax. And then they sit up very slowly with a straight back, but looking down on the floor.

We go through the dance together from the beginning. And, the lesson finishes. The children return to their classroom to change.

I believe that I have delivered the lesson successfully. Unfortunately, the assessors do not agree. Arguing my case, nobody is keen on accepting and acting on all the points I raise, even when I provide written evidence for every fact I give. They insist my lesson showed little progression.

Josie, my friend, suggests that I comply with the assessor's opinion regarding my final lesson, and prepare to be re-assessed. A miracle could happen in my favour because we are in a different country now. I agree, but prefer to have a different assessor this time around. I suspect this process could nullify the teaching qualification I obtained in South Africa. Therefore, I decide not to proceed with the re-assessment.

I'm determined to pursue this issue as far as it can go, hoping someone reasonable might see sense in this, and defend me. My mind is made up.

I feel courageous as I sit down to write my story to present to the Educational Tribunal. I'm hurt, and find this difficult to do. So, I obtain lawyers, and one, Mrs Matthews, happily accepts to take on my case. She knows her job very well, and is popular. Her office is always full of people needing help. The firm charges a high fee to cover the cost of preparing the documents, and for actual personal representation I'd have to pay more money. So, we agree for my lawyers to help me prepare the documents which I'd present at the tribunal.

The tribunal-hearing day arrives. I put my aide-mémoire into my bag, and call a taxi. I travel to the National Education Head Office building in the city where the hearings are held.

I stand outside the door for a while, to reassure myself before knocking. I hear loud voices, and listen carefully, noticing they speak Afrikaans. I can't understand them very well. I usually lip-read to aid my understanding of fluent Afrikaans speakers. But I can't do that now. I hear laughter again, but then knock at the door immediately to avoid being caught spying on them. A loud, deep voice says, *"Kom binne,"* meaning come inside – in Afrikaans.

I turn down the door-handle quietly, while pushing the door away from me to enter this big room with a long rectangular table in the middle. Three men, all quite mature-looking, and a younger woman, probably in her twenties, all of European origin, are sitting on both sides of the table. A chair for me is left just by the door. "You can sit down, Miss Baker," says one of them, pointing to the chair by the door.

"What is your problem?" Mr Van Vuuren asks, appearing to be unenthusiastic about this business.

I rise up, take out my notes and read them, slowly and clearly, pausing to enhance clarity of my speech.

"Do you want us to address you in Afrikaans or English, Betty Baker?" Mr Van Vuuren exclaims loudly in his rough voice, and in a manner that was very unsympathetic.

I'm glad that they have recognised my good command of both foreign languages. I remember Lottie telling me about a senior government officer who refused to consult the natives to ask them about their preferred medium of instruction in schools. He argued that it's to the benefit of the natives to learn both languages, to enable them to communicate with any 'Baas' who can only speak one of the languages.

I stand there ready to defend myself confidently.

"I can understand Afrikaans, Sir, but on this occasion, I would prefer you to speak in English," I reply calmly, staring at him.

"Right. Firstly, I must explain what our role is, and then you can decide if you want us to continue dealing with your query. Do you understand, Betty Baker?"

I reply, with great respect, "Yes, Sir."

"The purpose of this meeting is to decide whether your concern is not at all justified, partly justified or fully justified." He continues, "To help us make this decision, we have already considered whether the Star Academy followed its own procedures correctly. We have also considered if they made reasonable decisions in all the circumstances."

My throat tickles, and I cough gently. He pauses for a little while and then says, "In considering your case, we have taken into account all the documentation you and the Academy have provided. We asked you to comment on the Academy's response to your case. Bear in mind, our decisions do not necessarily refer to all the documentation provided and points raised during our review. However, we have considered all the materials provided, which we consider necessary in making an informed decision about your case."

He pauses, and stares at me in a way that I find makes me

uncomfortable. Our eyes meet. I struggle to breathe, and my hands sweat. I feel dizzy, as if my body is about to drop down. I hold onto the back rest of the chair for support, as he continues to speak:

"Let me remind you, Miss Baker, we cannot interfere with the operation of any institution's academic judgement. We have no mandate to do so. We cannot put ourselves in the position of examiners in order to re-mark work, or pass comment on the marks given by your assessor, who according to the Academy is doing her work very well. For your benefit, and for us to be seen to have done justice, we can just look at whether the Academy has correctly followed its own assessment, marking and moderation procedures. We can investigate whether there was any unfairness or bias in the decision-making processes. What's your view about all this?"

I remain silent for a while, considering whether it is worth going through this grilling period.

"What would you like to do?" Mr Van Vuuren asks.

"I'd like you to proceed with the hearing, Sir," I reply confidently, regaining my composure. Mr Dirkie Van Vuuren, who seems to be the senior member of the Tribunal, says, "Colleagues, the Star Academy provided us with a copy of their complaint procedure. It shows all internal stages of dealing with students' concerns."

He lifts his head up and looks at me asking, "Are you aware of this official document, Betty Baker?"

"Yes Sir," I reply.

He says, loudly, "Firstly, the Line Manager, within a maximum of thirty days, investigates the case. Secondly, the Academy conducts a hearing, chaired by any senior staff with four or five other staff members present. The student must attend this meeting. The process is expected to be completed within a week. Should the student be dissatisfied with the outcome, they can move on to the next stage. Thirdly, the principal or deputy principal must chair this meeting with the student in attendance. It must be done within two weeks. Fourthly, and finally, we here take into consideration the facts gathered from previous hearings. This is done by the Board of the Academy. At this stage, the student and other parties are not consulted. At all stages, the student can only proceed to the next stage after providing written representations detailing their concerns, and the resolution they seek."

No one speaks for a while.

"So, Betty Baker, you have gone through all these stages, and you are unsatisfied with the outcome?" Miss Swiss, a brunette with a high-pitched voice asks, sweeping her fringe sideways before looking at me.

"Yes, Miss," I respond.

"You mean you aren't happy with the decisions made about you?" Mr De Kok enquires, putting his spectacles on the table.

"That's correct, Sir," I say.

"Colleagues, let me give you Betty Baker's background, as this is very important in this investigation, as you might know," Mr Van Vuuren says. "Betty Baker is a 'qualified teacher' from South Africa."

Miss Swiss smiles, and rolls her eyes up to the ceiling. I feel ashamed with this reaction, wondering what the problem with qualifying in South Africa is.

"She enrolled on the upgrading programme for teachers, and was not trained by us here. Her start date has been deferred. I can see from this other letter that her Mathematics standard is quite low. She didn't actually meet our entry criteria, so she needed to sit our Maths exam, though she did so, successfully," she concedes.

The comment about Mathematics annoys me, as I recall the reason for getting a low grade in the first place. I remember Lottie telling me about the Educational Officer in South Africa who queried the purpose of teaching Mathematics to the natives, 'when they would never get the opportunities to use it practically in the right context'. Therefore, the policy was based on the fact that the natives do not require a high standard of Mathematics.

"What is this programme all about exactly, Dirkie?" Miss Swiss asks enthusiastically. Before Dirkie answers, Mr Burgher explains, "It's kind of a conversion programme, which enables teachers from other countries to be assessed against our standards. When we are satisfied, we give them a licence to teach. They can then seek work in our schools, but only when we experience some shortages."

"Do they train like our teacher-trainees here?" asks Miss Swiss, refusing to let this issue pass.

"No, there are various ways of doing it. They can get full time training or just teach part-time while being assessed. To undertake the second option, the student must firstly be employed by our government as an unlicensed teacher and accept to be paid less money. They aren't allowed to make a comparison with other teaching colleagues – those doing the same job for more money. This has nothing to do with the Academy, or the school rules. It's our initiative. The students make their choices, and there is no pressure on them."

"And what does the Assessor do for a part-time assessment programme?" Mr Erasmus, who has been listening to the discussion all along, asks. His voice sounds a bit croaky, perhaps due to smoking the pipe that's in front of him in the ashtray on the table.

"It's up to the Assessor, really: there is no prescription, Mr Erasmus. However, whatever they choose to do cannot be disputed. They represent us," Mr Van Vuuren responds, fidgeting with a pen. "We ensured this clause is included in all the training programme documents because Assessors are on the ground, facing all sorts of people. So, we must protect them and their judgement."

I'm listening to all of this discussion, and I understand how my case has been handled. I'm happy to know this information. My knees feel weak though so I sit down, feeling pity for myself, for having taken this issue so far, and I lose in the end. *Betty – it's okay,* I say mentally, encouraging myself.

* * *

At morning coffee time, I'm asked to wait outside, while the Tribunal members are having their drinks. I carry my chair to sit in the corridor, and shut the door behind me.

A woman who seems to be in her thirties appears at the end of a long corridor, pushing a trolley with cups, coffee and teapots into this room. She's wearing a pink apron, and her hair is tied in a bun and clipped behind with hair grips. She seems to be of the Baster racial group from Rehoboth. She stares at me, knocks slightly, peeps through the door, and goes in.

I hear another roar of laughter as they chat to each other loudly. I don't know what to do. I feel like screaming, "No!" to release my anger and frustration. I feel my knees shaking. I take a deep breath, and then let it out, several times. All along, I'm holding tears that have flooded my eyes, suddenly. I wipe them off with my tissues.

"Come in," the voice from the room says. I push the door slightly, and it flings open. I put my chair back to my place, by the door again. My head throbs.

Mr Van Vuuren continues, "A letter from Ben Schoeman Primere Skool confirms that Miss Baker will be employed in a full-time teaching post. However, this school terminates her contract soon after commencement. Miss Baker was subsequently employed at Arthur Benson Infants' School later in the same year. Do you agree with all this?" asks Mr Van Vuuren, unexpectedly.

"I refuted that decision, because it was unfair, Sir."

He pauses while looking at me. I'm puzzled. I don't know

whether to respond with a "Yes, Sir" or whether just a nod would be sufficient. I nod a "Yes."

"Her contract with the original school had been to teach older children, while Arthur Benson offered her a post to teach the younger ones. She's covered the whole age range."

"Hmm, that's good," Mr Erasmus agrees, nodding his head repeatedly.

They are trying to paint a picture, in order to understand my concern in detail. I sit quietly, allowing them to get on with it. I feel thirsty, but daren't ask for water, or to go to the toilet. "Subsequently, the Academy confirmed by letter to Baker that she has been successfully registered in our scheme for part-time assessment in the Infants' School. The duration of the programme is six months. Baker was deemed to have failed the last lesson observed by two teachers."

I notice that he doesn't talk about all the lessons I passed, and I wonder why. He only emphasises the fact that two observers failed my lesson.

Mr Van Vuuren, clearing his throat, continues to read the report:

"The Academy instructed Mrs Arno and a colleague to conduct a repeat observation of the failed lesson, giving Baker the opportunity to complete her course."

I stare at him when hearing this, thinking of how I didn't want Mrs Arno to be involved this time. This report misses this important aspect of my case, and I'm disappointed with what I hear. However, I keep quiet, biting slightly on my lower lip to ensure I stay in control. Mr Van Vuuren continues:

"On the scheduled assessment day, Arthur Benson School was closed for teacher training or something, and the Academy re-arranged the assessment for a later date. However, on the agreed date, Baker called in sick, and her appointment contract with the school ended shortly afterwards."

Yes, I confirm this in my mind.

"And then Baker formally raised her concerns, detailing excessive lesson observations, an unconsidered Portfolio of Evidence, ill health due to pressure of the observations and portfolio re-organisation, and the refusal of the Academy to recommend that she receives her licence to teach here. The Academy's Head of Education replied to Baker, stating, 'It was clear that you were on the part-time assessment programme, and as such would only be assessed, and not mentored by our representative.' The Head of Education explained that additional lesson observations were required, as Baker had not met the 'required standards'." Mr Van Vuuren raises both index fingers, and wiggles them to indicate open and close inverted commas, as he read the final words.

My attention is drawn to the 'required standards'. I remember what Lottie said about the authors of the Apartheid Laws in South Africa, regarding the education provision for the natives. Actually, they meant my mum, dad and then me. They had some reservations about us achieving a 'certain standard' of academic education. They must have been concerned that when the natives received a 'high' standard of education, no one would be available to do manual labour in their communities.

However, what does this have to do with my 'required standard' to obtain a licence to teach here? I quickly dismiss these thoughts as they fail to give me answers: I must have drifted away for a while. I try to listen attentively to Mr Van Vuuren's deliberation:

"So it was necessary to gather more evidence of her competence in these groups. The Academy offered Baker an opportunity to defer her programme in light of her ill health, to allow her to find an alternative school and complete the assessment fully in a different context."

The Academy seems to be portraying itself in a way which makes it look great. This report is worded in such a convincing way that everybody reading it would believe them.

"Baker notifies the Star Academy that she was unhappy with this outcome of the early investigations. The case proceeded to the second stage and a hearing took place after two postponements by her. However, the case review panel found no evidence that Mrs Arno had not supported Baker. The tutor had given advice beyond the requirement of the part-time assessment route. I can see plenty of evidence to support the Academy's views," adds Mr Van Vuuren.

As they continue flicking through these massive folders, I start feeling drowsy, and I hurt inside.

"Baker should have known all the assessment requirements of the Academy without being told. She did not request a change of assessors. There were problems with her Portfolio of Evidence about which she had been advised several times, for goodness sake! The number of observations was not excessive: it was just right for her."

I try to keep myself awake, pinching the back of my hand slightly. I feel like screaming, "Liars! You ignored all my requests earlier on!" but I can't. I listen to them misinterpreting everything deliberately to justify their findings. I can't stop them, argue or clarify the information they are presenting. I am very hurt. This is unfair.

Mr Van Vuuren continues, "The Academy suggested again here, that an experienced mentor, with no previous connection to Baker, assess her. She must provide medical evidence of fitness before any further employment in a school. The Academy was also willing to assist her transfer elsewhere for assessment if she wished."

At this point, Mr Van Vuuren stops and stares at me asking, "So, what did you actually want, Baker? What are you doing here? Have you come to waste our time?" Mr Van Vuuren then scans around the panel members, asking, "What do you think of this, colleagues?"

I feel tears gathering in my eyes, ready to flow down my

cheeks. I try to hold them in, but fail, and they start rolling down my face. I reach out for my tissues, and wipe myself discreetly.

Mr Van Vuuren should not treat me like this. He knows that I won't reply. He seems to be provoking me to anger so he can cause more trouble for me, and maybe get the police involved. I bite my lower lip hard this time, ensuring I keep quiet.

"Baker's lawyers indicated that she wished to proceed to the third stage of her case. The hearing took place, and Baker attended with her Teachers' Association representative. Why she got these people involved, I can't tell. What powers do they have? They are there to cause trouble. They know we don't recognise them, yet they won't give in. They can't meet our set objective - to prove that they represent a two-thirds majority of the teachers here."

"They are powerless, Dirkie," Mr Burgher responds, laughing.

Mr Van Vuuren, flicking through the documents again, continues, "The outcome of this stage was notified to her lawyers. The Appeal Panel found that the previous panel had cleared the Academy. It confirmed the Academy to have followed appropriate procedures, and upheld its findings. No evidence of bias was found, and the Appeal was not dismissed. It reiterated the offer made during the second stage to enable Baker to complete her assessment, and achieve her teacher licence. Regardless, Baker proceeded to the fourth stage with her concerns. Why did you do all this?" Mr Van Vuuren asks, aggressively this time. "You are very stubborn. That's not a characteristic of the good teacher you claim to be. You should be meek, and accept our criticisms."

"Sir, I believe I have adequate written evidence to prove my case. Should anyone of you have time to look at it, and compare the contradictory statements made by the Academy, you would see that they are wrong, and I am right."

They seem to lack understanding of my main concern, I remark internally.

"You sound bold, young lady," says Mr Burgher.

Mr Van Vuuren says, "This report involves the Star Academy's Board, later that year. Again, Baker attended with a representative from her Teachers' Association. It suggested that an Independent Assessor should review Baker's performance. However, by that time she was outside the government rule that a licence must be gained within a certain period. This outcome was notified to Baker by letter, which asked her to respond to the offer. Why did you ignore this opportunity, Miss Baker?" Mr Van Vuuren asks harshly.

"Firstly, I needed the Academy's responses to all my concerns. Secondly, I expected them to accept their mistakes, offer me an apology, and then emerge with a reasonable, achievable solution. It was unfair to expect me to comply with the Academy's proposal prior to addressing my needs."

"Unrealistic, Baker – your dreams misled you," Mr Van Vuuren says, shaking his head in disagreement. They talk among themselves softly in Afrikaans. I can't hear them, but there's no reason to worry about it, as I will be told the final outcome.

"Finally, the Academy sent Baker a Completion of Procedure document," reports Mr Van Vuuren.

I feel exhausted. I want to have a break, and a glass of water. I've had enough grilling, but I can't ask, and I'm afraid of what they might say.

Mr Van Vuuren goes on to explain the responses of this Review Panel.

"Baker's scheme application and a copy of Completion of Procedures were received by this office with no other enclosed documents or details of the case. The Scheme Application Form stated that certain lawyers were representing her, and would shortly provide the details of the case. They did not do this until our office sent a chasing letter. The lawyers then indicated that she was no longer their client. We received copies of her documents that did not set out her case details. We wrote to her seeking these. She responded, giving her explanation, and we were able to commence our review, and issued its draft decision. The Academy confirmed it as being accurate. Baker commented on the decision."

"Did we consider Baker's comments, before we made our final decision?" Mr Erasmus asks, appearing concerned at this stage.

"No, there was no need, Mr Erasmus. We don't allow people to defy our authorities here. This matter shouldn't have reached this stage in the first place. Our Assessors take decisions about who to let through, and which students shouldn't join our teaching staff. This is simple to understand. Not every native should be a teacher. I hope you will agree with me in this. You know the 'complications'. For your own information, Ben Schoeman Skool offered Baker a teaching assistant-ship after finding a suitable teacher for her post. She rejected it."

I know what they're talking about, and I'm surprised that they know about it. Who informed them? I remember my dad's warning: he always said, "Betty, you can never win."

"After lunch, Mr Burgher will take us through the details of how we reached our conclusion about this case. Baker, be back here for three o'clock," Mr Van Vuuren commands, piling the documents on the table.

"Yes, Sir," I say, blankly. I pick up my handbag, sling it over my left shoulder, open the door, and walk out, following the exit directions through the long corridor. My mouth is dry. Anger flashes in me like a hot wave. I feel dizzy. My God, I shouldn't pass out! I have never felt an emotion manifesting itself in such a drastic way.

All my childhood pressures come to the fore. I have no desire to continue this kind of life. I need change. I want a life I've never experienced before. But who will give me, it? I want to be recognised, and treated well. *Greg, you're my only hope.*

With a dry throat, and feeling rather hungry, I walk to the nearest café, and buy myself some sandwiches and a can of coke. I go to the park, sit on the bench and eat. The weather has changed, and it feels chilly. I look at my watch – it's half past two. I return to the office, and this time Mr Burgher leads the hearing:

"I'm going to give you a summary of the evidence that we gathered to inform our decisions. Should anyone wish to speak, do let me know," he says. "Betty Baker complains that the Academy failed her assessment for upgrading her teaching qualification to teach here within the required timescale." Mr Burgher pauses, looking up at me. "You still feel the same, Baker?" Everybody is quiet as they wait for me to respond. I've missed the question, as my mind has wandered off.

"Y...yes, Sir," I reply, my eyes widening with apprehension.

And then Mr Burgher continues reading their report:

"The Academy states clearly that Baker was given plenty of opportunities to undertake reassessment of the failed lesson, and proceed to final assessment, well before she was out of time under our rules. The Academy warned her about running out of time. We, the government representatives, have carefully considered the information and evidence provided by Baker and the Star Academy. I note that at the time of the failed lesson observation, Baker was within the time limits for achieving her licence. The Academy rearranged an opportunity to retrieve this lesson observation within a matter of days. Unfortunately, this was missed twice."

I distract myself by thinking about Greg, the man who respects and loves me. I imagine our happy days together under difficult circumstances, and remember that some people are genuinely kind.

Mr Burgher continues with the deliberations:

"I note that Betty Baker failed to meet the required standard to pass the lesson observation in question. This was a matter of academic judgement. I understand that passing this observed lesson was required in order to carry on with the next stages of this assessment. I also understand that the requirements of the licence to teach are set by our government. The Academy has a duty to ensure its students meet the necessary standards."

I accept all has gone against me, just as my dad said it would. I feel a sharp pain within my body, as of trapped wind. I guess the sandwiches with raw onions caused it. So, I rise up gently for a stretch. They all look at me, perhaps wondering what I was doing. I sit down to hear their final judgement.

Miss Swiss takes over, saying, "We are satisfied it was reasonable for the Academy to require that this lesson observation be passed for the process to continue. We are also satisfied that the Star Academy acted reasonably in repeatedly offering Betty Baker opportunities to retrieve the failure. She could have opted to accept such an offer, and complete her assessment within the time limits. However, she chose not to, as she wished the Academy to complete her final assessment without her having to do another lesson observation. Essentially, she wanted the Academy to override or disregard the judgement of Assessors. I have not been persuaded that there is a compelling reason why this should have been done. Had Betty Baker acted on the Academy's offer, my understanding is that she could have received the licence within the recommended timescale. I'm not persuaded that the Star Academy is responsible for her failure to do so."

She sneezes, picks up a glass of water and drinks slowly. After wiping her mouth with a tissue, she remains quiet for a while and then looks at me, perhaps expecting my comment. I maintain my silence.

"For the above reasons, I don't find this aspect of this case justified," says Miss Swiss.

I attempt to explain my case again for the last time, hoping they might understand me. My voice starts to vibrate with anger and frustration. "Excuse me, I informed the Academy of the problems I faced, and it failed to resolve them. It hurt my feelings badly and caused me stress which led to illness in the week of my assessment. That's how I missed the assessment opportunity. Can't you see this isn't my fault?"

Miss Swiss speaks, ignoring my comments, saying, "Mrs Arno was Miss Baker's assessor, and not her mentor. She was not appointed to train her. The Academy can't alter the professional judgement of an Assessor, since this would undermine the quality of the assessment process." She pauses, and then continues, "The minutes of various case hearings show that the Academy dealt thoroughly with the issues. I have seen from the papers provided that Betty Baker raised concerns with the Academy, that Mrs Arno's role in assessing her was different from what she was told earlier on."

I ask, "What really was Mrs Arno's role meant to be in this process?"

Miss Swiss, shaking her head with wide eyes, says, "Our role today, is not to investigate the detail of this case afresh, but only to review the Academy's handling of it. We're here to investigate whether its response was reasonable, and in accordance with its regulations, and not anybody else's. I note that Mrs Arno assessed Miss Baker with another teacher who participated in the decision to fail Betty Baker. However, she has only taken issue with Mrs Arno's judgement; why is that?"

"Betty Baker, could you explain this?" Miss Swiss asks.

I look at them again, saying nothing. I've decided not to defend myself anymore. It's pointless: they have already made their decision. They keep saying 'we', and I wonder who I am dealing with, here.

"Miss Baker suggests that the Academy's investigation was biased, and that the procedures used were time-consuming and ineffective. But we dealt with this case in accordance with our procedures; Baker caused many delays." Miss Swiss raises her voice at this point.

These words ring strongly in my ears. It hurts to observe that this panel assumes I blamed the Academy for my own mistakes.

Mr De Beer then takes over the lead. "We have summarised the case earlier in these proceedings. I note that the Star Academy does appear to have complied with the processes it set out. We have not seen evidence of bias in the decision made by the Academy's panels. Just like Mrs Arno, all panel members are connected, in one way or another, to the Academy, but they are all unknown to Baker. This was good, to ensure that our services are not challenged."

I keep looking at my watch, wondering when they will finish. This is not what I expected, just to obtain an outline of what the Star Academy said. I realise the fairness I'm seeking is far from being achieved. This has been a futile exercise. I draw my own conclusion that my interaction with the Star Academy was an unfortunate incident.

"We have considered all the evidence of complaints set out. We consider the final decision of the Star Academy to be fair and reasonable in all circumstances, and do not find your case to be justified. We, therefore, make no recommendations," concludes Mr De Beer.

"Do you have any other comment, Betty Baker?" Mr Van Vuuren asks.

I remain silent; and then Mr Van Vuuren utters his final remark: "The Star Academy, and Mrs Arno, in particular, must receive an Award in recognition of their excellent services this year. Make a note of that, Miss Swiss." And he brings the hearing to a close.

"They deserve it, definitely," agrees Miss Swiss, beaming with a smile while putting the documents together into her briefcase.

I look at them for a while with tearful eyes, and then say loudly and clearly, "I thank you all for providing this opportunity to hear my case. Thank you all for your precious time."

They look at each other. I receive no response this time

around. I can tell nothing I said could influence them to change their minds. Bargaining with them is practically impossible, and a waste of my valuable time. I need help to adjust to this predicament I find myself in, without further trauma and unnecessary pain.

I rise up and open the door. Before I leave, I give them another look – a friendly one, perhaps one they will remember for as long as they live.

I release my internal pain as I walk towards the staircase. I look down, and the drops of my tears leave an invisible trail that only I know of. It's good that human tears are colourless, I think to myself. I distract my mind as I think about Greg, his love and promises.

I walk down to the bus station, singing my favourite songs to myself. This continues as I wait for the bus. It arrives after ten minutes, and I board to look for a seat. Usually, I sit in front unless all of the seats are full. Today, I leave the vacant front seats to sit at the back, hoping not to meet familiar people. I get off and walk home. *Betty Baker, you should not cry again,* I say to myself.

I reach my front door, turn the key and go in. I throw my handbag on the floor, and go straight to the mirror to look at my face. With my eyes red and swollen from crying, I realise I still have hope for a better future, but somewhere else. Life is wonderful! I must enjoy it with Gregory, from now.

"Baas Jimmie's bullets missed me that night. I miss Mark."

from Betty's Diary, 10th January, 1968

Chapter 10

Abroad

May 1974

The aeroplane lands at Heathrow Airport at 7.30 a.m. I get out and follow the other passengers boarding the bus to the terminal exit. I join the queue to the passport control, and get cleared. Finally, Gregory had arranged the visa. I collect my luggage and follow the directions to the underground station to catch the tube to Euston railway station. From there I will get my connection to Leeds. At Leeds railway station, there are many trains to Skipton, my final destination.

At Euston station, there's a little wait before the 10.35 a.m. train pulls into platform 13. This gives me time to walk around, cooling my nerves. I imagine what it is going to be like, meeting Greg after all these years. I have some concerns. *Will he recognise me? How is his appearance now? Am I really physically attracted to him, as I was six years ago? What will happen if I find him less attractive or vice versa? That would be a dilemma. No... a disaster!* I smile, walking through the gates to platform 13.

Suddenly, the train approaches, and the doors open. Before I board, I check the name on its side to confirm it's the right train for Leeds. Yes, that's it. Feeling relaxed and encouraged, I sit next to the window to have a clear view. More passengers get on the train, taking all the available seats. The train departs exactly at 10.35 a.m. from Euston station. It is packed; some passengers are sitting on their luggage, just by the entrance. I'm fortunate to get a seat; I think to myself, as the train is speeding, heading towards the north of England.

I look at a little old lady with grey hair who is sitting next to me. She is so short that her feet cannot reach the floor. I glance at her secretly every so often, hoping she will speak to me. She doesn't. She is coughing constantly, and her heavy breathing makes a loud sound as if she is snoring. She appears uncomfortable, as she blows her nose.

Suddenly, there is an announcement, "Attention, passengers. The shop selling refreshments is now open at the end of carriage B. Please make your way to the front of the train, if you want to buy cold and hot drinks and snacks." I wish to have a hot drink, but due to my tiredness, I give this a miss.

After a while the train stops. It has reached the first station. Passengers get out as others come in. I dismiss my thoughts of having someone to talk to and resist the feeling of having a nap. I stay awake and enjoy my journey to Leeds.

I get off and go straight to the Enquiries desk to ask for train times and the platform for Skipton. I'm conscious of time. I want to travel on the next train, but queues are very long. I explore an opportunity to push in order to get served quickly. I see other passengers joining from the back. Feeling embarrassed, I wait patiently for my turn. I've been reciting my question mentally already, so I ask him, "What platform is the next train to Skipton, please?" The man looks at the time and, without looking at me, he says, "In 10 minutes. Platform 2b, love. Next please!"

Saddened by his attitude, I hurry to the platform. To my disappointment, the first carriage is full of passengers. Struggling to carry my heavy luggage, I continue walking up to the end of the train. All the carriages are overflowing. 'What shall I do?' I ask myself. 'Shall I push in, and keep standing all the way? How far do I have to go? I don't know.' I stand still, unable to decide.

I look to my left and see a metal bench similar to those I used to see when I was a child. My thoughts bounce back to early-childhood memories. I wonder if African natives are allowed to sit on those benches.

A feeling of utter despair overwhelms me. I drop my heavy suitcase, and sit down on the bench. For about ten minutes, the train is stationary. Appearing to be bored, some passengers are gazing through the windows. It's worth waiting for the next train, I decide. I would be unable to stand all the way because my feet are throbbing due to tiredness from travelling all night.

I hear an announcement, "The 13.45 train to Skipton is delayed by approximately fifteen minutes." This delay doesn't worry me. I'm waiting for another train anyway. I hear another announcement. "The engine of the first train has broken down. Please board the next train."

That's the train I'm waiting for. Soon, it arrives. I board this train, sitting by the window again. All the passengers from the train that has broken down also come in, filling every vacant seat. The doors shut, and the train departs slowly towards the north. All the passengers are quiet. This is unusual to me. It's difficult to tell whether anyone is looking at me or not. They are all of European origin. I sit confidently, pretending to know my destination. I look outside through the window as the train departs from the station.

Having travelled through the dense sprawl of North London the train passes through embankments with thick bushes towards Skipton. I guess people are quiet due to tiredness from work. The landscape becomes fascinating. There are green fields, stone-built farm buildings, and some farm animals grazing in the fields, just like in South Africa. A village appears in the distance. I really admire the countryside.

The atmosphere in my compartment appears tense, and no one chats. I wish someone would speak to me so that I can establish how far away Skipton is. The train arrives at the next station, and more people get off. I pass the time looking through the window, admiring the blue sky. The train goes through the tunnel, making my ears pop. I look at the passengers, estimating their ages to be between 20 and 35. I wonder where the older folks are.

The sky darkens, and clouds seem to be gathering rain. I rehearse 'Skipton' in my mind. The train drives over a small bridge, passing deserted old buildings, and some more villages. It seems to be heading for the horizon. The journey is never-ending.

I must have fallen asleep for a while. I wake up as the guard announces the next station but it's not Skipton. Many passengers have left. On my right-hand side and behind me, I see many vacant seats, and I'm a bit frightened. However, I continue looking outside. Farms exist in England, after all, I think, as I see many fields with stone walls round their outside. This must be hard work, I guess, to build them all.

"The next station is Skipton. This train terminates here. Please take all your belongings with you," the guard announces.

My heart begins to beat faster. I start having mixed feelings, a mixture of excitement and fear. My hands sweat, and my body feels hot with butterflies in my tummy. I wonder if Greg will be at the station to meet me, or will I have to take a taxi?

Whatever happens to me doesn't matter anymore. I've followed my heart to look for Greg, the man I fell in love with, some years ago. The train stops. I take my massive suitcase, travelling bag and handbag, and get off the train, following the 'way-out' signs – something we don't have in South Africa.

Many passengers rush out of the station. Walking slowly, I admire the station itself, with its attractive baskets hanging from the rafters. I walk past an old market wheelbarrow tied to a pillar also full of flowers. Finally, I've reached Skipton - but where is Gregory? I sigh, stopping my rumbling tummy.

Greg recalls

My journey to happiness is a walk to the unknown. It's now about 4 years since my forced return from South Africa. I'm at Skipton railway station. In a world of my own, I wander forward towards the platforms. As I look around, my eyes catch a beautiful apparition. It is as if I'm in a dream, and nothing else exists.

In fact, without doubt, she is the most exquisite creation of womanhood I've ever chanced upon. I look across, admiring her hourglass figure. Her head lifts up, and we make eye- contact. It's as though I'm on a conveyor belt. In a moment, I'm pulled towards her. I have no control of myself. I ask her, with my hands fidgeting, "Excuse me. I hope I'm not getting this wrong, are you Betty Baker?" She looks at me, and smiles.

"Yes, I'm Betty, Betty Baker," she replies, with her calm, tender voice. We haven't seen each other for many years, although we have recently exchanged letters and pictures.

The bright sunlight from out of the station illuminates the outline of her sensuous figure, as she stares sat me magnificently, like a goddess of Greek legend. Her lips stay apart. My heart pounds, and my blood rushes through all parts of my body. I hug her, whispering, "Betty, you're mine – you're my woman, the one I love. I waited for you!" I pull her closer to me, giving her a good kiss.

"No, not here, please," whispers Betty, pushing me gently away from her.

"Don't be worried, about the people passing by," I reassure her. Some passengers rush onto the platform to board the train.

The train cleaners probably overhear us, and give me a smile.

I look at her from head to toe, preparing what to say next. I catch her fabulous smile. Her brown eyes roll over to look at me, and her long brown curly hair cascades at the back.

"Greg, my darling, Gregory!" Betty shouts, appearing very excited. She is so loud that it suddenly goes quiet. The British are a very reserved people in comparison. "My Angel!" she says, throwing her arms around my shoulders. Feeling a bit embarrassed, I move closer, holding her tightly towards me for a long time, just like the day I left her in South Africa in tears, badly heartbroken because the *1949 Mixed Marriages Act 55* and the *Immorality Act 23 (as amended in 1957)* prevented me from loving her.

"Here you are, standing in front of me, looking so pretty! My Betty," I say, excitedly, looking directly in her eyes. "I have a lot to share with you. I guess we both have loads to catch up on," I continue.

"Yes, definitely," she replies in a soft tone, the one I'm familiar with.

Betty recalls

I look at Greg. He grips my attention: I can't take my eyes off him again. That's my Gregory. He is wearing jeans torn at the knees, and a greenish t-shirt, his usual casual style. He looks similar to how he was in South Africa. His eyes are the same as those engraved in my memories - the eyes, with long eyelashes, bushy eyebrows and a well-trimmed beard. All this allays my fears instantly.

I've known him since I was in my late teens and he was in his early twenties. I want to hear more from him about his background. Who is he, exactly? What does he find attractive in me? This can happen when we are relaxed, in a good atmosphere. I know he is in love with me.

We walk together, heading towards the town centre, with everybody seeing us. No one seems bothered here. We turn to the right, and go straight into the alleyway. We go over the bridge, walking towards the residential area. On this side of Skipton town, the houses are terraced, built on the slope with stones. Chimneys protrude through the roofs. The streets are bare; no cars, or people passing by. I wonder why? We pass a cinema; the word, 'cinema', is written in big, red letters just above the door. My mind is engaged deeply with these thoughts; sadly I miss what Greg says. He notices this, stands still, and stops talking. I am not sure what to do.

"Sorry, Greg, my luggage is very heavy; do we have a long way to go?" Greg must have noticed that I'm struggling.

He looks at me, saying, "No, we don't have a long way to go. My home is over there." He is pointing further away. He is right; it's not a long way from the station, but I feel uncomfortable; my feet hurt from wearing high-heeled shoes all day. I try to ignore the pain. They are my Sunday best, and I've worn them to impress Greg. My ear lobes hurt from the weight of my new earrings. I tolerate this discomfort too. We talk all the way, stopping for a drink at a café.

"What would you like to drink, sweetheart?"

"What's available?" I ask Greg.

"Cappuccino, latte, espresso, ground coffee, or what?" he says.

"Mmmh," I say, not sure which coffee to choose. He notices this and says, "Could you tell the waiter what we want, while I use the toilet?" These names sound unfamiliar to me. I'm not keen on asking the difference, so I confidently make my choice. "Espresso...yes, espresso, please."

Greg returns, and we continue talking as we wait for our drinks. The waiter brings very small cups with strong coffee. I look at Greg and laugh. I take a sip to taste it.

"Ugh, it's awful! I can't drink this. Could we ask for hot water to dilute it?"

"Certainly," says Greg, raising his hand to attract the waiter's attention. The waiter comes over to our table straight away. Greg asks for an extra cup, and water. The waiter disappears into the kitchen, returning with a jar of hot water.

"Thanks, mate," says Greg. I halve my coffee, reach out to the jar, and dilute it. I take another sip. There is no difference.

"No, sorry I can't drink it still," I say, pushing it away from me.

"Not to worry - try the latte," suggests Greg, desperate to cheer me up.

He goes to the counter, orders, and pays. The waiter – an English man - possibly a Yorkshireman - brings it on a tray. "Thank you," I say, and show no surprise. I drink my coffee, and it is nice. I'm getting to grips with non-racist England. We finish our drinks and leave.

Greg puts his hand around my back, offering me assurance. He couldn't do this in South Africa. I feel a bit uncomfortable as I'm also very exhausted. I beg Greg to take me straight home.

We soon arrive at Greg's home where he had lived with his mum all his life. I go in and sit down in the living room.

"Betty, this was my mum's house, and now it's mine," says Greg bluntly. I take a deep breath of relief that he has got a good house to live in, but I still sense something is not right. Instantly, I scan through the whole darkish, living room, with tall, wallpaper-decorated walls. A long brown settee with three cushions is positioned in front of the gas fireplace. The carpet matching the blue patterns of the wallpaper looks old, with some holes. A massive gilded mirror hangs on the wall to the left side of the fireplace. An old, dusty piano stands behind the door with ornaments displayed on it. Opposite, there's a bookshelf filled with all sorts of books. They are arranged neatly; I see adventures, books on sports, diet and religion, and on the wall hangs a big black-and-white portrait - that is his mum. She is wearing a white shirt with a Chinese collar, and is wearing pearl studs. She has long brown hair resting on her shoulders, and a fringe on her forehead. The wooden frame of the picture is thick, and the glass is full of dust. The picture looks old, as if it was taken before the Second World War.

I sit on the sofa, which is covered with a cream throw, facing the door leading to the dining room. A big table covered in a cream cloth and surrounded by eight chairs is visible. Thick curtains which match the carpets are closed, making the room darker.

"Yes, I like it," I say with appreciation.

"What?" asks Greg. I say nothing for a while, just scanning the house. He sits next to me, and puts his arms around my neck, saying, "I love you so much; don't worry, we will be all right."

I nod, saying, "Okay," and then smile.

He continues, "I want you to be happy."

It is for the first time, as far as I can remember, that I have had so much hope. I want to share my past life, but I do not know where or how to start. I can feel I am close to breaking, but I do not want to spoil this moment. So, I ask, Greg, "What news have you got?"

As he begins to speak about his family, I notice a change in his appearance. Sad memories of the past engraved in his mind come to the fore, causing his gorgeous smile to fade. Greg says, "My mum returned to live in this house after my dad had an affair with Annie. Do you remember her?"

"Yes, your stepmother. She was a nice lady, wasn't she?"

"I don't know much about that. I lived happily with my mum for so many years," he says. His voice slurs, slowing down as his eyes water. I wonder what I'm about to hear. I can guess, and it's heart-breaking.

I'm careful not to interrupt him. My eyes go all over the living room, searching for clues. There is no sign of a woman living here. Greg is unaware of my fluctuating mind. He clears his throat and continues, "I told my mum about you, and our South African encounter. I showed her your photo, and told her you were the woman I was planning to marry."

"What were her views about you marrying me?" I ask.

"Firstly, she doubted our relationship would last. And then she asked many questions, probably to test my determination: are there no English women to marry? Will I cope with mixed racial children? Would I tolerate 'stares' from people, who might be unfamiliar or disapprove of mixed-race relationships?"

"What did you say to her?"

"I answered all her questions positively. I realised that my mum was less well-informed about people of other races. I showed her the picture I drew when I was fourteen-years-old. Remember Betty, that time I also had no clue about the African continent."

Greg disappears upstairs onto the landing, and brings a big frame with my picture next to the drawing he is talking about.

"My mum looked at my drawing alongside this photo you sent me from South West Africa. She confirmed that you were the woman I drew." I look at both pictures in surprise.

"How could this have been?" I ask, still staring at both pictures. I confirm their likeness. "Well," I say, amazed by such a coincidence. "This looks like me!" I'm excited, and relieved, still holding the pictures.

"In the end my mum was pleased that I had found the woman I love. She was persuaded we'd get on well, and she blessed us."

Struggling to talk, holding back tears, Greg frowns. There is an instant silence. This drags on; his heart definitely aches at the thought of his mum. I wait for him to continue his explanation. I can't stand seeing him cry, but he remains quiet.

"So, your mum was a Christian?"

"Sort of - in this country we don't normally discuss religious views."

"I'm sorry. I didn't know that," I say, wondering what is

wrong in discussing Faith. I do not pursue this topic. *This could be his cultural views,* I thought.

"Where is your mum now?" I ask, sympathetically, refraining from jumping to a conclusion about death. She might have re-married, or abandoned him. There's a silence again, and then Greg continues:

"She prolonged her life, tolerated the pains, refusing to let go. However, on this particular day, she reached a decision. 'Gregory, call the ambulance,' she pleaded. I reached out with urgency to the phone, and dialled 999.

"Sorrow gripped me. I felt her pains. My throat dried up, and I swallowed my saliva, holding back my tears. I gave them our address, and some directions to our house. 'Hurry up, please!' I said, before hanging up. I rushed upstairs to be by my mum's side.

"She seemed to be asleep: her eyes were shut. As I sat down on her bed, her eyes opened gradually. 'Gregory,' she called. 'Mum – speak: I'm listening.' 'Look after yourself. I love you.' It didn't take long. I heard the ambulance sirens. I peeped through the bedroom window. The blue emergency lights were flashing as the ambulance pulled into our drive way. Two paramedics rushed in, passing me by the door into my mum's bedroom. They put her on a drip, and carried her downstairs on a stretcher to the ambulance. They rushed her to the hospital. I followed, waiting for news. The doctors admitted her into the Intensive Care Unit, and she lost consciousness. I visited her daily. She couldn't recognise me; I spent almost every day sitting by her bedside, holding onto her hand for two months.

"The specialists tried their best to save her life, but the cancer had already spread throughout much of her body. They couldn't do any more for her." Greg struggles to keep up the momentum of his account. His pauses interrupt the flow of speech so often. However, he demonstrates his bravery, by continuing, "The hospital arranged a transfer to a hospice, but I wasn't keen on that. 'I'd rather die in my own house,' - that was my mum's wish. She always said that, while she could speak. This was the best thing for me to do for her. I requested her to be discharged, when it became clear that she wouldn't recover. The ambulance dropped her back home with her medication to ease the pain. Her doctor and nurses paid her regular visits so she still received good care. Sometimes she was in severe pain: I could sense it. I gave her various prescribed pain relief tablets."

I look at Greg, sharing his grief. I want to ask him to stop talking; I can anticipate what he is about to say next, and I don't want to hear the sad ending. But I do not want to offend him by interrupting. So I just let him talk.

"At midday, that Sunday, her Vicar visited, and gave her Holy Communion. I held her hand and supported her neck as she swallowed the last drop of wine. Her upper lip twitched. Her eyes opened, and gradually closed. Her chest moved as she breathed in and out. She died peacefully in her sleep that night." Greg looks up, keeps quiet for a little while, and then says in his tearful and shaky voice, "It was cancer."

Suddenly, Greg's face appears red. He puts his hand around my shoulders, pulling me towards him for comfort. He looks dreadful; this talk seems to have triggered memories he had buried in his mind. I share his grief and close my eyes in response. He apologises for the distress he might have caused, emphasising that he didn't mean to upset me. I watch him cry like a baby, non-stop. I understand, feel sorry for him, as he tries to recollect the details of those events.

Greg says, "I never grieved properly for my mum. A lot of things were going on in those days. Her death left a deep hole in my heart. She was a good woman. And I love her."

"I'm so sorry to hear this, Greg," I say, soothing his right hand gently, and brushing a tear from his cheek with a tissue. I roll over, giving him a comforting hug. He starts to be emotional, and cries again. I listen to him. I want to hear everything.

I refrain from telling him anything about my past struggles since he left me in South Africa. This might be too much for him to bear. He isn't ready for it, I can tell.

"Not to worry, Betty, I'm okay now. I have you. Isn't that right, darling?"

We hug each other for some time. I put on my flat sandals, and we go for the tour of this big four-bedroom house. In my mind, I record the changes it needs: new wallpaper, fitted kitchen unit and bathroom, brand new carpets and sofas. I'll be happy to have these done as I don't expect Greg, the bachelor, to do much.

Greg prepares me a bath. I get in and soak my body before he joins me for a further conversation. I feel very tired, nearly falling asleep. I jump out of the bath, dry myself and go to Greg's bedroom. I take out my clean bed sheets from my suitcase and make up the bed. I spray around, giving the room a fresh smell. We go to bed, and sleep for the whole night together for the very first time.

The following morning, Greg and I have breakfast. Later that day, we visit his neighbours. They are a friendly bunch, and are pleased that I'm here at last to keep him away from the pub every night. Then he takes me to Skipton town. It's small, but interesting for shopping.

We walk to the park just to relax. I look at the green lawns and beautiful flowers:

"Sweet, it's appropriate for us to sit on that bench, isn't it?" I ask just to please myself, and despise the old days when I couldn't even enter the park gates in South Africa.

"Come on, we're in England. We can go anywhere we want together," Greg says, putting his arms around my waist.

As we arrive at the park, the memory of European couples sitting on the benches in Burgersdorp enjoying the sunshine in beautiful parks with green lawns and colourful flowers, like roses and bougainvillea, flashes back to my mind.

I remember the sign that could have been on that park if we

were in South Africa: Europeans Only – *'Slegs Blankes'*, in Afrikaans. I dismiss my thoughts decisively, look at Greg and smile. By this time, we are inside the park. We sit on the bench.

Again, I think briefly about the Apartheid Laws aimed at restricting the natives. I realise that's what they meant. As if Greg is reading my mind, he clings onto my hand, saying, "I'll never let you go again."

We talk about many things, sharing joyful tears, and releasing frustration built up over many years. As we cry, we try engaging in serious conversation, discussing beliefs. Ours are similar in many ways. So many surprises are unveiled: Greg and I share a birthday – the 20th of December. Greg holds me very close to himself, and gives me a deep and soothing kiss. I feel frightened again.

"No!" I shout, trying to free myself from him.

"Darling, we're safe here, believe me. Will you give me a kiss, please?"

I still feel uneasy. It's hard to believe what I hear.

"Could we go and sit somewhere privately instead, please?" I ask, politely.

Greg replies, "Okay, let's go to the café for a drink, Betty."

"Thank you."

We walk hand-in-hand to a café, talking all the way. Greg appears so thrilled when I welcome his suggestion of coffee. We order our tea and scones and are relaxed. We enjoy them as we sit together, talking for a while. We both discover that we like adventure holidays; Greg promises to go camping with me, and we can explore caves. He doesn't know how much he has brought excitement into my life. We walk back home, and a few weeks pass.

* * *

Greg works in a firm, five days a week from 9.00 a.m. to 5.00

p.m., and earns enough money to give us a comfortable life. He likes surprising me with gifts. On this particular Friday, he returns home about 3.30 pm.

"Greg, anything wrong?" I ask.

"Nothing."

"So, how come you're home this time?"

"I just need some time to sort things out," he says going into the cupboard, below the stairs. He takes out the tent in a bag to the living room. And then returns to bring more stuff out; sleeping bags, gas cooker, water bottle and a big box with plastic plates and cups.

"We're camping this week end?"

"Yeah, we need to get out of here - just for a break," he says looking at the heap of things covering the sitting room floor. We both carry the first lot to the car; and I continue doing this, while he is loading everything.

Greg drives us to the Dovedale campsite in Derbyshire. We talk all the way, while admiring the landscape. We arrive and quickly pitch our tent together. After off-loading everything, we make cups of tea, and then go for a walk along the banks of the river. The evening is cool. We come to a big rock called Lover's Leap and stand there for a little while talking.

And then, Greg kneels in front of me saying, "Betty, will you marry me?"

Living in North Yorkshire

After the wedding we manage to live quite a lavish kind of lifestyle, because we have enough money coming in, and we don't have a mortgage to pay. The insurance paid off the house balance when Greg's mum died. We only pay insurance cover for our house, car and the utility bills. As Greg talks me about his responsibilities, there is a brief silence every now and then, perhaps he is giving me an opportunity to respond, and I am careful not to interrupt him. I almost smile, forgetting the old days in South Africa, when I felt, life was horrible. I cover those images, with the new ones, letting my face beam.

Later the following year

Greg leaves me alone in the house all day, and I soon get bored. We arrange that I meet him in town for lunch and I love this to begin with but, later, I can't keep up with it.

"Love, I'm bored doing nothing all day. I should be working and bringing home more money for us. I'd like to go back to teaching. Do you think I should apply to teach here?"

"Honey, why don't you go back to college and get a British qualification?"

"But I'm a qualified teacher, you know that."

"Yeah, but it's from South Africa."

"So, what's the problem with that?"

"We don't recognise their qualifications. I'm sorry if no one told you this," says Greg.

"'Qualifications' – again?" I exclaim. "Could you get me a prospectus? I'll do a degree course then."

"Of course. I'll pop into College after work."

Greg remembers to bring me the prospectus, and I call up for the application forms. Soon, they arrive through the post, and Greg helps me to complete them. Weeks pass, and I almost forget about it. Then I receive admission confirmation. I'm enrolled at St David's College of Education to do my Higher Education Degree. Greg pays my university fees.

Betty returns to College

In September, I embark on the Bachelor's Degree course. I find it hard in the beginning, and I have to do lots of reading to catch up. I have to read more than other students in my class to familiarise myself with the education system and literature. I like all my tutors; they are kind and supportive, and the same applies to my classmates. We go out on fun trips, and have dinners together.

We do presentations in our class. Out of fifteen primary school teachers in my class, fourteen are English, and I'm the only native South African. When I set foot into our lecture room it feels a bit strange being in the minority. With time, I hope to get over this feeling.

One of our lovely tutors, Mrs Vivian Fowler, seems to understand my situation, and gives me more attention. She instructs the class to conduct team presentations, but as I have been through a different education system that no one knows or understands, I have to do mine on my own.

I'm happy with this arrangement, although at first I think it's a joke. "How on earth can Mrs Fowler expect me to stand in front my classmates and deliver a paper? I can't believe this," I say to myself, releasing my anxiety. Two days pass without me planning for this presentation.

As I walk into a lecture, Mrs Fowler asks, "Betty, how are you getting on with your presentation?"

"I don't think I can do it at this point," I reply.

"Come and see me after the lecture so that I can give you some resources," she says.

"Thank you," I respond, although I'm not really happy about meeting her. I feel more anxious and tearful. I excuse myself, and go to the toilet. By the time I reach the door, I'm sobbing. I shut the door, and cry for a while.

Then, I wipe my face, refresh my make-up, and regain my composure. I say to myself, 'I will do it.' At the end of the lecture, I go to see Vivian in her office, and she gives me resources to help me prepare for my presentation.

I complete my planning, and show her it. The presentation day comes, but we run out of time so I have to do mine the following day.

I'm reasonably comfortable with my presentation, using the overhead projector to give some visual aids. I use an illustration to explain the concept of a broad and balanced curriculum. As I draw a model on the acetate sheet, to explain the importance of providing the learners with the whole curriculum, suddenly, my classmates clap their hands in appreciation of what I've said. I'm pleased with myself. From this day onwards, I continue with my course confidently, and graduate successfully.

Sophie, our first-born, is born before the graduation. I take a break of two years bringing her up. As I have no pressing need to work, I return to university full-time to do my Postgraduate Degree in Education.

Wayne, our son, is born a year later. Greg is proud to be a dad of two, but now we are a family of four, Greg's salary needs topping up. One evening after tea, I ask Greg if I can look for work, to top up his income.

"Of course you are free to look for work," he says, and then asks, "What work do you want to do?"

"I'm keen on pursuing teaching. Now that I hold British qualifications, and I am familiar with the system, I should get in easily – teachers are always needed."

"You have all my blessings – go ahead," says Greg, disappearing into our bedroom to sleep.

Betty's job search

I get up early the next day, and by 10.00 a.m. I'm on the phone enquiring about jobs from the Department of Education. The secretary asks in her Yorkshire accent which I find a bit difficult to understand, "Are you a qualified teacher?"

"What, sorry?"

"Are you qualified to teach here?" she repeats.

"Teacher, yes, I'm a teacher."

There is a silence, as I try to figure out what she says. She realises this.

"Do you have qualified teacher status?" She speaks slowly and clearly this time.

"Yes, I'm qualified," I reply.

"For primary or secondary?"

"For both."

"What's your D-of-E number?"

"D-of-E number?" I remain quiet for a moment as I try to work out this abbreviation without success. Eventually, I ask, "What's that, please?"

"The number you get, when you qualify as a teacher. You need our qualified teacher status to teach here. It's like a kind of licence." Her patience is running out, I can tell from her tone of voice.

"I don't have it. I wasn't given one."

"You can't teach here without it."

"But I've just graduated here."

"You still need your British teaching qualification from the Department of Education."

"How do I get it?" I ask her, frankly.

"Go to the institution where you trained and ask them."

"Okay. Thank you for your help," I say with my flat and lifeless voice, putting the phone down. I have tears in my eyes. I doubt if I heard her correctly. I feel very strange in my body. I know I am crying, inside, and I walk aimlessly in the house, unblocking my nose with a handkerchief that is wet from my tears. A sharp pain grips me in my stomach. I sense that History is repeating itself. Holding tight onto a cushion on the sofa for comfort, I cry. The more I cry, the worse the pain increases. In the end I am crying, but with no tears coming out of my eyes.

I realise later that this isn't as easy as she makes it out to be. She could have said she is referring to initial teacher training, and for me, I hold the South African Certificate, that is not recognised here by law.

* * *

I make my way to St David's College to ask for this qualification and number. I enter the School of Education building that I left some time ago. A friendly receptionist receives me and, while speaking to her, one of my ex-tutors passes by. I'm pleased to see him, and I hope he will remember me and be sympathetic, knowing the amount of work I did. I'm very wrong. "I'm afraid your degrees don't give you qualified status and the number you need. They are courses for teachers having the status already," he says.

"Why did you take me in then, when I applied?"

"You provided your South African teachers' qualifications, so you met all the entry requirements for that year."

"I'm looking for teaching work. What can I do to get this recognition?"

"Sorry, I can't help you. We have new guidelines from the government."

And off he goes on his way.

"Excuse me, Mr Wilkes!" I run behind him, calling his name, hoping to regain his attention. He appears to be slowing down, as he hears my footsteps. I narrow the distance, calling gently, "Mr Wilkes, could I have a word, please? I need your help!" Helpless, he looks at me over his right shoulder and continues down this long corridor, until he is about to disappear behind the double doors, leaving me puzzled to the point of breaking. A lady, probably a teaching colleague or other staff member, comes towards us through the dual doors. Tommy stops to talk to her. I stand a bit too far to his right for him to notice me. Without saying a word more to me, he rushes off again.

It's 'the Government Directive' again! I think, standing still and confused. My eyes flood with tears, making it difficult for me to see my way; I wipe my eyes gently with the back of my hand as I watch his back in a blue shirt vanish behind a set of double doors.

Pain grips me as I walk slowly towards the door, thinking about the money that we spent on my training. I remember the discomfort, sleepless nights and frustration during the courses. So, I apply to be a teaching assistant. To my disappointment, this never works out: all my attempts are unsuccessful.

After many enquiries, I speak to someone who explains how the English educational system operates. In no time, I get a temporary teaching post at Summer Hill Primary School, where I hope to be supported through the recognised initial teacher-training programme.

Greg returns home after work on that day. I meet him at the door, "Good news?" he asks me, patting my face, looking at my eyes.

"Yes - thanks for asking. I have a temporary contract at Summer Hill Primary School."

"Wow, well done! When are you starting?"

"On Friday. I will collect my books, and everything I need, and prepare to start properly on Monday."

Betty remembers October 1978

Summer Hill Primary School is about five miles away from Skipton. It's a small school, and the governing body, my management, colleagues and other school staff are excellent, supportive and welcoming. The whole environment is generally friendly, although I still feel a bit isolated. As I teach here, I shall be doing my initial teacher training.

The parents drop their kids in the morning and rush off to work. After speaking to them in the playground, I quickly establish that they will be happy to drop their kids at 8.30 a.m. and above all realise that would give the children an extra twenty-five minutes of reading for enjoyment before the school starts. I discuss this venture with my headmistress, Mrs Melody

Brent.

Every morning I stand by the entrance at 8.30 a.m. to receive the children. I do this voluntarily, just to give them more time for support. Children enjoy interacting with their parents during this reading time.

I've brought a new culture to this school. The children's love for reading and writing develops gradually. Most children in my class are now making good academic progress. They desert the play-corner, and it finally closes. The children choose other areas for learning, like the writing table and the reading corner.

I introduce a new concept in the class of 'learning for a purpose'. The children often say, "We come to school to learn." And all the children look forward to playtime, when they play games together in the playground.

I quickly learn that some children have no one to help them with homework, as parents are at work. I send home the work to reinforce what I've taught. I work in partnership with the parents, and encourage them to be involved in their children's learning, especially the lone parents, who work all day.

As the learning culture is growing, I set up the 'extra work corner' for all children who finish the set activities. They are free to choose from the activities suitable for all abilities. My children enjoy making their own books or cards, and doing worksheets. Other stimulating areas are for listening and storytelling. We also establish the 'Quiet and Thinking' area. Our phrase, or slogan is, 'We've got to catch up'. My children enjoy this, and I sometimes hear them tell it to their parents. I've witnessed happy and motivated children. My children enjoy 'buddy reading' the most, as well as reading to me. What a wonderful experience I have to give to the children - to direct their minds to learning for pleasure while they are still young and easily directed.

Disruptions are reduced until I have very few. The parents trust me; I tell them the truth about their children's academic

performance, and we work together to improve their performance where necessary. I point them in the right direction, and
parents appreciate this. They are just children who need my care
and support. I take full responsibility for their future while in my
hands. I receive excellent reports from the parents through the
Management Team. The Team visits my class and observes my
teaching. I create an environment which is highly conducive to
learning. My displays are vibrant, and enhance learning.

The Management makes me the Head of Art. I hear many
stories from the parents outside school hours. I remember
meeting one of the parents in the market square. He said, "Mrs
Davies, you know Sarandip surprised me. We don't eat pork in
our family. However, as I had to rush back to work, I bought him
some cold meat from the fish and chip shop. He said, "But dad, I
can't eat this. It has pork. Can't you read, p-o-rk?" We had a
laugh.

My school received recognition for being the most improved
school in the area, and the governing body informed me of their
appreciation of my service to this school.

Betty's contract ends

On Friday afternoon, during my 'non-contact period', I'm sitting
in the staff room drinking a cup of tea while planning lessons for
the following week. The door opens and Mrs Brent walks in,
appearing sad. Today she is dressed in her brown suit, and is
wearing a pearl necklace that matches her ear-rings.

"Betty, I'd like to see you in my office," she says, slamming the
door behind her.

Fine! I think as I get up, following her. I feel butterflies in my
tummy. I start thinking, *what have I done wrong?* But can think of
nothing. We arrive at her office and she shuts the door behind us.

Sitting at the table opposite me, she says, "Betty, since I have
known you, your work has been excellent, and your character

exemplary. However, legally, you can only teach under certain conditions." She declares this emphatically.

"Yes," I say, nodding my head gently, waiting for her to continue.

"Since your initial teacher training is from South Africa, your current post with us is actually classified as 'unqualified teacher' or 'overseas qualified teacher'. I hope you remember that you are, in fact, employed on a temporary basis. I'm sorry to inform you that the authority has recently instructed me of my duty in respect to your appointment. I have now found a British trained teacher for the post you hold. However, I could help by employing you as a teaching assistant, and remunerate you accordingly. I have this letter prepared for you," she says, stretching her arm and dropping a white envelope in front of me. "You can read it now if you like."

I gradually raise my eyes to look at her face. I cannot find what I am looking for - sympathy. *Surely, she has made up her mind*, I think, staring at her eyes. I look at this envelope, and shake my head, saying, "No." Whether this utterance was audible, or in my mind, I cannot remember. My eyes are blurred. For a little while, there is a silence, as I contemplate my next move. I swallow, and then clear my throat. I get up, push the chair under the table, straighten my dress with both hands, and pick up my letter in its white sealed envelope. My tears want to come out, but I don't want to cry in front of Mrs Brent - why should I make her happy? My head starts throbbing. I drop my letter into my handbag, turn around, open the door, and shut it behind me. I walk past the receptionist, who is smiling, and I respond with a lively grin. I stagger all the way to the staffroom, trying to see the way through my flooded eyes. I push the door, and it flings to the inside. I sit down at the table, tilt my head forward, resting it on the table while pressing down with my middle fingers on the veins that spurt a wave of pain into my head. Fortunately, there is no one in the staffroom. So I let my tears flow freely from my eyes, letting them soak into my tissues. I replace each one with a dry one, as long as this is necessary. After a while, I calm down. I open my letter, which reads –

Dear Mrs Davies,

Your letter of appointment sent to you by this local education authority, made it clear your appointment is temporary, because your qualification is unrecognised here. People with your qualifications can teach, but only under certain conditions.

It was hoped you would complete the initial training programme while with us. However, as this has not happened yet, this places us under a duty to establish whether a suitable teacher is available, by advertising from time to time the post you occupy. So, your employment will terminate when a teacher who qualifies is appointed. I cannot avoid my duty in law, and this letter serves as a notice that we must advertise your post.

We are very grateful for your service to this school. We will make it our great effort to be of service to you, in preparing for your uncertain future. Please be assured the above decision arises due to our duty to conform to the regulations. It should not be interpreted as reflecting on the quality of your service.

With all good wishes,

Mrs Melody Brent
Headmistress,
Summer Hill Primary School
7ᵗʰ November 1977

Immediately, I fold the letter and put it back in the envelope, and then drop it in my handbag. I remind myself that sometimes, things can get worse in life, generally. My stomach rumbles; I dismiss this strange feeling, by allowing my brain to engage in deep thoughts again. I think about my childhood, living with my parents in Skoonfontein; I think about my life in Swakopmund when I could not find Thomas, and Caroline took me into her home. I think about my wedding: life is not that bad after all. Episodes of good and bad times come and go. I could have given up long ago - but I made a decision not to. This episode is also going to pass, probably very soon. I think about what is best for me to do. I decide to go back to college to do the recognised initial teacher training. I get up, sling my handbag and drive home. All the way home, I think about what Greg will say about this new set-back.

He has to spend more money on my training again. Knowing him very well, he won't deny me the opportunity to achieve my ambitions. I collect our children on my way home, and try to dismiss my troubled thoughts by doing the chores until Greg returns from work. Greg arrives and finds me in the kitchen.

"Hi, Betty, did you have a good day?" He always greets me this way when he returns home.

"Not really," I say, giving him the letter.

He reads it silently, and asks, "What are you going to do then?"

"I guess, I must apply to go back to do the same teacher training I did donkey's years ago. Anyway, as a Commonwealth citizen, this shouldn't be too difficult to achieve. I should get someone to support me."

A month later

"Greg, this is becoming ridiculous!" I scream as I go through the college's course structure.

"What is it, Betty?" he asks.

"This College won't accept my mathematics qualification from South Africa."

"Why is that?" asks Greg, staring at me until his forehead creases. And then shakes his head.

"They say it is below the British standards."

"Fair enough, Betty, they are telling you the truth. You should accept that, and improve on it."

"So, this is what Lottie and Nancy meant about the Bantu Education system?" Surely, I am unable to embark on the British Initial Teacher Training under these circumstances? No College or University will enrol me. So, I ask the College to defer to my registration, to allow me time to take the British O-Level Maths Examination. St David's College kindly postpones my studies for another year, while I register at St Theresa College to study Maths in the evening. During this period, I hand in my notice at Summer Hill Primary School.

St Theresa College is far away from home; this makes it difficult for me to drive our car to get there. The train is quicker; I prefer using it rather than having to drive through the traffic jams in busy roads, during rush hour, to reach the College before the class starts at 6.00 pm, every Wednesday. So, as soon as I hear the bell ring for the end of the school day, I walk my class quickly to the 'Dismissal Area' in the school-ground, and then run to the bus stop for about half an hour, to board a bus to Keighley train station. I then board the train, which is usually full with commuters. I finish my journey with a fast walk, for ten minutes to St Theresa College.

I like Miss Peterson, our Maths lecturer: she is very friendly. I like everything about her, her tiny voice, her lesson delivery, and the jokes she makes during the lesson. I often laugh out loudly. She helps me to remember those equations I learned many years ago, and I also learn some advanced trigonometry.

The syllabus is revised so often that, unless you're actually teaching secondary school maths, it's easy to forget things, and get behind. I continue attending the classes. Greg contributes a great share in bringing up our children. Sophie has just turned five, and Wayne will be four years in March, next year. My little girl is very tall for her age. She has dark brown, long hair, and sandy eyes, resembling her grandma on her dad's side. Her face is round and plump - a bit like my mum's. She likes playing with her toys, and hugging the baby. Wayne, who was born prematurely with me at eight months gone, is rather fragile, and reserved. He is the spitting image of Greg - very light-skinned, with a sharp nose, brown eyes and curly hair. Like most babies, he cries, displaying a sharp temper tantrum, when he is hungry or uncomfortable. I see this as his strength. I hardly see them some days. Sometimes, I return from college at midnight due to train delays to find them asleep. Very early in the morning, Greg drops the kids at the child-minder, who walks them to school. After school, they go straight to the child-minder, Katleen, who walks them to school, as a 'Social Enterprise Business'. She lives half a mile away from school and has a licence to run a 'Walking Bus Scheme' to and from school, from Monday to Friday in her home. She is so kind to all the parents, always wearing a smile, and she doesn't mind having them there on Saturdays, 'giving mums and dads a bit of a break, while off work'. We call her Katie.

The man with a balaclava

It's in the evening after lectures. It's freezing outside after a snowy day. I say goodnight to my classmates, and walk out of the college premises onto the footpath, cutting through the bushes on my way to the railway station. Suddenly, I hear footsteps from behind me. Frightened to look back, I increase my pace until I start running. The more I run the closer sound of the footsteps sounds behind me. *Am I being chased?* I wonder as I increase my speed. I look back to see who is running behind me. He looks more like a young man, but he's all covered up and wearing a balaclava, so I can't see his face.

I run through the bush as fast as I can, looking backwards every so often. The distance between us narrows. I feel a stitch in my chest. Struggling to run, I reduce my speed and resort to walking, still panting heavily. At this point, the sound of the footsteps seems to have disappeared. As I turn into the main road, I can see the station lights at a distance, but that doesn't help me by any means. I run again, crossing the road. I hear the footsteps like before. I look back, and this person follows me across the road. The road is unusually quiet – no cars or people in sight. That's it; I'm done. 'Anything can happen now,' I say internally.

He gets closer and closer. I stand still, expecting the worst.

"Hi, you're fast, man," he says, breathing heavily. "I've been trying to catch up with you. Have you dropped anything?" I put my freezing hands into my coat pocket, searching.

"Yes, my red purse, with my rail ticket!" I raise my voice in shock, still struggling to breathe.

"Here you are, love," he says, handing it over to me. Immediately, joy fills my heart as I look up at the face covered with a balaclava.

"Thank you, thank you very much," I say, still panting and regretting being suspicious of him. He turns around and walks back, leaving me alone. I stand there for a while, shocked. He disappears into the bushes.

"Aah, some people are kind and helpful here."

I arrive at the station and go straight to the waiting room. It's cold, so I move closer to the heater, placing my feet over it. There is an announcement about train delays. I sit there for another thirty minutes, waiting. "Ouch!" I burn myself, having dozed over the heater.

I hear other trains come and go, but not mine. There's a second announcement, "The train to Skipton is delayed by 40 minutes." I sit there feeling very hurt from my burn. My train arrives, and there's hardly anyone on board tonight. I begin to cry.

I get home after midnight, freezing to my bones, feeling frustrated, and guilty at neglecting my family. I put myself to bed, and turn out the light, hoping to sleep: I don't. I spend the next three hours of the early morning tossing and turning, thinking about many things: my love for my Maths lessons, my happy family, and my parents in South Africa. And then the Apartheid Laws that brought about the system of Bantu Education for the South African natives, that is notorious worldwide for being narrow, and thereby carrying a 'stigma'. I realise, regardless of how hard I try, correcting all the damage the Bantu Education Curriculum caused will be hard to achieve. I begin to cry again until I fall asleep.

Greg suggests that I should go on a holiday – I deserve a break. This time I chose South Africa.

I have enjoyed teaching with Betty. She is enthusiastic and willing to take on board advice and this in turn results in good working practice. Miss Baker has also demonstrated an ability to teach across the primary age range. She demonstrated sound effective planning in the lessons I observed. Her assessment and record keeping goes beyond the school's requirement, and provides a useful tool for her to address the many different needs of the children she teaches. Her manner and delivery of lessons are calm, considered and focused, and she is readily able to give feedback to develop each child within her class.

As the Deputy Head Teacher, I've worked alongside Betty addressing challenging behaviour and curriculum issues. I am very pleased with the progress individual children make, and the ideas she suggests for helping our children. It is clear from her practice that she demonstrates a sound knowledge of the curriculum. She can create a stimulating and effective learning environment through interactive displays, and the organisation of her classroom.

Betty works well with all her colleagues and the parents. She shows consideration to all, and this is reflected in the positive feedback I receive from the parents of the children she teaches. The children make progress both emotionally and educationally. Please contact me if you need further information about her.

John Smuts
Deputy Headmaster
Summer Hill Primary School
7th November, 1979

Chapter 11

Big Decision

November 1980

I have just returned with British Airways from holidays in South Africa. It presented some happy opportunities for me to be with my family and friends again. However, it's nice to be back with Greg and the kids. At Heathrow Airport I move from the immigration clearance counter for International Passengers, through the automatic sliding doors, following the slow queue behind other passengers, pushing buggies, luggage trolleys, and pulling their suitcases. Across, on the Arrivals Meeting Area, many people are waiting.

Some are carrying babies and others are holding up name-cards. As soon as I approach, Sophie shouts out loud, "Mummy!" and runs towards me, leaving Greg holding onto a card written, 'Mummy, welcome back – we missed you!' It goes quiet for a little while, before people start chatting again.

Holding onto my hand-luggage with my left hand, I let go the handle of my suitcase I am holding with my right, open my arm widely, bend my knees to hug her tightly, and kiss her. We walk towards Greg and Wayne, who is strapped on his pushchair. Behind the card, Greg has a surprise for me – a white rose. With my heart bubbling with joy, I kiss Wayne, and then look up at Greg, who is beaming with a smile. He gives me the rose. I bring it to my nose.

"Mmh, it smells fresh!" I say, looking at his eyes. I feel his hand on my back, as he pulls me towards him. Our lips meet, and we give each other a good kiss.

"Did you have a good trip, darling?" he asks, reaching out to the handle of my suitcase.

"It was great - although tiring, as you know it. Is everything all right?"

But after the happy reunion my mind is soon pre-occupied with my desire to obtain the teacher status recognition and continue working. Following the successful completion of my Mathematics course, I'm now ready to proceed with the upgrading of my initial teacher qualification at St David's College.

I submit my mathematics certificate to St David's College, expressing my intention to resume the course. A tutor contacts me, and we briefly discuss the training programme due to begin. Towards the end of the second month of my course, things start going wrong. It becomes impossible to complete the training. Continuity becomes difficult when the member of staff who has taught me leaves the College, and new ones take over, as this required a repetition of the work already covered.

I get very desperate seeking a solution to sort this matter out once and for all. So, I speak to Greg and ask his opinion.

"Betty, the route you are considering is not easy," Greg warns.

"Don't worry, honey," I say. "I will argue my case again. I need to prove to others that the qualification I hold deserves recognition."

"Who cares, Betty? How many people are out there, with good qualifications, and no jobs?"

"Get lost, Greg - that's enough!" Furious, and filled with a burning sensation, I look at Greg with my eyes soaked in tears. I walk away from him in a rage, and throw myself on the bed, crying. But I later return to Greg and show him my reference letter.

"Read this, please. Who wouldn't like a good teacher like me in their school?"

"So, what? There are many other good teachers out there."

Greg sagely confirms what I already know.

This discussion provokes me. I look at Greg, thinking, *can't he see my point of view in all this?* I'm trying to raise the awareness of the stigma attached to the Bantu education system. I want the whole world to see that it is upgradable.

While in deep thought about my situation, I hear a knock at the door. I peep through the security hole, and recognise the postman. I open the door, receive a big envelope, and then sign for it. It's from Abdul Hassan, my solicitor in London. I open the envelope with enthusiasm. It contains the copies of my academic records, and the rest of the documents are details of my enrolment. There's a lot to go through. I'm curious, but I feel anxious at the same time. I believe there is enough information here to support my case, should I decide to seek legal advice. I weigh the pros and cons of taking this route.

Then I decide not to pursue this matter, as I remember the South West African experience.

Betty relates well to other members of staff, and always works to promote the best impression of the school in the eyes of the community.

Mrs Ann Rogers
Head of Junior School,
Summer Hill Primary School
8th February, 1979

Chapter 12

The Last Mile

June 1981

This time, I return to South West Africa for a short holiday. All the preparations are easier, as Greg takes a lead in doing the bookings, and also taking me to Heathrow airport. British Airways fly directly to Windhoek airport, in South West Africa. The flight lands at 10.45 am. I collect my luggage, and go to the arrivals, to meet, Mariaan, my friend. She has agreed to pick me up.

At about noon, I hear a tap on my shoulder. It's her.

"Betty!"

"Mariaan, it's lovely to see you again."

"How's your husband? And your children?"

Before I could respond, Mariaan asks many questions.

"No, stop." I try to slow her down, so that we can get into a serious conversation. I'm dying to hear the news, since I left the city. Mariaan calms down, and we soon engage in a talk and have a laugh about many things. She drives me to her home in Ludwigdorp.

"Betty, have you now given up on Mark?"

"I'm glad he appeared to have fully recovered from the events surrounding the murder. But, do I still love him? No, no, no."

"How are things with Gregory?"

"My husband?"

"You married him?"

"Yeah, it was time – we're in love."

"I had wanted to speak to Mark, the last time I saw him, and this didn't happen."

"You're right, a 'Hello, Betty!' or just a wave would have been nice."

"Obviously, he saw me. Could anyone have specifically instructed him to ignore me? Maybe, yes; I don't know."

"It's too late now, Betty you're Greg's wife – forget him."

"Of course, I'm settled with Greg now."

I meet up with my friends for coffee, almost daily. We catch up with life stories from since I left them. I soon realise that I'm at peace with South West Africa. Before I realise, two weeks holidays is over, it's time to return home. I board my flight back to Gatwick airport in England. And I'm back to Skipton.

* * *

It's great to be with my children and around their dad, Greg again. I missed them massively, when I was away. Greg welcomes me back home, and asks many questions about my family, believing the purpose of my trip was genuine– to see them. His commitment amazes me. From the first time I met him in South Africa he has remained true to me.

Days pass

"So, Betty, what's up?" Greg asks me one evening, after dinner, as we watch television in the living room, by which time Wayne and Sophie were asleep, in their bedroom. I run out of words, as I feel his presence next to me. He cuddles me, rubbing his lips against mine. By this time, his hand is moving gradually, touching me, sending a gentle electric current up my spine to the brain, and then down to my feet.

"Well," I reply with my slurred voice, finding it difficult at the moment to think about anything, specifically. "Mmmmmh." That's all I'm able to say, enjoying everything he does. After having fun sharing intimacy, we go to bed. I think about Greg's question, as I drift into sleep in his arms. Hearing him breathe deeply, I know he is fast asleep. I fall asleep on his arms.

The next day

At 6.00 p.m. the following day, Greg returns from work. I serve him a cup of tea. Sitting next to him, I say, "Sorry, love, you asked me a question last night. What, actually, do you want to know?"

"I just wanted to know your thoughts."

"My thoughts - about what?"

"Your plans for the future - I mean things like work, or that kind of thing."

"Oh, that's what you're on about? It's good for you to ask. Actually, I was intending to ask your views about completing my training. I think I can give it a final push, and succeed, within the next six months. What do you think, my darling?"

"Of course, you know I'll support you, Betty. I know how much you want this."

I'm by now more relaxed about the idea of being at home temporarily. I get up, and help the kids to get ready and drive them to school. After the school-run, I spend time on myself, steaming my face and pampering it. Some days I go to the gym; I have membership for a year. I soon get to know other community members.

I do gardening, and other chores also, along reading in preparation for re-training. I have been considering the college or university to go to.

Fortunately, as I open my bed drawer, to pack our linen, I find my diary, with the McTate Foundation contact details. My colleague, Gary, gave me the number, before I left Summer Hill School, 'in case I needed it'. I'm pleased Greg is supporting me to qualify.

The following day I call the McTate Foundation. An extremely friendly and very professional lady answers the phone.

"I'm Betty Davies. Is it possible to speak to the Director, please?"

"What is it about, if I may ask?"

"I'm wondering if you have a vacant place to take me on for assessment."

"Assessment for what, sorry?" she asks.

"I'd like to gain the qualified teacher status for teaching here in the UK. My case might be different from other recruits. That's why I would prefer to see the Director first, if possible, and then we might take it from there."

"I'll put you on hold, while I speak to him, if that's all right."

"Yes, thank you," I respond, holding my breath.

The lady returns after about two minutes:

"Hello, are you there?" she asks.

"Yes, thank you," I say anxiously, unable to guess the news I'm about to hear.

"Mrs Davies, Mr Roberts is willing to meet you at eleven o'clock tomorrow morning. Will that suit you?"

"Yes, thank you very much." My appreciation comes from my heart. I can hear her saying, "Mrs Betty Davies," as she books an appointment for me. "Hello, Mrs Davies, do you know where we are?"

"Are you still at 247, Keighley Road?"

"That's correct."

As I enquire, it's hard to believe that I've found them. So, tolerance does breed its own reward, as I'd been taught.

"Yes, we're in room 44, on the third floor. Just press the buzzer. We'll open for you. You're fortunate, you know. The Director doesn't normally work on Fridays," the secretary says. I wonder if she is aware of the courage she's giving me. "You're booked in now."

I feel like saying, 'at last'. I respond with a polite chuckle instead.

"You may come ten minutes earlier, and have a cup of tea, before speaking to the Director," she says.

"See you then. Good-bye for now."

I hang up. I sit down, motionlessly, thinking. *That's a different response altogether from what I've had in the past. The secretary is so kind, and very polite. What a difference from my treatment in South West Africa. Greg will certainly be pleased with this news.* 'Oh, it's time to collect the kids,' I suddenly think to myself, and drive off.

Greg returns from work, I meet him by the door.

"Hi, love," I say, greeting him with a new optimism.

"Hi, darling, have you got good news?" Greg responds, throwing his arms over my shoulders, pulling me towards himself, and giving me a pleasant kiss.

"Well, I'm meeting the director of the McTate Foundation tomorrow."

"Wow! And – what is it about?"

"I'm amazed with the reception I received over the phone. Mara, the secretary, even asked me to come in earlier and have a cup of tea - unbelievable!"

"Well done, honey! You never know - this could be your time to get teacher status."

I get up early on Friday morning. I take a shower. I put on

makeup, my navy blue pair of trousers, jacket and a matching shirt. I select a hand bag to match my shoes. I take two folders containing the most important documents regarding my application to show the Director. I help my kids to get ready to go to Katleen our child-minder, who has agreed to do the school-run for us today. Greg drops them at Mavis' after taking me to the railway station to catch the 8.35 a.m. train.

At the railway station, Greg reverses the car, and drives off. I stand there waving at them until they disappear around the corner. I buy my ticket, and hurry to the platform. The train arrives. I get on and find a seat. The seats fill up so quickly with people commuting from Skipton to Keighley and Bradford. Some passengers have no seats. Soon, the train arrives at Keighley station. I get off, and it's a straightforward route to the McTate Foundation office. I get there on time. I ring the buzzer, and listen. I hear, "Hello?" I recognise the voice immediately as that of the secretary.

"Hello. I'm Betty Davies," I say. "Is it possible to speak to Mr Roberts, the Director, please?"

"Third floor," she says, abruptly. I find my way up to this floor in an old lift that takes time to ascend. I have to give it one bang, and it responds to that, but it is noisy all the way. On the third floor, the lift stops, and the door opens. I come out of the lift into a corridor. And outside the offices, there is a big banner, with 'McTate Foundation' on it. I knock at the door, and push it open.

The secretary appears from behind her desk to greet me, with a firm handshake, and wearing a broad smile on her face. She directs me to the side with the sofa, and towards a jar of mints on the table. I feel relaxed here, as she says, "Please take a seat, Mrs Davies." As I sit, she asks me, "What drink do you prefer?"

"Tea, with milk and no sugar, please," I say. I look around, admiring the paintings on the walls. There are three working areas with desks. The staff are already getting on with their work. The secretary returns with a hot cup of tea.

"Thank you." I receive it with a big smile.

While I'm drinking, I look up at the notice board opposite me. There is a poster of a bird in a pond, attracting my attention. This bird has long legs, and a sharp protruding beak. Inside its mouth, it has something looking like a frog. The head has disappeared down its throat, yet the body is in its mouth, almost eaten up. Strangely, this animal has its fore limbs around the bird's neck, strangling it. How ironic, I think!

"When you're ready you could come through for your interview, Mrs Davies."

"Yes, thank you."

I get up and proceed to the office. Mr Roberts rises to greet me with a handshake, beckoning me to my seat opposite him. Opening a folder, he says, "Right, Mrs Davies. My secretary has briefed me about your intention. Could you fill me in on the details?"

I narrate my story positively, showing him the supporting documents in my folders, and end by asking if his Foundation could assist me to complete the process of getting English accreditation as a teacher.

"This is possible, Mrs Davies. I'd like to see you teach in the classroom for one lesson. You have enough evidence to prove your competence. You need to register with us first, and we'll do the rest."

Filled with joy, I smile, nodding. Mr Roberts continues:

"We've got an arrangement with a few schools in the area, to observe the foreign teachers for this kind of assessment. When would you like to start with us?"

"As soon as possible, Mr Roberts. This process is long overdue."

"That's all right," he says, and then calls his secretary.

"Would you register Mrs Davies, and contact one of our schools, to arrange a slot for lesson observation, please? Keep all her folders together, if you would."

Mr Roberts turns around to speak to me. "We've finished now. We'll confirm your placement by telephone, Mrs Davies. Thank you for coming. Should you wish to speak to us between now and then, just give us a ring?"

I grab my bag, feeling even more excited, as I leave the office. Walking down the road, back to the station, I hum softly my favourite song, 'All I have needed, Thy hand has provided –great is thy faithfulness, Lord unto me.'

The following Monday

As I walk down stairs, the telephone rings. Picking it up, I say, "Mrs Davies speaking, may I help you?"

"Hi, I'm Mara, I'm glad to find you, did I call at the right time?" she asks.

"Yes, thanks," I say a bit concerned with what I was going to hear.

"Is your family all right?"

"Yes, thank you." I then remain quiet, hoping she will tell me her reason for calling

She is so chatty as if we have known each other for ages. She then confirms my placement for Tuesday at Wellington Primary School. She asks me to prepare a lesson for a Year One class. I choose Maths.

On Tuesday, I arrive in time for my observation. After signing the Visitors' Book, the secretary takes me to my classroom for the day. The school starts with Assembly and Collective Worship. The Maths lesson is first. Mr Roberts comes into the class, together with the Head Teacher. They both sit down at the back and observe me teach. At ten o'clock, the children have playtime. Mr Roberts gives me the observation report, before leaving the school. The overall grade is A.

I return home feeling tired, but overwhelmed with joy. I share my good news with Greg, as usual saying, "Mate - it went well!"

"And then?" Greg says, prompting me to continue.

Taking a deep breath, I say, "Greg, it did work well in the end."

"What went well Betty?"

"My final assessment and everything that goes with it."

"Pardon me."

"Yes, I am a qualified teacher."

"Good for you."

"And for all of us."

"So, what next?"

"I forgive them."

"Forgive - who?"

"The authors of the Apartheid Laws."

"Mmh, Betty, what happened to make you change your mind?"

"Yes, Greg, I now understand: they were doing their jobs, and they had to do it professionally, like everybody else, to earn their income."

Six months later

I receive my Certificate of Accreditation through the post. It is in a brown A4 envelope, supported by a hard card, and labelled, *Do not fold*. I show Greg, before putting it away in my folder, for safekeeping. This folder also contains other important documents about me.

In The Folder:

Reference

I have the privilege of teaching with Betty Baker. She has a thorough and dedicated approach to the paperwork side of the job. She instils in the most able pupils a love of literature that has stayed with them. She can see the potential in her pupils, and strives to bring out the best in them. Her infectious faith and enthusiasm radiate. Betty cares for the pupils in her charge, many of whom have deeply troubled lives and whose behaviour is very challenging at times. Betty believes passionately in the importance of our young people's achievement. She also brings the balance of her sports training to the job.

I'm happy to recommend her.

Joseph Cane
Head teacher

THE PRIZE
THIRD PRIZE - Gladys Mountain SECOND PRIZE - Charlotte Brays and FIRST PRIZE is - Betty Baker!

My annotation:

We all walk to the front to receive the book prizes, nicely wrapped in brightly-coloured wrapping paper. I look at my nametag, in disbelief: 'Betty Baker'. And then walk back to my row. This recognition I will always remember.

THE PRIZE
Betty Baker!
EXCELLENT STAFFROOM CLEANER
For cleaning the Staffroom well, and reaching out to the corners.

Commentary:

Betty deserves this prize - a box of chocolates. She never murmurs when collecting used tissues left on the teachers' tables. She polishes the tables and chair-backs with 'Furnigloss', leaving them shining.

The Cards
From a parent and her daughter, expressing their appreciation.

This card reads:

To: Miss Betty Baker

Thank you for looking after me for the whole year. Lots of love,
Miriam & thanks from Mrs McAnthony

A card with a picture of a teddy bear carrying a basket full of red
roses reads:

To: Miss Betty Baker

Thank you, Teacher!

Best wishes!

Lots of love,

Hovesh

The Notes:

Dear Mummy,

I have no words to describe the wonderful person you really are.
You are very caring, kind and warm. Your love and tender heart
are something I'll always remember about you. You are my
greatest gift from God. You are the best mum among all the
millions of mothers in this world.

Your loving daughter,

Sophie

Dear Betty,

I'm glad to be the man in your life. You keep my life at peace, my
woman.

Your husband for now and for ever,

Greg

x

The End

Appendix

THE APARTHEID ERA IN RELATION TO THE SOUTH
AFRICAN TIMELINE 1948-2013

1913: Betty's dad was born.

1914: National Party founded.
Betty's mum was born.

1919: South Africa administered South West Africa.

1948: National Party won elections and adopted Apartheid Laws.
Mark Douglas was born.

1948 -1998: the 50 years of the regime that impacted on the life of
Betty Baker.

1949: Prohibition of Mixed Marriages Act 55 passed.

1950: Betty was born.

Group Areas Act segregating the natives from Europeans.
Population Registration by Race Act 1950.
Immorality Act 21
African National Congress (ANC), led by Nelson Mandela,
organised opposing campaigns.

1951: Bantu Authorities Act 68

1952: Natives Pass Laws Act 67

1953: Bantu Education Act 47
Reservation of Separate Amenities Act 49

1959: University Education Act 45
Promotion of Bantu Self-Government Act 46

1960: Sharpeville uprisings and massacre. ANC banned.
International pressure against government starts. South Africa
excluded from Olympics Games.

1961: South Africa leaves the Commonwealth.

1966: Prime Minister and Apartheid architect Dr Hendrik
Verwoerd assassinated.

1970: Bantu Homeland Citizens Act
Betty's South African citizenship renounced automatically.

1976: Students protest against Afrikaans language being used as
the medium of instruction. Soweto uprising.

1989: FW de Klerk becomes president.
Public facilities open to all races. ANC unbanned.
Nelson Mandela freed from prison after 27 years.

1991: President de Klerk repeals remaining apartheid laws.
International sanction against South Africa lifted.

1994: Non-racial elections.
ANC wins the elections. Nelson Mandela becomes president.
South Africa rejoins the Commonwealth and the United Nations.

1996: Process to reconcile the former political enemies start.
The Truth and Reconciliation Commission start hearings on human rights crimes committed during the Apartheid era.

1998: The Truth and Reconciliation Commission Report presented to the government.
Apartheid declared a crime against humanity.

2013: Dec. 5, Nelson Rolihlahla Mandela died peacefully at the age of 95, having led his beloved country from European rule under Apartheid to the Rainbow Nation that it is today.

About the Author

H. N. Quinnen is a successful British Politician, who grew up in South Africa. She was a school-teacher when she realised that despite her achievements, she wanted to affect change in people's lives on a bigger scale. Through public speaking, she empowers and motivates people, focusing strongly on individual achievement. This is her debut novel. She lives in England with her family.

**TOP HAT
BOOKS**

Historical fiction that lives.

We publish fiction that captures the contrasts, the achievements, the optimism and the radicalism of ordinary and extraordinary times across the world.

We're open to all time periods and we strive to go beyond the narrow, foggy slums of Victorian London. Where are the tales of the people of fifteenth century Australasia? The stories of eighth century India? The voices from Africa, Arabia, cities and forests, deserts and towns? Our books thrill, excite, delight and inspire.

The genres will be broad but clear. Whether we're publishing romance, thrillers, crime, or something else entirely, the unifying themes are timescale and enthusiasm. These books will be a celebration of the chaotic power of the human spirit in difficult times. The reader, when they finish, will snap the book closed with a satisfied smile.